MW00681499

ALL THE TARGETS

a novel by Noah Bond

ALL THE TARGETS

A NOVEL BY NOAH BOND

First Edition. Published at Fort Lauderdale, Florida, by Mission Investments, Inc. Cover and dust jacket design by CityStreetz, Oakland Park, Florida. Printed by BookMasters, Inc., Mansfield, Ohio.

Library of Congress Catalog Card Number: 2011936608

ISBN 978-0-9673551-3-9

Noah Bond continues to provide the rest of us with intellectually stimulating page-turners without foul language, profanity or obscenity. Also by NOAH BOND:

THE LOST TESTIMONY OF BONES LeBEAU

The plot to assassinate President John F. Kennedy from inception through implementation, as explained by a witness whose testimony had been lost. The witness is fictional. The rest is truth. Finally, a coherent explanation of the conspiracy without all the conflicting reports and theories.

THE DOORSTEP OF DEPRAVITY

A tale of lawyers, heirs, greed, deceit, lust and death. The young heiress is not what she appears to be. The one-woman law office representing her takes on the biggest firm in town on her behalf, but there's no getting around the requirement that she must be married to inherit. Negotiations escalate from unorthodox to lethal. People die. Money vanishes. Then the unthinkable happens.

NOMAD/Y THE MOON BASE PROJECT

Faced with the probability that a Cosmonaut would walk on the Moon before an Astronaut would, NASA moved the goal posts. The winner of the space race would now be the first to establish a base on the Moon. An international suspense thriller about the greatest cover-up in history and the astonishing events which it generated. Visit *www.moonbaseproject.com* for a free preview.

To read the reviews and find more information, visit *www.noahbond.com*.

Dedications and Expressions of Gratitude

This novel is dedicated to my wife Susan.

Thanks to:

Vera K. Randall, my senior English teacher.

Screenwriter Michael de Silva.

Copyright attorney, Barry L. Haley.

The friends who proof-read the manuscript and hopefully made it a better story.

Special mention:

The Upper Arlington Golden Bears Class of 1960.

Most of all, I thank He who made this book possible.

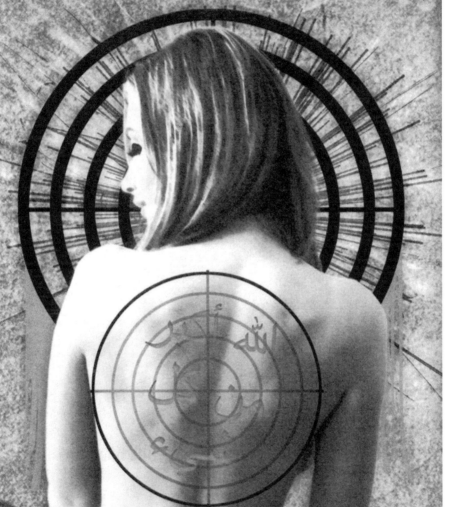

ALL THE TARGETS

A NOVEL OF INTERNATIONAL INTRIGUE
BY NOAH BOND

Men and nations will always do the right thing in the end --- after they exhaust every other possibility.

— *Abba Eban*

PROLOGUE

Dallas, July 4, 1967, 6:47 PM CDT

Elizabeth Redondo was in Parkland Hospital, more than ready to deliver her first child. Like so many others, she had crossed the border for the event in order to bestow the blessing of dual citizenship upon her child. Unlike most others, she had flown in from Monterrey on a corporate jet. Her husband, Luís Redondo, was the vice president of the Latin American division of a new "big box" retailer.

Elizabeth still wasn't clear about the dual citizenship. She was Canadian, from Calgary. Her husband was Mexican, from Puebla. Both had U.S. resident visas at the time. Did that make their son a citizen of three countries?

At 7:04 P.M., Marco Patrick Redondo was born into a life of privilege --- but it wasn't enough.

CHAPTER 1

Cheyenne Mountain, Colorado
Friday, May 25, 4:37 PM MST

The new red Corvette ate up the smooth mountain road toward the North American Aerospace Defense Command (NORAD) Headquarters, tires squealing on the turns. The weather was fantastic: 52° and not a cloud in sight. The windows were down. The sound system was up. Johnny Rivers was simultaneously afflicted with the *Rockin' Pneumonia and the Boogie Woogie Flu©*. It was catching. It was Friday afternoon, the beginning of the long Memorial Day weekend. Life was good for the junior U.S. Senator from Texas.

Marco Redondo smiled as the security officer needlessly checked his identification. "I'm sorry, Senator, we're not allowed to make exceptions," the officer explained.

"It's a good rule," Redondo replied. "You can't let in just any member of Congress." He was one of the best known men in the Americas. His official campaign for the Presidency had recently begun, financed to a significant degree by his family wealth.

Marco Redondo was tall, but he was not thin. He had worked on his father's ranch outside Monterrey during the hot summers. The rest of the year, he would exercise when he could. That had been easy when he attended the University of Texas, but more of a challenge during his years at Georgetown law. His eyes were dark brown. His full head of hair was brown. In the sunlight, it had a reddish cast which he attributed to his mother's Irish ancestry. (It never hurt to broaden one's constituency.) As always, he was immaculately groomed and dressed. He was single, but engaged. America hadn't elected a single man to be President for more than a century. He wasn't going to buck that trend.

Credentials returned to him, he placed the lanyard holding the Special Visitor's pass over his head and drove up toward the entrance. It never failed to amaze him. A barbed-wire topped chain link fence leading to what appeared to be a large culvert sticking out of the side of a mountain. Deceptively unimpressive. It didn't look like the entrance to a magician's chambers, but, in a way, that's what it was.

Of course, one could not just pull up to the entrance. For one thing, internal combustion engines were not permitted inside because the air scrubbers could not handle the emissions. For another, any such vehicle approaching would be efficiently rendered irreparable.

Air Force Major Luís Fox came forward to greet him as he pulled into the VIP parking lot. He was a bit shorter than the Senator, solid but not quite stocky. His jet black hair was short, in military fashion. The temples were beginning to grey. He looked like an average Mexican-American in uniform --- until the piercing black eyes caught you. Luís Fox had been raised upper class, but left without resources when his father died young without insurance. He had joined the Air Force to continue his education. It had worked out well.

The Major stopped about six feet from the driver's door, crossed his arms and greeted the Senator with "Word of the gas crisis hasn't reached Washington?" He spoke with a soft Texas drawl that had authority behind it.

"It's a hybrid! I'm going 80 on the Interstate and the engine shuts off! It's downright spooky, Luís!"

"Then I'm glad they don't build hybrid aircraft," he observed dryly. "Ready for the tour?"

"Not just yet, amigo. Let's enjoy the open air a few minutes more."

"You haven't become claustrophobic, have you?"

Senator Redondo smiled and indicated the negative by shaking his head, as he began to walk toward the perimeter of the parking area. Major Fox fell in beside him. After a few moments of scanning the dramatic horizon, the Senator spoke.

"You know I'm running for President...."

"News came on the last wagon train. Counting on the Hispanic vote?"

"That's what I've always liked about you, Lou. You cut to the chase. You don't mince words."

"*En la boca cerrada no entran las moscas.*"

"Indeed. Flies don't enter a closed mouth. Loses something in translation, doesn't it? We were both raised to keep our mouths shut. I seem to have gotten over it."

"Comes with the territory, I suppose."

"Some reporter always wants to know my thoughts."

"I hope you don't tell them."

A wry smile came to the Senator's face. "I haven't said 'Where'd you get that awful tie?' or 'Your dress fits like shrink wrap' yet."

Luís nodded his approval. "So what do you want to talk to me about?"

"I'll need a military aide to brief me --- and advise me." He looked his friend directly in the eyes. The question was implied.

"And keep you out of trouble, I suppose."

"Goes without saying, Zorro," the Senator replied, using a childhood nickname.

"What if...."

"I don't become President? Well, that's a possibility. But I'm not hiring just yet. You've got the job if you want it."

"Then count me in." Just like that.

It didn't surprise either of them.

"You could have asked me over the phone," the Major commented.

"Too important. Besides, I need to be up to date on the military. This place ranks at the top of the list. Some Senators still think it's outlived its usefulness." Then "Why'd you have me come up so late in the afternoon?"

"Had VIP visitors earlier," the Major commented smugly.

"My competition?"

"Hope not. Denver Nugget Dancers. Didn't want you distracted."

"Really?"

"Wore their little dance outfits. Did a little routine." He paused and closed his eyes and sighed. "It was a heartwarmin' spectacle."

"No. I meant, you show them the nation's primary

defense system?"

"Couldn't very well discriminate against them after we gave the hockey team girls the tour. The Avalanchettes or something."

"Next time, I'm driving right through the check point."

"Wear a helmet. There are actually a few guys in the Air Force who can fire a hand gun. Congress won't buy us all Sidewinders. When are you going to get on the Appropriations Committee?"

The Senator's mind still retained the image of red fiberglass exploding on all sides of him, decided he didn't care for it. "I prefer to remain on the Intelligence Committee," he said absently.

"Well, don't get all disappointed that you missed the dancing girls. With the assistance of the Dear Leader, we may have a little show of our own for you."

"North Korea?"

"They rolled four missiles into place yesterday. They don't do that unless they intend to fire them. Taepodong doesn't have the climate of Cape Canaveral."

"Only the leader is balmy."

"I've got to work on my timing. That was my line."

"Sorry. The difference between a politician and a stand-up comic is measured in millimeters."

"Glad to hear there's still a difference."

"But I'm a statesman."

"Whatever you say." The Major rubbed his hands together and suggested they go inside. This time they did.

CHAPTER 2

Cheyenne Mountain, Colorado
Friday, May 25, 7:14 PM MST

Senator Redondo and Major Fox stood before the Situation Screen, nursing their surprisingly good *cafes con leche*. The room was well occupied. The facility was on a high state of alert.

The Major spoke. "We never know what the little bastard's going to throw up. Our satellites tell us all the ones on the pad are Taepodong IIIs."

"Three-stage ICBMs."

"Right. He's shown that he can send them right past Hawaii. What we don't know is what he's been aiming at. But he's got the distance."

"If he's aiming at Chicago and hits Detroit instead, it's still a problem. What about the payload?"

"These aren't real big rockets. But they could carry a small nuclear warhead. So far they don't seem to have done that."

"Not multiple warheads, though."

"Not yet. We think he's having trouble acquiring the technology."

"What about the Chinese?" the Senator asked.

"They want North Korea to be a diversion, not a threat."

"What happens if Kim doesn't play by the rules?"

"That's why we're ready. By the way, I'm in command right now. Let's hope you don't get to see my skills put to the test."

"Showtime?" The Senator pointed to the huge electronic map that covered the South Wall of the room.

"Ahh. They've lit one up. Let's see where it goes."

After a flurry of comments, the room fell silent. The short red line emerging on the green screen began to assume a vector. As it lengthened, it pointed Northeast.

"Alaska?" asked the Senator.

"That map is an Air Force version of Mercator Projection. As you will recall, the planet is sort of round. It's too distorted to tell visually. In a minute, the map will show a projected flight path and rearrange the geography accordingly. Watch."

After a short time, a broken red line appeared which showed the missile passing directly over Seattle. The line stopped over the Salton Sea in Southern California.

"We used to do that by hand."

"Bet it wasn't that fast."

"It also wasn't that accurate. Computers can be contrary, but they still work miracles."

"They're aiming for 29 Palms?"

"No, Senator. The projection line is programmed to end at the estimated limit of the missile's maximum range. Since there are no potential targets South of that, it doesn't matter if we've underestimated the range. The target will be somewhere on that line."

"That narrows it down to Seattle," the Senator observed. "I don't mean to be an alarmist, but we're watching an ICBM headed for a major U.S. city. Shouldn't we be doing something?"

"The Secretary of Defense should be watching a similar display right now. It's up to him to keep the President informed. Since shooting down a missile is a far cry from killing people, several people --- including me --- have the authority to give that order. Naturally, our scientists want to study the flight as long as they can...."

"So we don't wait for them to give the order?"

"Exactly." The Major pointed. "See those numbers at the lower right of the screen." He waited until the Senator found it. "Those are the number of interceptors in the air, the aircraft types and armaments."

"Do I see Navy?"

"Yes, you do. Most of those scrambled from carriers. The aviators from the Pacific and the Aleutians scramble first. The Canadian Air Force should show up soon. RCAF."

"What can the interceptors do?"

"They can shoot it down --- theoretically. The tests haven't been that encouraging, but we're successful on our own rockets about forty-five percent of the time. The more shots we get, the better the chances are of intercepting it. But we've never shot at a Taepodong III."

As they watched the red line pass East of Sakhalin Island, the Senator asked "Why not?"

"It is one thing to destroy an incoming missile, but we're not authorized to interfere with a test. Could provoke an international incident." From the terse manner in which it was stated, it was obvious the Major thought this was nonsense.

"So we wait until the last minute to save our cities, in the hope that it's just another test?"

"Standing orders, though I must say your interpretation is pithier."

The Senator just shook his head.

The red line continued to grow, like a living thing --- a monster set upon the destruction of cities and lives, American cities and American lives.

A new figure appeared at the lower right corner: 1420ke.

"The payload's estimated to be 1,420 kilos," the Major advised. "That's not good."

"Big?"

"Big enough for a nuclear warhead."

"Doesn't mean there is one."

"No. We knew at some point they would have to test their rocket for this size of payload. This is the first time."

"Do we know it's a test?"

"No. They don't announce them. All the others have been tests --- we think. Maybe some have been provocations. But it would be stupid to test a rocket for the first time with a nuclear warhead on it."

"And we don't think Kim Jong-il is stupid. Just crazy." He gave the Major a meaningful look.

"Yes. But our nation's defensive strategy is based upon underestimating the enemy's nerve."

"Pearl Harbor."

"Hickham Field to the Air Force."

Everyone watched the red line pass well South of Kodiak Island.

"When do we panic?" the Senator asked. He was sincere.

"It's an individual choice, Senator, but I'm waiting a while. We've seen them come this far before, then fall into the sea."

"I'll trust your judgment."

A young lieutenant entered the room, walking straight to the Senator. "Urgent call from your office, Senator. You can take it across the hall." Cell phones had never worked inside the facility, but they had been banned as well when they began to sport cameras.

Senator Redondo nodded, then turned to Major Fox. "Nothing like an urgent call to relieve the stress," he observed wryly.

The room across the hall and the telephone were the same color: Air Force uniform blue. It's peculiar what one notices under duress.

"Sorry to bother you, Senator, but you said to let you know immediately if this ever happened." He wondered if his aide could know about the missile. She continued. "Seven Hundred Million euros were transferred into one of Kim Jong-il's private accounts in Monaco yesterday. This has been confirmed. We haven't been able to positively identify the source, but Iran is the prime suspect." She fell silent, wondering if this had been important enough to have interrupted the Senator.

"Thank you, Marcy. Keep checking and keep me informed." He hung up. "God help us." It was a silent prayer, not an exclamation. Then he quickly returned to the Situation Screen across the hall.

CHAPTER 3

Cheyenne Mountain, Colorado
Friday, May 25, 7:32 PM MST

"Shoot it down now, Luís." The Senator was discreet, but adamant.

"What?"

"I said shoot it down! Now! Don't wait for the chain of command. Just do it!" Seeing that his friend wasn't moving, he added "Kim Jong-il just received Seven Hundred Million euros, probably from Iran."

"*¿Estás seguro?*"

"Absolutely. There can be no mistake."

To the Senator's amazement, Major Fox picked up the nearest phone and punched in a two-digit number. Then he conversed rapidly in a whisper. Before he replaced the telephone receiver, he said loudly "Yes, Sir, I understand. Immediately, Sir." Only Senator Redondo could see that the Major's hand held down the switch hook during the entire simulated conversation. The Senator was sure the Major would fit right into his administration.

"Attention!" shouted Major Fox. "Highest authority. Orders are to engage and destroy the Taepodong III missile we are tracking. Initiate now!"

It is incredible how efficient people can be when they're ordered to do what they've always wanted to do.

Once he saw the aircraft moving into position on the screen, the Major turned to the Senator. "If you're wrong, maybe I can be your gardener."

"I'm not, Luís. And thanks."

"I should be thanking you. I may be a hero." He hadn't meant it seriously, but suddenly it seemed possible. It was an interesting concept.

"Don't run against me."

"Never." They returned their full attention to the map just as a second red line appeared from the Korean peninsula. "Never shot one off when another was still airborne. That supports your attack scenario."

"You indicated that it might be an interesting afternoon."

"Yeah," he replied dryly. "Interesting."

Then Major Fox turned to the room and announced that all inbound rockets were to be intercepted.

The same officer appeared before them, holding a white bottle with no cap.

"Thank you, Lieutenant." The Major took the bottle and shook out a small pink tablet. He popped it into his mouth and chewed it quickly. "Chewable aspirin," he explained. "For the blood pressure."

"Didn't know you had high blood pressure."

"I don't. Nor do I want to. Take one. Can't hurt."

The Senator began to decline, but then changed his mind. He could feel the blood in his temples.

"Intercept imminent!" someone shouted. All eyes

returned to the display, where pinpoints of light briefly surrounded the leading edge of the missile track for just a moment. "Direct hit!"

But as the red line continued, it became clear that the missile had not been stopped. Nor had it changed course.

"Probably too low. Missile's still in the stratosphere," the Major said softly.

"Intercept imminent!"

The room watched in silence as the bursts of light appeared at the head of the red line. The missile was unaffected.

"This is like watching the barrels disappear under the water in *Jaws*," the Senator offered.

"They'll have a better shot when it gets lower." The Major was calm as the red line of death inched toward Victoria Island.

The display suddenly zoomed in, showing a smaller area. The interceptors could be seen as blips. Several were closing in on the missile at once.

"Intercept imminent!"

The bursts were brighter, but the red line continued.

"What are those planes doing down by Portland?" the Senator asked.

"Those are the Near-Impact Interceptors, the last stand. They're programming their flight paths to intersect the missile's trajectory."

"*Kamikazes?*" The Senator was incredulous.

"It could turn out that way, but...."

"Intercept imminent!"

Three planes this time. One right after the other in tight

formation. Dozens of bursts appeared on the screen.

    The red line stopped moving --- then disappeared.

    People began to cheer, and whistle, and hug each other. There were tears and laughter. Smiles all around.

    Until the display returned to full size.

CHAPTER 4

Near Midway Island
Friday, May 25, 7:37 PM MST

The B-2A Spirit Stealth Bomber streaked West across the Pacific Ocean at ten miles a minute. Its four F118GE-100 turbofan engines were mounted inside the body of the wings to reduce the thermal signature. The exhaust temperature control system further minimized it. The North Koreans might be expecting it, but they still wouldn't see it coming.

It had left Guam when the first Taepodong III missile had lifted off. It would make the round trip without refueling. At nearly ten miles high, the crew of two, seated side by side, could see the curvature of the Earth. When they looked up, the sky was the darkest blue imaginable --- frozen midnight. As the consumption of several tons of fuel lightened the aircraft, it could approach an altitude of eleven miles.

It had begun as a routine mission. When they left Andersen Air Force Base, no one had known what Kim Jong-il had in mind for the day. As a result, it carried a variety of weapons in its rotary launcher and two bomb-rack assemblies. Among the devices was a Boeing GBU-57A/B Massive Ordinance Penetrator, an earth-penetrating non-nuclear bomb for use against hardened buried targets. Guided by a precision

GPS system, the 20-foot long, 15-ton device was capable of penetrating 200 feet before exploding. The B-2A was also carrying four AGM-129 advanced cruise missiles with a range of 1,600 miles. These would be used to destroy the gantries and any rockets in place. Maybe that would be all they needed to do. That would keep them out of the North Korean Air Defense Identification Zone.

The radio didn't crackle to life, as in the old days. Instead, a clear voice came over the Milstar strategic and tactical relay satellite communications system. It instructed them to destroy the missile base and all missiles --- missiles first.

"We're going in close and heavy," the pilot remarked calmly. His co-pilot forgot to breathe for about thirty seconds. Then he began to prepare for the attack. They had just been ordered to take out the underground nerve center of the Taepodong Missile Facility.

CHAPTER 5

Cheyenne Mountain, Colorado
Friday, May 25, 7:40 PM MST

The second Taepodong III missile was already South of the Bering Straits. It was another red line bringing destruction to America. Like a cobra, it mesmerized its prey.

"Intercept at once!" barked Major Fox, breaking the spell. Everyone scrambled. "Projected path?"

In a moment the broken red line appeared, accompanied by a voice. "Projected path firm, Major."

This time the target was as obvious as it was symbolic: America's party town.

The missile aimed at Seattle had taken them by surprise. By the time the threat was recognized, the ICBM was just minutes away from its target. The room had simply observed the glowing map in disbelief. This time was different. They had already assimilated the incredible fact that the United States was under attack --- probably nuclear. No other reason to waste a good rocket. Reaction was immediate.

"Las Vegas," several voices intoned in disbelief.

Major Fox read the looks in their eyes and reacted. "No calls!" he bellowed. You could tell who had friends or relatives visiting Las Vegas. They froze. At least a quarter of the people in the room just became immobile. "Get back to work. We need to stop this one."

The Major walked to the telephone on the wall. "Security, this is Major Fox. Seal this facility at once. Level 4. No unofficial communications. No one goes in or out. Cut contact with the gate and all other facilities that could use cell phones. This is not an exercise. And send a guard here now."

"My daughter...," a woman moaned.

The Major then addressed a lieutenant. "You have anybody in Vegas now?"

"No, Sir!"

"Then make sure that door stays closed until the guard arrives."

"Yes. Sir!"

"When he gets here, tell him no one goes through it without my personal permission. Then you keep watch on this side."

"Yes, Sir!"

"Intercept imminent!"

All eyes returned to the display. The missile was approaching Canada. The bursts appeared, but the missile track continued.

"What's the payload?' barked Major Fox.

"Same as before. Could be a nuke, Sir."

The terrible red line inched its way across British Columbia, seemingly pursuing the projected line to Las Vegas.

All told, twenty-two interceptions were attempted before the Taepodong III missile passed over Lake Tahoe on the final leg of its historic journey.

Twenty-six miles North of the Luxor Hotel, one of the

Near-Impact Interceptors managed to explode a shell within several feet of the incoming missile. Everyone held his breath. But there was no cheering as the missile continued South.

"Could have damaged it," Major Fox commented to the room.

The Taepodong III missile entered the luxury tower of a new hotel at a steep angle. It tore through each reinforced concrete floor like a rifle bullet through flesh. The concussion blew out all the floor-to-ceiling windows, which sliced through pedestrians a half mile away. What remained of the tower collapsed immediately after impact, creating a rush of superheated air through the casino. Everyone and everything that had been inside the gaming rooms were blasted into the parking lot. Poker chips became bullets. Limbs were nearly severed by laminated playing cards. It would take days just to separate the bodies from the slot machines.

"We just got lucky," Major Fox observed in a whisper. "It should have been an air burst."

"It didn't explode...." Senator Redondo couldn't believe it.

"Back to work!" Major Fox shouted. "Hendricks, make sure Clark County knows they might be dealing with a nuke. Don't want some gung-ho deputy triggering it now."

"How many more do they have?"

"Two more in the gantries, probably ready to go."

"Why wouldn't they launch them all at once?" the Senator asked.

"Overwhelm our defenses? They would if they could."

"So we wait just wait for the next one?"

"We're not just waiting. We're retaliating. We just can't

see it from here."

CHAPTER 6

The Democratic People's Republic of Korea (North Korea)
Friday, May 25, 8:06 PM MST

The Lockheed Martin radar warning receiver blinked blue, indicating that hostile radar was scanning. Both men watched to see if the LED would change color to indicate they had been located. When it didn't, they breathed just a bit easier as they approached North Korean air space. The cockpit display showed the two remaining rockets on the pad. These were the primary targets, but the whole compact facility was to be destroyed as well. It would be done with conventional weapons, including the Massive Ordinance Penetrator for the sub-levels reported by Langley.

The display flashed as one of the rockets ignited on its pad. "Cruise! Now!" the pilot barked into the headset. "Damn!" The co-pilot initiated the launch of a cruise missile at the rocket now lifting off. The radar warning receiver blinked red as the North Korean air defenses acquired the signature of the cruise missile. Their cover was blown.

The ground erupted with scores of anti-aircraft missiles aimed in the immediate vicinity of the Stealth bomber. But the pilot had already put the bomber into a dive, banking to the left at the same time. Two minutes later, it was approaching the

Taepodong missile complex from the Northwest while the North Koreans attempted to fill every meter of air space with anti-aircraft missiles. The Stealth's rotary launcher loosed a hail of precision-guided munitions on the launch area, followed by the giant bomb. In a matter of seconds, the Taepodong Rocket Complex was seriously out of business.

But the cruise missile did not intercept the launched Taepodong III. It had already risen from the gantry. It would be the last opportunity for Kim Jong-il to earn his euros today.

The next phase of the plan called for a deviation of course before bombing the capital, Pyongyang. But the B-2A was recalled before that happened. That was the President's idea. At least three people thought this was a good decision. Two of them were on the recalled bomber. The idea of appearing exactly where they were expected had little appeal for them.

CHAPTER 7

Cheyenne Mountain, Colorado
Friday, May 25, 8:12 PM MST

There was a collective groan as another red line appeared on the display. The stress was exhausting. But relief soon came as a flash appeared at the beginning of the missile track, indicating the destruction of the launch facility. "Permission to cheer!" shouted the Major. The room erupted into shouts, whistles and clapping.

"Did something blow up?" asked the Senator.

"The B-2A got through. There won't be any more missiles for a long time," Major Fox explained. "Too bad it wasn't a minute sooner."

As the red line that represented the third missile crossed over the Sea of Japan, the room fell silent again. The instant the projected path appeared, everyone knew it was aimed at San Francisco.

"Intercept imminent!"

The interceptors began their attacks in Russian air space off the Kamchatka Peninsula. Either the Russians had given permission or they were tolerating the situation. Every base in Siberia was on highest alert. MiG 22 fighters patrolled the coastline, but did not interfere with the American effort. Even the planes sent to spy on the American defensive tactics kept their distance.

The red line kept getting longer, closing on California.

"Intercept imminent!"

Groups of interceptors attacked the missile in turn.

The red line inched toward Mendocino.

"Intercept imminent!"

Senator Redondo watched the Near-Impact Interceptors position themselves over the Silicon Valley. No one spoke. The attempts to intercept were so closely spaced that they weren't announced anymore.

The terrifying red line extended from the destroyed rocket base at Taepodong to Marin County. A dozen Near-Impact Interceptors raced to meet it head first.

No one in the room drew breath as the speeding dots representing the desperate fighter pilots converged on the ominous red line. It was the last chance to stop the incoming missile.

CHAPTER 8

San Francisco, California
Friday, May 25, 7:33 PM PST

It was the year 100 in North Korea, where the calendar starts with the birth of Kim Il-sung. In honor of that chronological aberration, the one-megaton nuclear warhead of the Taepodong III missile exploded in the night fog exactly one hundred meters above San Francisco Bay off Treasure Island.

A guard at Alcatraz saw a great yellow flash, which immediately turned orange as the X-rays burned up the air. Before he could react, a blast of superheated wind rendered him into flying body parts, which were instantly consumed by fire that needs no time to burn. There was no ash; ash is unburned residue. Everything burns at Ten Million degrees. The proper term to describe his demise is "vaporized."

The same fate befell Fisherman's Wharf, the Moscone Center, Union Square, the Bay Bridge and everything else east of Fillmore Street. The TransAmerica Tower did not fall; it simply ceased to exist. The seventy-seven square miles of waterfront land that had been created by filling in San Francisco Bay over the previous 166 years was liquified by the shock wave and sank below the sea. The great city which had grown from the Mexican village of Yerba Buena was no more.

What little the blast left, the water erased. A wall of radioactive water eighty-five feet high passed over the Embarcadero, carrying everything in its Westward path with it to the Pacific Ocean --- less than seven miles away. Nothing North of the San Bruno hills was spared. Waves nearly as high raced over Sausalito, Tiburon, Oakland and the other bayside communities. A giant wave tore through the Golden Gate, ripping away the bridge supports, and began crossing the Pacific Ocean as a tsunami.

Other walls of water sped South to inundate the Silicon Valley and North to overflow San Pablo Bay and the Carquinez Strait. The Petaluma River reversed course and flowed upstream for seven miles. Sacramento drowned. Entire Bay Area Rapid Transit trains shot from the tunnels like aluminum champagne corks, their passengers crushed by the force of the water.

Then, without pause, the wind did something that no laboratory wind tunnel has ever accomplished. It instantly reversed course while maintaining its force. It raced back to the detonation site to be sucked into the vortex of the forming mushroom cloud. Billions of radioactive airborne drops of San Francisco Bay were swept upward for several miles to become nuclear fallout. Everyone outdoors in the Bay area received lethal doses of gamma radiation. Only a handful would live until morning --- and they wouldn't want to.

When the Westerly winds returned, the radiation would be spread past Lake Tahoe to Salt Lake City. As the clouds climbed the West face of the Rockies, the radioactive droplets would be released. No one would ski at Vail or Aspen again. The radioactive dust would remain in the air, spreading cancer and birth defects across the Great Plains and into the Midwest.

But they would survive. Whereas, Northern California from Carmel to the Napa Valley already was, and would for a dozen lifetimes be, a graveyard.

Within minutes, specially trained Army units from Texas and Southern California were on their way to restore order and bring relief to the Bay Area. It had been a military decision taken unilaterally by the President. Only after they were on their way, did someone call FEMA — that agency which had disgraced itself after Hurricane Katrina. Within hours, civilian governmental agencies, charities and private individuals would be mobilizing aid for San Francisco.

But the Americans still did not grasp the cunning of their enemies. Just as the highjacking of four commercial aircraft had been only the beginning of the September 11 events; so had the nuclear explosion been the prelude to further disaster.

CHAPTER 9

Cheyenne Mountain, Colorado
Friday, May 25, 8:34 PM MST

The room was silent as disbelief turned to shock. For the first time in over six decades, a nuclear weapon had been used in warfare. The city where the United Nations Charter was signed had been destroyed by an atomic warhead. Millions of Americans were dead and dying. The unthinkable had happened, and had to be faced. But first, it had to be absorbed. Someone began to softly sing "I left my heart in San Francisco," but broke down after the opening words.

The Major cleared his voice. "You're all going to remain in this room for a little while --- not more than an hour. The President will need to sort this out and address the nation. In no event will anyone ever speak to the press about what happened today. We have nothing to hide except the same secrets we had this morning. As long as there is no alert, you may talk among yourselves or watch CNN. No telephone calls yet." He started to turn away, then stopped. "God bless America!" he shouted. He and the Senator promptly left the room. Behind them came singing from the room. "God bless America, Land of the free, Stand beside her, and guide her...."

As they walked toward his office, the Major asked "What

would you do right now?"

"As President?"

Major Fox nodded.

"I would meet with the Secretary of Defense and the National Security Council before taking any retaliatory action, but I would be inclined to obliterate Kim Jong-il and his cabinet at the first opportunity. It is clear that we must respond decisively and quickly, before the rest of the world tries to tell us what should be done. On the other hand, I don't see any benefit to nuking Pyongyang. The North Korean people have enough problems already. I reserve judgment about Iran until we're sure of the source of the funds. What would you suggest?"

"Strike back now. Take out the regime without too much regard for the collateral damage. Everyone will expect that. But I agree that a conventional response is the way to go. Let the enemy have the sole claim to nuclear evil. Besides, Pyongyang isn't much of a target."

"Like swatting a fly with a Buick?"

The Major almost grinned. "Something like that. More damage was done to Tokyo by conventional bombing than Hiroshima suffered. People forget that."

"Most civilians never learned it."

The Major grunted in acknowledgment. "You can use one of the phones in my office," he said as they approached the door. Stepping inside he announced his guest. "Yolanda, this is Senator Redondo. He needs to make some calls."

The young woman in the tailored Air Force uniform snapped to attention as they entered the office. "Yes, sir," she said briskly, and turned her eyes to Marco. "Welcome, Senator."

Although he was eager to get to the telephone, the politician in him made him look into her eyes. Unexpectedly, they were deep green. They were out of place in her latina face. "Thank you, Yolanda," he beamed, despite the circumstances. He allowed himself just a moment to take her in. She was tall, mostly legs it seemed. She had *mestiza* skin and shiny black hair, but the rest of her said "MADE IN THE USA." He recovered. "Which phone should I use?"

Second Lieutenant Yolanda Herrera showed him into a small conference room adjoining the Major's office and offered to bring him coffee. He accepted so she would come back. He wanted to see her again. There are some constants in the universe.

CHAPTER 10

San Francisco Bay Area, California
Friday, May 25, 7:43 PM PST

"What's that?" Sheila Grant shouted to herself upon hearing a tremendous blast in the distance, sharp then rumbling like thunder. Immediately, a series of beeping alarms went off nearby. She was a pre-med student who had accompanied her boyfriend to the geology lab to check on an experiment. Then he'd wandered off into another part of the basement. The walls of the old brick sub-structure confined the sounds and sent them ricocheting. She turned to the source of the beeping noise and looked at the display. The straight ink line on the seismograph had turned into peaks and valleys. The mechanical pen was jumping across the paper as if possessed. Although she recognized the device, her first thought was that the Earth was having a heart attack.

Then the floor began to shake violently. She reached for a table, but it moved away. She fell to the floor and stared up at the ceiling. The ancient wooden beams were splintering. She managed to get to her feet and scramble toward the exit. Bricks fractured; the support beams began to break. Then, the first floor became one with the basement. The experiments were abruptly terminated. So was Sheila's boyfriend. Sheila was sealed inside the stairwell where she would be found barely alive five days later.

The building, indeed the entire campus of Stanford University, was moving South in a violent series of short thrusts that were unnoticed amid the overall motion. The two plates of the strike slip fault named San Andreas were moving past each other at several millimeters a minute --- warp speed for a geological event.

Having witnessed the explosion from a distance, the California Highway Patrolman had taken it upon himself to stop Northbound traffic from entering San Francisco. The spot he selected was the bridge where Interstate 280 crosses the Crystal Springs Reservoir. Beneath that bridge is the very structure which created the reservoir by damming up the exposed rift of the San Andreas fault. It had seemed like a splendid idea at the time. There was a crossover at that point for official vehicles. His quick thinking had saved at least forty lives before the dam collapsed, taking the bridge span down with it. The bridge approach and the patrolman's motorcycle soon followed. Without a flashing light, he found himself ignored, and several drivers sped past him into the void. In desperation, he stood waving before a school bus which managed to stop only after running him down.

The Crystal Springs Reservoir, which had made life possible in San Francisco, became a narrow tsunami, erasing everything in its path.

The tectonic plates continued to grind against each other as they headed in opposite directions, releasing the pent-up energy stored since April, 1906. At that time the displacement had been 21 feet. This time it would be greater --- much greater. It would be measured in miles. In 1906, the effects of the earthquake did not spread South beyond Black Mountain, where the San Andreas fault makes a nine degree turn. Now, the 3000-foot mountain crumbled under the grinding forces, as the energy sped South to release centuries of accumulated pressure. Water mains burst, high tension lines snapped, cell towers toppled and bridges fell all the way to Los Angeles.

Then all Hell broke loose.

The Puente Hills blind thrust fault runs twenty-five miles, through Beverly Hills and into downtown. It unleashed a torrent of seismic waves that stirred the foundation of the city. The venerable brick buildings collapsed first, as the mortar became fluid. The non-ductile reinforced concrete buildings shattered next. Finally, the steel framed skyscrapers succumbed to the relentless swaying, a few actually toppling over onto neighboring buildings --- like dominos.

Los Angeles was constructed upon a tangle of faults from the Haywood in the North to the San Jacinto in the South. As the seismic waves smashed into them, they all became active, spreading the event throughout Southern California. The Salton Sea vanished into the desert floor in mere minutes. All along the coast, the palisades crumbled. The surf covered Malibu Beach, breaking 30-footers across the crumbling Pacific Coast Highway. Further South, Balboa Island liquified and Laguna Beach simply slid into the ocean. Fires erupted from broken gas mains. The sound of sirens filled the night, but the streets were impassible.

The devastating earthquake had lasted forty-three

seconds, by far the longest on record. In less than a minute, a quarter million Angelinos had been killed or mortally wounded. California was closed until further notice.

CHAPTER 11

CNN Center, Atlanta, Georgia
Friday, May 25, 11:24 PM EST

The bearded man with the improbable name of Wolf was at the center of controlled hysteria in the CNN Situation Room as reporters called in on cell phones to describe the devastation. "To recap for those of you just tuning in, there has been destruction on a massive scale throughout California tonight. It began with a tremendous explosion in, or just East of, San Francisco, which some reports are saying was an atomic bomb. As yet we have no confirmation of that. Whatever it was, it was followed by an unprecedented earthquake along the San Andreas fault which spread all the way to the Los Angeles area. We are receiving thousands of calls to report damage and injuries, but --- perhaps ominously --- there has been no contact from anyone in San Francisco. If, and I want to emphasize that this is unconfirmed speculation at this point, but if there was an atomic explosion, our technicians advise me that it is possible that all communications devices within the area would be inoperable."

Senator Redondo and Major Fox were watching in disbelief. "Is that caution or denial?" asked the Major.

"Probably both. They'll have it right by the time the East

Coast wakes up."

The program continued. "... flooding has been extensive all around the San Francisco Bay area, but the cause or causes are not known yet. CNN has been trying to contact the seismological studies unit at Stanford University, but communications are down. The Seismological Institute in Uppsala, Sweden has reported that a major earthquake registering 10.8 on the Richter Scale occurred in the past hour in the Bay area." He turned toward an unseen source of information and read. "We remind you that the Richter Scale is a geometric progression, which means that each succeeding number is ten times the number before it." He looked into the camera again. "This is by far the strongest earthquake to ever hit the United States. It will be some time before the damage can be fully assessed."

Wolf stopped and cupped his right hand over his ear. He paused for a moment, then "The Secretary of Defense has just confirmed to CNN that the explosion in San Francisco was a terrorist attack! Casualties may be in the thousands. Everyone has been requested not to attempt to place any calls to --- or within ---California. Land lines and cell towers are down throughout the state. Those lines that are working are reserved for emergency services. The President will address the nation tomorrow at Noon Eastern Standard Time. CNN will cover that and keep you updated on this tragedy through the night."

This was what they did. When the rest of the world was immobilized by events, the journalists and the reporters had purpose, a clear mission. Rather than discuss what story might be worth airing, they were rapidly processing diffuse raw data into information that could be understood. The adrenalin was flowing at CNN, at the BBC --- and at *Al-Jazeera,* which arguably had the most coherent coverage because they had begun working on the story three hours before it happened.

CHAPTER 12

Cheyenne Mountain, Colorado
Friday, May 25, 9:39 PM MST

The Major was walking the Senator out to the parking lot.

"Why'd you pretend to speak with someone before ordering the intercept?" Senator Redondo suddenly asked.

"Ah! I should have known you'd catch that. It's called authority enhancement. There's never an argument if the President ordered it."

"And since you had the authority anyway...."

"No harm done."

"You won't be that devious in my administration, of course."

"Won't have to. I'll just holler to you down the hall."

"Or send someone from your staff to wake me up."

"Speaking of which, I'd like to bring a few of my own along --- to avoid the retraining process."

"Makes sense. Does that include Yolanda?"

"It certainly does. Strong-willed woman with great instincts. Watch out for her, Marco. She's had commando training."

Senator Redondo was intrigued. "Not just another pretty

face, then?"

The Major stopped and looked the Senator in the eye. "I know you've never taken my advice in these matters before, but I have to warn you. Yolanda takes romance very seriously."

The Senator considered this. "Is she married?"

"Her husband died unexpectedly."

"Line of duty?"

"No. Shot. Hunting accident."

"That's pretty rough. How did she take it?"

The Major hesitated, considering his reply. Then simply answered "She wasn't convicted."

"*¿Verdad?*"

"True. There was an anomaly. I liked that term."

"Anomaly?"

"The gunshot hole in his vest was considerably smaller than the entry wound in his chest."

"I guess that could happen...."

"That's what her attorney guessed too. But the prosecutor thought he'd been shot up close without his vest. Then he was dressed in his vest and shot again from a distance in the same spot to make it look like a hunting accident."

"That would be some second shot."

"Exactly," Major Fox concurred. "And the tests were less than convincing. Of course, her husband hadn't been especially discreet about his cheating. And Yolanda does have a garage full of marksmanship trophies. The prosecutor had a truckload of surmises, but no evidence. Anyway, it's a long story for a happier occasion, and at least several *cervezas*."

"Next time we're in the same State, then."

"For sure, Senator."

There was no music on the drive back. The Senator was considering the options available to the President to deal with the act of terrorism and preparing a clear response to each option. Only when he neared his destination did he wish that Yolanda were waiting for him instead of his fiancee.

"Oh well," he thought. "I've made my bargain with the devil."

The devil in this reference was Paul Carnegie, a wealthy Easterner with abundant Ivy League and Wall Street connections. Carnegie was credited with electing two New England governors and several members of Congress from the Northeast. Now he wanted to make a President.

All he'd wanted from the Senator was that he be married to a respectable WASP before the convention in August. Political marriages were as old as recorded time, probably older. Jack Kennedy had married Jacqueline Bouvier in order to acquire the respect of rich Eastern Democrats. In the spirit of the moment, Marco had proposed marriage to Paul Carnegie's only daughter. Meghan Carnegie was an attractive tall, thin blonde with a political science degree from Columbia, who spoke fluent French, Spanish, Italian, German and Arabic. She looked like a model. Her demeanor was not inviting, but rather, challenging. She radiated "You can't afford me." Her own father had described her as being "austere."

How could her father have known that she approached sex as a competitive event?

Politics and madness are not mutually exclusive. In fact, quite the opposite.

CHAPTER 13

Washington, D.C.
Wednesday, June 13, 12:02 PM EST

The Willard had always looked to Marco like a European Palace, located conveniently on Pennsylvania Avenue, a place where governance occurred in non-traditional ways. It was true that you could zip past it in a taxi and never see it, but that would not happen once you knew it was there. He was here to confirm his political future, to stamp his passport for destiny.

His destiny suffered a detour through the hotel lobby when he was dropped off at the wrong entrance. "Man plans; God laughs," he reminded himself, citing the expression old enough to be common to both Hebrew and Arabic.

He entered a Spartan office with rental furniture. A wealthy man, Paul Carnegie saw no need to impress with anything but his talent. A woman wearing wire-rimmed glasses peered over her computer screen at him, then pressed a button on her desk. It was typical of Carnegie efficiency. Paul Carnegie appeared at once to greet the Senator.

They went to a small conference room, where they took two of the four chairs around a simple oval table. To one side of the table top was a clear cooler with ice and cans of soda.

"Need a glass?" asked Carnegie.

"No, thanks. I'm already dazzled." He took a Dr. Pepper and popped the top.

"I tried one," Carnegie admitted. "Wasn't bad. I may try one again sometime." He opened an unflavored iced tea to confirm that this wasn't the time.

"Dr. Pepper is the unofficial non-alcoholic beverage of Texas. It comes with the politics. Will I have to switch for the national market?"

"To what? The unofficial beverage of Georgia? In public you drink whatever they offer. But your image should be coffee --- which includes espresso and Cuban, but not latte or cappuccino."

"Nothing with whipped cream on top, then?"

"Heavens, no!" Then Carnegie smiled. "That was good. You found the button and pushed it."

"There must be tougher issues...."

"Nothing is unimportant to the public. H.L. Mencken said 'No one ever went broke underestimating the intelligence of the American public.' They will seize upon the least significant thing and make a major issue of it."

"Like my race?"

"Sure. Let's dance into that particular minefield for a moment. You may lead."

"My father traces his family back to Spain, but they arrived without women. So the wives came from all over. Not just Mexico. There were Creoles from New Orleans and Havana, for instance. At one time, Acapulco was the major trading port with Asia. There could be *Filipinas*."

"African?"

"The Spanish considered all the native populations to be

their slaves; so, there was no need to import them. Is that good or bad?"

"Who knows? Your mother?"

"Irish by way of Canada. Kind of the opposite of my father. It was the men who mixed up the blood: Scots, English, even Vikings kidnapping Irish women to become their mates. And the English themselves represent most of Western Europe."

"Any Visigoths?" Carnegie asked dryly.

"We were never sure about Uncle Alejandro...."

"So, who's going to vote for you at this convention? Who do you think you can count on?"

"Hispanics, Texans, Irish, Catholics. That's my core constituency."

"Don't assume that will work like it did in Texas. You are going to have to be a chameleon. You need to be the son of Mexican immigrant when you switch to Spanish to address the delegates from Laredo. You need to be a strong American to address the Cubans from Miami --- in English, by the way. You must profess to be a devout Christian without scaring the Jews and Muslims. And always remember that most American Christians either fear or loathe the Roman Catholic Church. So do quite a few Catholics after the revelations of molestation in New England. Don't take anything for granted. Hell, there are people who believe it is un-American to even know another language." Carnegie thought for a moment. "Do you speak any languages other than English and Spanish?"

"No. Do you speak any other languages?"

"Not really. But I did pick up the ability to understand Scots from a great uncle. Unfortunately, the only practical application seems to be BBC comedies."

"So I should keep my Spanish speech writer."

"For now anyway. So what will you say about San Francisco?"

"That I am outraged by the North Koreans. The initial response of destroying the Taepodong missile complex was a good measured response at the time. But it should have been followed by more decisive action. Madame President may have precluded unilateral retaliation by seeking a coalition. In the first few days, she could have done anything. The rest of the world would have sympathized. Now everyone thinks we're incapable of taking action by ourselves. That, by itself, is enough reason to replace her."

"Would you go to war?"

"I would not consider sending troops anywhere that we don't already have them. Nor would I take any action which would broaden the present dispute by involving more countries. The United States can handle North Korea alone."

"What about the Chinese?"

"We literally feed the Chinese. We are by far the biggest customer for their manufactured goods. They are heavily invested in our Dollar. We need each other. Besides, they understand that we must punish North Korea in some fashion, if only to discourage similar attacks. We must do something or we will lose respect. President Bush understood that --- although he got carried away with Iraq."

Carnegie nodded, then asked "What about Iran?"

"We need to complete the task of assembling the evidence to prove the Iranian role in the attack. Then we will take appropriate action. There is less urgency, since Iran lacks the ability to attack us directly. But there must be an appropriate response."

The discussion continued through deli sandwiches. Then, shortly after 7:00 PM, a tall and slim woman entered. Her long blonde hair was pulled back and up. She wore low heels, wire-rimmed glasses and a black pants suit. She walked straight to the Senator and kissed him lightly. Then she turned to Paul Carnegie.

"Hello, daddy."

"Welcome, Meghan. We've just finished. Join us for a drink."

"If you insist." She removed the glasses, let her hair down, unbuttoned her jacket and the top of the blouse --- and became desirable. Playing with the next button, she smiled innocently at both of them and said "We don't have the votes in the West."

"What?" in unison.

"It's like this," she explained. "Too many Mexicans went home after the earthquake. They haven't come back. There's a lot of unemployment. Then there's the fact that California is now the fourth largest state, right after New York, which has lots of Puerto Ricans --- who don't necessarily love Mexicans. Then there's Florida, the second most populous state, which has lots of Cubans, who consider themselves superior to other Spanish speakers for some reason. Spanish is not a very unifying language, is it?"

Senator Redondo had to ask. "What about the Russians, the Persians, the Chinese, the Japanese, the Vietnamese?"

"They vote Anglo in California."

"The Blacks?" Senator Redondo was stunned.

"The Blacks like to think the Hispanics took their jobs. In places like Florida, that was the great excuse for Black unemployment. Then came a wave of Jamaicans, who were even blacker, but it was said that their British accents gave them an advantage over local Blacks. Then came the Haitians, who didn't even speak English, but they too demonstrated upward mobility. So the Blacks went back to resenting the Hispanics."

"The Jews?"

"The Jews who admit to voting Republican love your competitor for the nomination. Matt Chambers does a wicked *hora*." She moved her arms and swayed in hula fashion. "Still think you can make me the First Lady, *mon cherie*?"

CHAPTER 14

Boston, Massachusetts
Wednesday, August 8, 6:48 PM EST

The tension in Suite 3206 of the Westin Boston Waterfront Hotel was tangible. So was the heat. There were too many anxious bodies in the room. The convention was ending its third day. The platform was in place. The speeches by the Old Guard were thankfully over. It was time to pick the candidate.

Seated in the center of the living room of the suite were Senator Redondo and his wife. They had been married two weeks before in a private ceremony at her father's estate in the Shenandoah Mountains of Virginia.

Approaching them was campaign manager, Paul Carnegie. "It's California, Marco. Governor Chambers has the California delegation," explained Carnegie.

"I've still got Texas and Florida, though."

"But he's got New York, Pennsylvania and New England, not to mention his home state of Illinois. The math is against you.

The Senator grinned, then shrugged. "Go see Chambers."

"It's the wise thing to do at this time. As Vice President,

you'll be the logical person to succeed him."

"If he gets elected...."

"With you on board, it's a sure thing."

That improved the Senator's outlook. "O.K., Paul. Now convince Chambers."

"That's the easy part. You convince my daughter. You told her she'd be the wife of the President."

He looked at Meghan. "She will. Just not as soon as we expected."

"That's the spirit, Marco. I'll go over to Chambers' suite. Won't take but a few minutes. I'm sure he'll want to see you."

"But will he want me as his running mate?"

"I don't recall saying that I would give him a choice." With that, Paul Carnegie, multi-millionaire, kingmaker and father-in-law, rose and walked to the door filled with purpose. Nobody in the room doubted that he would succeed.

Meghan Redondo rose and joined her father, saying "I wouldn't miss this for the world." To her new husband she added "Wish us luck, Pecos." Pecos was her new pet name for Marco. He hadn't decided whether to like it or not.

Matthew Chambers was man of quick wit and even temper. With his mane of silver hair, he looked every bit the father figure his campaign manager insisted he was. Chambers had slipped away from his own suite to a room he had secretly rented on the floor below. Once his bodyguards had checked it, he had them wait outside. He had given himself plenty of time to stretch out on the sofa. He was exhausted, but would not close his eyes. He took a mental inventory of his aches and decided that the feet were edging out his back for first place. If elected, he would be seventy years old by the time he was inaugurated. What had he been thinking?

To get elected, he had to appear younger than he felt. Spry alone wasn't enough. He had to be vigorous for three more months without actually killing himself. He planned a brief vacation after the convention. A reporter had asked what he would do then and he had replied, "I'll tell you when I wake up." Everyone thought that was hilarious. Chambers thought everyone was a lot younger than him.

Pauline, his wife of forty-three years was back home with her legs propped up to ease the swelling. She'd tried, but her heart wasn't up to life on the campaign trail any more. He hoped she could fly in for his acceptance speech.

The knock on the door came too soon, like everything else recently.

The meeting was short. Governor Chambers had already determined that he needed Marco Redondo on the ticket. Besides, they didn't have any major policy differences. Each had campaigned on his record and experience. The older man had more experience.

There were only two surprises. Paul Carnegie told him that Senator Redondo demanded a high-profile role in the conduct of international affairs. This was accepted without discussion. The man was certainly qualified. Mrs. Redondo expressed her desire to work as a political aide to the President. This was not required by the Senator; so Chambers simply told her that he would welcome all the help he could get.

"Go ahead. Marco will be waiting," Meg said to her father. "I'll be right along."

As soon as he'd left, Meghan turned back to Gov. Chambers. "You're in need of a Middle East expert who can speak Arabic. I graduated at the top of my class at Columbia...."

"I've seen your work on your husband's campaign. I'm already impressed."

"I can't wait to get to work. There's so much we can accomplish!"

"There's still an election to win."

"I'll help with that, too."

Realizing her value, he said "You get us in the White House and you'll get your chance to sort out the Middle East."

"It's a deal." She stuck out her hand and he shook it. "Don't forget to tell your staff I'm on board."

"As soon as the nomination is final," he promised.

CHAPTER 15

Boston, Massachusetts
Thursday, August 9, 9:00 PM EST

"If I could have your attention, please. There has been a change to this evening's program." The amplified voice filled the great space. The delegates in the Convention & Exhibition Center fell relatively silent. "It is my privilege to introduce the Honorable Junior Senator from Texas, Marco Patrick Redondo."

"Yee-ah-HOOO!" came from the Texas delegation. It was quickly adopted as the appropriate response to the introduction by hundreds of other delegates, some of whom had obviously never uttered this particular greeting before and should not have chosen this occasion for the first attempt. Nevertheless, there followed that brand of exuberance which is endemic to such gatherings. A brass band struck up "The Eyes of Texas Are Upon You." Delegates, having partaken of a surfeit of caffeine, alcohol and adrenalin, hooted and waved signs in the air. More than several ten-gallon hats were launched toward the ceiling. A few even attempted to dance to the music.

Marco smiled down at them as if they were his beloved unruly children. When the band stopped playing, he yelled into the microphone "Any Texans out there?"

It started over, but this time the band played "Are you from Big D?" There were fewer cowboy hats in the air, in part because those who had previously been so moved had yet to recover theirs.

With a comedian's timing, he relit the fuse with "Any Republicans out there?"

Of course, that was a sure winner. Everybody was included this time. Six and one-half minutes later, it had run its course. The Senator then spoke again. "This is a great night for the Republican Party!" Braving the cheers, he continued. "This is a great night for America!" He remained silent for nearly thirty seconds before continuing. "In fact, this is a great night for the civilized world!

"Tonight we change the course of history! Tonight we begin to restore this country we love to supremacy!"

This time he let the crowd react.

"I have a plan. All we have to do is to take control of our government back from the Democrats. Now everyone in this hall tonight knows the Democrats have no business running this fine nation of ours, but there they are. It's an enigma." He held his palms up to indicate there was no explanation.

Some delegates were not too sure what an enigma was, but they laughed anyway.

"To clear out the Democrats, we have to work together --- even if it's not convenient, not comfortable."

This sobered the crowd. It was almost still.

"I'm going to start that process right now by taking back all of the bad things I've said about Matthew Chambers!"

There were moans from the Texas delegation and sporadic cheers elsewhere.

"Actually, as you have noticed, Matt and I have been delivering the same message throughout the campaign. And I believe in that vision of the future. Just this afternoon, my political experts have advised me that Matt Chambers has the better chance to re-take the Presidency and implement our plans for America. So, rather than try to divide you, I urge you to vote for Governor Matthew Chambers as your candidate for President of the United States of America!"

"Chicago, Chicago." The band played it swing style, like Sinatra was going to be singing it. There was bedlam. When it finally died down, the Senator spoke softly.

"I'm still here." The crowd laughed, the Texans less than the rest. "I have spoken with Governor Chambers. I told him I would be looking over his shoulder and second-guessing his every decision in office. He told me that was the Vice President's job."

The delegates were trying to catch up with him.

"This may have been a casual observation, or a bit of humor on his part. But I like to seize an opportunity; so I accepted."

This evidently confused the band. After a moment it began playing a Scott Joplin rag. The Texas delegation didn't hear it anyway. The others were laughing at his explanation.

The Senator was savvy enough to leave on a high note. So having made it impossible for Governor Chambers to select anyone else as his running mate, he closed. "Thank you for your support --- and God bless the United States of America!"

The band was ready this time, with "God Bless America."

As he left the stage he recalled the tearful voices singing it at Cheyenne Mountain.

CHAPTER 16

Above Iran
Thursday, January 17, Noon EST

The pilot of the Israeli F-161 jet released his first "bunker buster" bomb over the nuclear facility at Natanz. At the same moment, others would be making attacks on Arak and Esfahan, but Natanz was most important. The fledgling ability of the Iranians to produce nuclear weapons was being terminated unilaterally by the nation that had already been identified as the prime target.

Crossing into Iranian air space from Kurdish Iraq, he had outrun the aging F-4 Phantoms the Iranian Air Force had put up. Now surface-to-air missiles were being launched at him. He hoped the Iranians were still deploying their newest equipment around the oil refineries and Tehran, as the Mossad had reported. However, the Tor M-1 mobile anti-aircraft system was, unfortunately, truly mobile. He consoled himself with the realization that he'd certainly be dead by now if Natanz had acquired such a defense.

If he survived the Iranian defenses, he still wasn't home free. His mission was no longer a secret. The shortest path home crossed the heavily defended Persian Gulf coast region. Since he did not have enough fuel for a different route, that was where he had to go next. On the other hand, his plane was faster and more maneuverable without its bombs. It was also more expendable.

In the distance he could view his handiwork. The nuclear facility at Natanz was engulfed in flames.

Surprise, world!

As the Israeli jet streaked across over the Persian Gulf, Matthew Chambers took the oath of office of President of the United States. Marco Redondo was sworn in as Vice President minutes later. Neither knew of the raid upon Iran, which the outgoing President kept secret until the news services broadcast it. Then she described it as her gift to the new administration. Even the majority who thought it was a good thing hated her for that.

She was too busy writing her autobiography to care what anyone thought. She was still smarting from her unexpected defeat at the Democratic convention. When she had been unable to carry a majority on the first evening of balloting, she had known she was in trouble. During the sleepless night, a minority candidate emerged as the only alternative everyone still liked. He was a respected Black television star, who had begun his career as a stand-up comedian. When he'd received the nomination, he'd quipped that he had more experience than the Republican comedian running against him. His campaign had generated the second largest Black voter turnout in history. It could have made the difference in a close election. But the public was ready to give the Republicans a chance again.

And the Vice President's new wife was radiant

throughout, smiling whenever she thought someone might be watching her.

CHAPTER 17

The White House, Washington, D.C.
Friday, January 18, 7:00 AM EST

"Good morning, Mr. President." Marco Redondo announced his arrival in the Oval Office with a forced smile. The President was sitting on a couch, sipping from a steaming mug.

"Good morning, yourself, Mr. Vice President. Now let's cut the crap and get to work. Our first Presidential Daily Briefing takes place at 8:00 A.M. Our first one, each person will be vying to present his case."

"Sounds intense, all right. What's your plan?"

"Tell them up front that our time is limited today. That usually works. By the way, I'm Matt and you're Marco in this office. That will save a lot of time over the next four years. Help yourself to the coffee over there. It's strong."

"I could use it. Broke curfew last night. Great party." He thought briefly about what had happened after the party --- when Meghan had emerged from the bathroom wearing only black gloves and black stiletto heels, insisting they have sex standing up. "Didn't get much shut-eye." It was an understatement.

"Yeah. I'd have slept later but for the Iranian bombings."

"What's the reaction so far?"

"Unofficially, everyone in the world is relieved. Officially, it's an outrage which could not have been perpetrated without United States complicity."

"Is that true? The part about complicity?"

"That's where it gets interesting. Apparently my predecessor was notified by Tel Aviv only after the planes were about to leave Iranian air space; so we didn't assist there. The Israelis did request that we not shoot down any of their aircraft that strayed into Iraq on their way home."

"Did any?"

"Every damn one of them! One after the other, like ducklings!"

"It still seems like a bargain...." Marco mused.

The President fell silent for a moment. "The truth be told, it's likely the bargain of the decade for the United States, but we have to choose between appearing to be accomplices or complete fools. And it was done in such a way that our administration can't take any credit."

"Could have been useful if the mission had failed." By now, Marco suspected that the President had as bad a hangover as he did himself. "Now we can concentrate on Kim," he offered.

"Good point. I like a positive attitude. You might want to remember that when I don't react favorably to it. How do we get him and his military henchmen without killing a lot of his innocent countrymen --- people who would kill him themselves if they could?"

"Rescinding Executive Order 12333 would be a good start. Why fight a war to dislodge one evil person?"

"If that's what we did in Iraq, then I agree with you. But there are potential problems with rescinding it. First, the world would find out too soon. By that I mean before we leave office. Second, we would be held responsible for every assassination plot in the world. But, with the Order in place, we can proclaim our innocence."

"So, we leave it in place and ... just ignore it?" Marco was trying to picture this strategy in action.

"Not quite. You see, the Order only applies to our government agencies, not to other governments or civilian contractors."

"Matt, I think you're on to something."

"I hope so. The CIA is afraid of leaks in the South Korean intelligence services. They're exploring alternate routes. Let's see what develops."

Since Marco considered himself to be the expert on international affairs, he felt challenged by the President's initiative. "The operation must appear to be Korean. We could try to contact someone like the Green Dragons, an East Coast Korean gang with connections on both sides of the 38th Parallel."

The President smiled for the first time. "I knew you were more than just a pretty face. I'll mention it to the CIA Director."

CHAPTER 18

The White House, Washington, D.C.
Friday, January 18, 3:45 PM EST

The familiar face peeked around the doorjamb of the Vice President's White House office. "You functioning already?"

"Zorro!"

"Mr. Vice President," responded Major Fox. "That still sounds spooky, amigo."

"Call me Marco, then. I see you survived the festivities. Did you find your office?"

"Yeah. Yolanda's getting it set up. Ordered me out, come to think of it."

"Let's get caught up. The Arabs have joined the Iranians in denouncing us for alleged complicity in the Israeli raid. Venezuela doesn't need a reason to denounce us. Oil prices have risen to $167.00 per barrel without any discernable collusion. Oh, and the OPEC meeting is tomorrow."

"What about the Iraqi oil we supposedly control?"

"The Shiites have turned the Eastern half of the country into an unofficial Iranian territory since we withdrew. The Sunnis still need us to protect them from the Shiites; so they're cooperating when it suits them. The Kurdish Sunnis are acting like they live in a country called Kurdistan and doing their own thing. But they are producing oil. It's just not enough."

"OPEC won't attempt an embargo, though. While they may be able to assure that one tanker will sail to one certain port, they can't really prevent all tankers from entering U.S. ports. They know that. Besides, they need the Dollars. The only effective tool they've got is production cuts, which punishes everyone --- including the producers."

"But mainly us," Marco reminded him. "So they can claim any other damage is collateral."

"In the past only Iran and Saudi Arabia have really cut production significantly. I suppose that's how it would be the next time."

"Those who cut production will shown themselves to be our enemies. That's how I see it."

"Even our allies?"

"Especially our allies. It's time to stop propping up the petro-terrorists just because we don't have the will to drive efficient automobiles in this country."

"Maybe it's time to do something about that too," Major Fox speculated.

"If gas prices don't finally do it for us."

"Come on down and we'll see if Yolanda has me organized yet."

"With pleasure."

When they reached the Major's new office, Marco was impressed with the lean, efficient look of it. Until Yolanda appeared from the adjoining room --- all legs, curves and flashing eyes.

"Good afternoon, Mr. Vice President." Her tone was cool, but her eyes were inquisitive. "I have a question."

"Just call me 'sir.' What's your question?"

"Are you in the military chain of command?"

He hadn't thought about it, but he was a quick study. "I am the CCIC — Contingent Commander in Chief."

There was no response.

"He can only deploy troops on February 30th," explained Major Fox.

"I see," she said, and began to return to her office. Unexpectedly she turned and met his eyes again. "Perhaps you would like to inspect the entire suite?"

"Go ahead. I've seen it," the Major declined. "Besides, it's a bit tight for three people."

Yolanda went first, standing behind her desk. His eyes surveyed the room, then landed on her.

"Permission to speak freely, sir?"

"Granted."

"*Mantenga los ojos en sus pantelones.*"

Marco was stunned. "Did you just tell me to keep my eyes in my pants?"

"That's correct, sir. It's an expression from East L.A. I'm sure you can figure out what it means."

"And apply that knowledge."

"Yes, sir. I would appreciate it. I don't engage in casual flirtations, casual affairs,... casual anything. I've been told that my disposition is too intense."

"Understood, Lieutenant. I apologize if I have upset you."

"You have not; so no apology is necessary."

"See you later then."

"Yes, sir."

She could not have inflamed him more if she had said "Rip off my uniform and take me here!" But, he reminded himself, she had said quite the opposite. Hadn't she?

CHAPTER 19

The White House, Washington, D.C.
Sunday, January 20, 6:30 AM EST

President Chambers had a rumpled look about him, although it wasn't his clothes. As Marco entered the Oval Office, the President began to unload his mental burden. "You may regret insisting upon an equal role in global affairs, Marco. It could happen in the next few minutes, in fact."

"I'll have my coffee and your news straight then."

"It's not just the Arab nations that are upset about the Israeli raid. Everyone thinks we encouraged or sponsored it."

"We sure as Hell didn't discourage it," Marco thought, as he sipped from the mug his wife had furnished him. The writing on it said "CAUTION! V-P with an attitude." The President thought it was a riot. Marco intended to disappear it as soon as the opportunity presented itself.

"It's the whole Muslim world."

"They'll get over it. They'll always hate Israel, but they need to keep doing business with us."

"Will they? The OPEC meeting is still in progress."

"Any new intelligence on Pakistan?"

"Only that the military is becoming more jihadist."

"Then it would be good to get some points on the board

with the Muslims before anything gets worse...."

"That's your way of letting me know you have a radical idea. I'm getting so I can read you better."

Marco just smiled sheepishly.

"Out with it!"

"Recognize the nation of Palestine on our terms, which might not coincide with Israel's. It's a *de facto* state already. Quite a few nations formally recognize it."

The President was momentarily stunned, but recovered. "Another ridiculous Mid-East Summit?" The idea obviously hadn't won him over.

"No, sir. In fact, just the opposite. Go to Jerusalem. Meet with the leaders of Israel and the West Bank --- separately. If you can get the West Bank Palestinians to agree to recognize the right of Israel to exist as a sovereign state and renounce terrorism, we promise them full recognition as a nation state.

"With what borders?"

"Basically, the West Bank as it was before the 1967 war."

"The Palestinian leadership can't agree to give up its claims for Jerusalem."

"So they don't. Before 1967, Jerusalem was divided. Those details will be sorted out afterwards. It can be done as long as the Arabs keep the Dome of the Rock and the Jews keep the Wailing Wall. The Arab quarters in East Jerusalem are a demographic problem for the Israelis anyway. As part of Israel, they make Arabs the majority of the population."

"That is awkward," the President observed. "The United Nations doesn't favor minority rule."

"Palestine won't be the only country with a claim on part of its neighbor's territory. Let them have their claim, as long as they renounce use of force to pursue it. As of now they're claiming all of Israel. I call that an improvement."

Chambers was a quick study. "The Israelis will never allow it."

"That's why we keep it secret. If we tell them what we're up to, they'll want conferences and votes. The leaders will be afraid of the backlash. So we spring it on them."

"They'll be furious."

"We trade the fury of the Muslim world for a few uncomfortable months with the Israelis. We'd be doing them a favor by excluding them from the process. Their leaders would have deniability."

"Like they excluded us from the Iranian raid?"

"Exactly. Who are they to complain?"

"So we accomplish what everyone needs, take a little flak and possibly eliminate the alleged cause of Middle East strife."

"Interesting choice of words: alleged cause," Marco noted.

"Flesh it out in two or three pages. Strictly BBR. Get it to me this afternoon." President Chambers stood and walked around the room. "I hope to Hell there isn't a downside we're missing here, because this is a very appealing idea, Marco."

"BBR?"

"Burn before reading."

CHAPTER 20

The White House, Washington, D.C.
Monday, January 21, 7:30 AM EST

"Marco, your idea is already in motion," the President said. "A routine announcement will be released to the effect that we are sending a low-level diplomatic mission over to introduce the new administration."

"That won't work, Matt," Marco interrupted.

"No, it wouldn't. But that's the story. It's been designed --- by the clever Mrs. Redondo, by the way --- to appear uninteresting. In fact," the President added, "I will be the person who is sent."

Marco considered that for about forty seconds. "I like it, but how will you get to see the leaders if they don't know you're coming?"

"We're insisting upon it as a condition to a continued U.S. role in the peace process."

"That should do it. What about transportation?"

"Air Force One is obviously out of the question. It will sit prominently in the hangar at Andrews during my absence. My helicopter will take us --- the President and Vice President, and our wives --- to a retreat at Camp David. Your wife and I shall be spirited away by the Secret Service in a delivery van to a waiting government jet, which will whisk us away in plebeian accommodations to Tel Aviv."

"My wife?"

"The plan details are hers. She should be there to observe them in practice. She will pose as my Arabic interpreter, since she speaks the language. Our embassy will provide one as well, of course. Both of us will use alternate identities to be provided by the Secret Service until we arrive at the meetings. I understand that I'm to receive a bad haircut and a cheap suit. Who knows what other indignities I will suffer for the sake of security? But the best way to avoid being targeted is to not present yourself as a target."

"And if it doesn't work, no one will know the difference...."

"There is that potential benefit," the President admitted, "but I'm not going through all this to fail."

"What do you want me to do in your absence, then?"

"You have the difficult job. You have to pretend we're in meetings all day at Camp David. As you know, I have a stand-in who looks enough like me to fool my mother. You'll be playing gin rummy with him. Only a few people will be in on this...." Searching for the perfect description in one word, he found none ready.

"Caper?" Marco suggested with a smile.

"Not what I had in mind for the history books," he laughed, "but it will serve for now."

"What about a stand-in for my wife?" asked Marco.

"It's being arranged. The plan calls for someone single, to avoid involving another person. You'll have to share a cottage, but we'll get you one with two bedrooms."

Marco pictured the First Lady. Pauline Chambers had not recovered from the campaign. Instead, she had become an invalid. The doctors who had said that she only needed some rest had been replaced by cardiac specialists. No need for a second bedroom for her. She'd be home convalescing. "Who's selecting my new bride?"

"Your present one, of course. She insisted upon being in on the final choice, seems to relish playing the matchmaker for you. Her selection may be a message to you. Or she could be a temptation." The President was enjoying this. "If the Secret Service doesn't have anyone who fits the physical description, they'll borrow from another agency for prospects."

"The FBI?"

"They're out of the loop on this...caper. The Secret Service has to be involved, but we can keep the other agencies in the dark to increase security."

"Matt, this is dangerous. Once you meet with anyone, your cover will be blown. Then you'll be a prime target with insufficient protection."

"That's true. We assume the danger is greater in the West Bank, but that a leak is more likely in Israel."

"So you plan to meet with the Palestinians first and get the Hell out?"

"It's the only choice, really. Furthermore, it avoids insulting the Israelis, who will understand it." The President shrugged. "You've got to take some risks if you want to change the world. Nevertheless, if you think of any way to make it safer, don't be shy."

"Can you meet the Palestinians at our embassy?"

"We ran around that idea several times. The bottom line

-71-

is that the Palestinians will not send their leaders to our embassy for a low-level diplomatic meeting. There is also some question whether the Israelis would permit it."

"Where do you intend to meet them then?"

"Bethlehem, the capital of the independent nation of Palestine."

"Even Arafat wasn't safe in Bethlehem," Marco observed. "If they won't let you out, what's the plan?"

"That's when we offer them East Jerusalem, I guess. But they have to let me out to complete the deal. These are statesmen, not Arafat or Bin Laden."

"Let's hope so. When are we going to Camp David?"

"Tomorrow afternoon. Take some books if you don't play gin rummy."

The Vice President was astounded. "Matt, you are indeed a man of action."

"I want to be remembered for my bold moves."

"As long as the action produces the desired result."

"You can't win if you don't play."

CHAPTER 21

Camp David, Maryland
Tuesday, January 22, 6:14 PM EST

It had been dark an hour before the helicopter carrying the Vice President and his wife landed on the helipad deep in the Catocin Mountains. The President would arrive later on Marine One. The flight would take half an hour. In the interval there would be other landings by Marine helicopters lifting off from the White House and flying to Camp David. Although these carried Secret Service men and Presidential advisors, they were known as decoy flights. The assumption was that there were not enough Stinger missiles in the hands of the terrorists to waste one on a helicopter that might not be transporting the President. Not only that, but the first missile fired would cause the remaining flights to be canceled. So far this tactic had worked.

Whereas winters in Washington tended to be of the damp and sleety variety affectionately known as "slop," it was usually ten degrees cooler at the Presidential Retreat. The obvious advantages of this in the summer were lost on Marco and Meghan as a Marine escorted them to the guest cabin which bore the name Rosebud, a rustic structure which had been seriously upgraded inside without losing its woodsy atmosphere. "Welcome to the Home for Wayward Spiders," proclaimed Meghan when they were alone. "Maybe this is supposed to make the Middle East look better."

"I think I should tell you now that *Diamonds Are a Girl's Best Friend* is not appropriate for a group sing-a-long by the campfire," quipped Marco.

"I, my dear, am not appropriate for a group sing-a-long by the campfire," she countered. "On the other hand, Vivaldi and champagne in front of the fireplace sound delightful."

It sounded good to him too. He knew she would have ordered champagne for the refrigerator; she was wonderfully efficient. So he looked around for a stereo system. Instead he found a Victrola with 78 records. He selected *Gulf Coast Blues©* by Ella Fitzgerald. This inspired him to prepare a fire in the stone fireplace.

"Did you find the champagne?" Meghan called from the bedroom.

"Yes, but no flutes --- only glasses."

She entered the living room wearing an oversized red plaid shirt and high heels. A champagne goblet was held in each hand, chest high. "*Buvez une coupe, monsieur?*" She often spoke French when she was feeling sexy. He had learned that "Drink a glass?" translated into "Would you like a drink?"

Marco had also learned to say "*Mais certainment*" instead of "*por cierto*" and did so on this occasion. He took the glasses from her and opened the bottle of Dom Perignon. Meghan restarted the record and danced slowly to the music, never taking her eyes off of him as he popped the cork. At the moment Ella uttered the unforgettable lyrics "a hand full of gimme and a mouth full of much obliged" Marco handed

Meghan her bubbly. She unbuttoned her shirt before accepting it.

"I don't want you horny when your new mail-order bride arrives," she explained as they lounged on the sofa before the fire. "It's a breach of etiquette to attack her immediately."

"So you think I'll like her?"

"She looks like me. What's not to like?"

"Right down to the birth mark on your left hip?"

"Beauty mark," she corrected him. "And no. That's an exclusive."

"You looked?"

"Of course. But touching was minimal...." Meghan assumed a thoughtful pose, as if reconsidering whether her inspection should have been more thorough.

"Well, is she smart?"

"A veritable whip."

"Then is she sexy?"

"That's subjective. But I told her to flirt with you when you're alone."

"And why'd you do that?" he wondered aloud.

"I also gave her permission to use her extensive martial arts skills to defend herself if you came onto her."

"Thanks for sharing that."

"Strictly non-lethal, of course."

"How considerate of you."

"Can't deprive the country of its Vice President," She stated flatly as she removed her shirt. "We don't have much time."

Then she jumped him.

When Marco and Meghan arrived at the presidential cabin, her hair was a mousy brown. She wore grey slacks and a blue blazer; both were unremarkable. A long, hooded overcoat obscured these changes. Other than lipstick, she wore no make-up. She had sensible walking shoes on. They were shown straight into the main room. It had a high beamed ceiling and natural woods throughout. There was an abundance of space which was nearly filled with furniture groupings and even a few rocking chairs. This cabin was known as Aspen Lodge or simply the Lodge.

President Chambers stepped forward to greet them. His hair had returned to its original dark brown and his eyes were now blue and tearing slightly from the unaccustomed contact lenses. His cheeks were fuller. He appeared to be in his early 50's. "The Marines have blocked the entrance from Route 77," he announced. "So we should be left alone for a while."

"To proceed with your caper," Marco added.

"Indeed. The caper advances on schedule."

"Then you will need a translator," Meghan said as she removed the overcoat.

"Is that really you, Meghan?"

"In the traditional State Department garb, Matt." She did a model's twirl for them. "GS-9 down to the skin."

"I believe that's my coat." The voice came from behind Marco. He turned to identify the source and saw another Meghan, slightly shorter and a bit sturdier than the original.

Aware that he had allowed too much time to pass before reacting, Marco drawled "You must be the mail-order bride."

"None other." She offered her hand. All eyes were on him. "My name is Meghan Redondo," she lied defiantly to his face.

Marco realized that this was going to be more difficult than he had envisioned. He automatically shook her hand.

"You two will have to do better than that in public," remarked the real Meghan. "You need to work on your intimacy."

"And what is your name, my dear?" the President asked the real Meghan.

"It says Erin Hill on the passport. How about you?"

"I'm Per Maarten. My grandparents were Dutch; my father thought I should remember my roots." The President shrugged. He was enjoying this charade. He'd been Matthew Chambers forever. "My cover document states that my name is spelled wrong on my high school diploma," he added.

"Which name?" inquired Meghan.

"I was hoping no one would ask that." They all laughed, but it did not release the tension.

Caper or not, it was still dangerous.

CHAPTER 22

Jerusalem, Israel
Wednesday, January 23, 10:26 Bravo (local)

Yusef Hoseni is a lineman for the East Jerusalem Electric Company. He is in his twenty-fourth year, single and a bit chubby. He has a limp which he hopes looks like a war injury. It is actually a birth defect. His right foot is skewed to the right. So the direction of his stride is about 30 degrees right of where it would normally be. When he takes a walk, pedestrians approaching from the other way frequently collide with him.

But that is not how he sees himself. At age seventeen he made his way to the terrorist encampment at Baalbek in Lebanon to offer his services. After minimal courses in explosives manufacture and placement, he was deemed unsuitable for further training. Hamas then made him into a servant for its leadership. Though insulted, he had remained until he felt he had learned all that he could.

He was given a job for the utility that most thought to be too dangerous, making emergency repairs to the insufficiently maintained lines atop the pocked-marked poles. He had mentally twisted foolhardiness into bravery and aspired to machismo. He knew himself to be a daring leader --- with no troops to lead save a few layabouts who might accompany him out of boredom.

Yusef had heard destiny speaking from his cell phone this morning. A small diplomatic mission from the United States was coming to Bethlehem tomorrow. The proposed route had been disclosed to assure that it would not be blocked by utility vehicles or public works. A small mission would have little protection. He would seize this opportunity Allah had presented to him. He would blow up the very road upon which the infidels rode. Yusef Hoseni would be a hero of the *Jihad*. A hero, not a martyr. He was acutely aware of the distinction.

In'shallah. If Allah wills it.

CHAPTER 23

Jerusalem, Israel
Thursday, January 24, 9:36 Bravo (local)

They were good bombs, Yusef thought. And a good plan. Allah be praised.

Yusef was wearing his uniform, which consisted of a cap that said East Jerusalem Electric on it in Arabic and an identification badge with his photograph and title in Arabic, Hebrew and English. He detested the Hebrew, but it was better than being shot by the Israeli police. He also wore his best light blue dress shirt to appear more managerial. He had even polished his boots for the first time. To this impressive display, he had added a silver whistle someone had brought him from a trip overseas. He didn't know that it was a London bobby's whistle.

His plan was to place explosives on or under the car, detonate them remotely and then depart in his company pick-up truck. Execution of this plan was to be dictated by the situation. He was flexible. Even if he didn't kill the infidels, he would be sending a message, striking a blow.

He had enlisted two others to stand on opposite sides of the street where traffic usually stopped at a busy intersection. Upon spotting the diplomatic vehicle, they were both to converge upon it as though crossing the street, and simply drop the improvised explosive devices next to the car as they passed it. As soon as his accomplices cleared the area, Yusef would detonate the explosives.

There were a couple details known only to Yusef. The time of detonation was to be determined by the time the car remained stationary, even if the bombers were not clear. *Jihad* needed martyrs too, Yusef reflected. Also, there was only one remote control device for both bombs. Yusef owned only one television set, which had provided the device. Yusef would use it whenever he thought best. If the second bomb was not yet in place, it would serve as a distraction. If the plan worked, Yusef's martyrdom would be limited to having to get out of his chair to change channels. This did not concern him, since he did not have a satellite dish.

By Western standards, there is not much traffic in central Jerusalem. But by Western standards, there is no real infrastructure in place to expedite the movement of automobiles. With someone's holy shrine every few yards, widening the street is impossible. And every shovel which enters the ground produces another archeological site. This is why Tel Aviv is the business center of Israel. So there it sat, a black Crown Victoria adrift in a sea of colorful (and occasionally white) Toyotas and Nissans. Yusef thanked Allah for the predictability of diplomats!

Yusef made eye contact with both bombers and nodded. Each began to cross the gridlocked pavement with a small plastic bag in his hand. The first bomber successfully dropped his parcel in front of the Crown Vic. Yusef fingered the trigger button on the remote control as he watched the traffic and the second bomber. All was proceeding well until it occurred to the first bomber that he might be expendable now that his assignment was completed. This moment of clarity induced him to break into a run to escape the expected blast. Had he not also covered his head, the Marine driving the Crown Vic might not have panicked. As it was, he immediately stomped on the accelerator in an attempt to break free of the traffic. The second bomber froze about fifteen feet away from his target. The diplomatic car was smashing through the smaller vehicles towards the sidewalk, passing over the first bomb. A white Toyota Corolla followed it until it could make no further headway. The Toyota's gas tank was now over the first bomb. Then a large American in uniform began to exit the passenger side of the Toyota. He would be in position to intercept the second bomber.

Unsure what to do in this changed environment, the second bomber looked at Yusef for guidance. Seeing Yusef preparing to press the remote control provided all the guidance he needed. He threw his parcel at the Crown Vic and ran the other way. Yusef pressed the remote control as the second bomb hit the pavement behind the Crown Vic. The Corolla was launched into the air almost ten feet by the combined blasts. Any threat from its occupants was instantly removed in a ball of fire. The force of the first bomb blew the Crown Vic forward into the sea of smaller vehicles. Its warranty expired in a steaming mass of crumpled hood, but the cabin was intact. "More explosives next time," Yusef muttered to himself.

Then Yusef ran through the traffic towards the disabled vehicle, blowing madly on his whistle. He wanted to see if the attack had been successful. He let the remote control fall among the cars. His knowledge that the explosions were over gave him an advantage. He was the first to reach the diplomatic car. To his dismay, the occupants appeared to be alive. The driver was bleeding, but would probably recover. Although dazed, the passengers did not seem to be seriously injured. Yusef knocked on the rear window, disappointed to find it intact. A man and a woman looked back at him uncertainly. Winging it, he pointed to his badge. The woman tried to roll down the window, but it wouldn't budge. Yusef forced the rear passenger door open and extended his hand. "You must leave. Now!" he said in Arabic.

The driver shouted to his passengers in English "Go with him. I'm stuck." When they hesitated, he added "Get out of here!"

Two minutes later, Yusef and his two American passengers were bouncing through the Arab Quarter in the utility truck. Yusef was trying to figure out what to do next.

"Take us to the United States Embassy," the President requested.

Yusef recognized enough of the words to respond. "*La!*"

Meghan shook her head to indicate that he had said "no."

Then she had an idea. "An-cay ou-yay eak-spay ig-pay atin-lay?" Meghan whispered to the President.

He grimaced, then whispered back "Es-yay."

In rusty pig latin she told him not to speak English because their driver might know enough English to figure out what they were talking about. She also advised him never to disclose that either of them spoke anything except English. He nodded to indicate that he understood.

Listening to this strange language had agitated Yusef, who had come to realize a number of important facts. He was unarmed. He was outnumbered. He couldn't leave Jerusalem because he'd be stopped at a checkpoint. He was in over his head. The woman was attractive. The Israeli police were looking for him. Time was running out fast. Immortality may yet lay within his grasp. He was in way over his head. Yusef's cranium buzzed.

He prayed silently.

Then he called his brother Abdul on his cell phone. Abdul had fought the Americans in Iraq for *Al Qaeda* until his right hand was shot off in Fallujah. He'd been given emergency treatment which consisted of two people holding him down while a third held his stump in burning coals. Then he'd been sent home, where many people thought his hand had been removed as punishment for thievery in accordance with the *Sharia*. He traced all of these indignities back to the American infidels who had the bad manners to shoot back --- with accuracy. Yes, Abdul would postpone all other recreation to help his brother deal with these hated Americans.

As they wandered through the maze of the Arab Quarter, his passengers began to doubt the nature of their salvation from the ambush. The President had suffered a concussion and was now bleeding from his left ear. "Hospital!" shouted Meghan, hoping to get anywhere that was safe.

"Hospital?" Yusef recognized this word. "*La!*"

"Yes, hospital," Meghan replied eagerly, pretending not to understand that he had said "no!" in Arabic. "Doctor!" she shouted. pointing to the blood trickling down the President's neck.

"*La!*" Yusef shouted back at her, as he turned a corner with too much speed. The truck skidded into a building. He had to back up to regain the narrow alley. She was telling the President to jump out at the next opportunity when the pick-up truck came to a screeching halt in front of a man with an AK-47 assault rifle. It was immediately pointed at the President's head. The man was Abdul. There would be no escape from the truck.

"Welcome, infidels," Abdul said with a grin. He stood before a low concrete block structure with a single wooden door that had once been painted blue.

"Take them inside," barked Yusef as he tried to slow his heartbeat.

"To hear is to obey," replied Abdul with sarcasm. This was Yusef's operation, but Abdul had granted himself broad veto powers.

Once inside the rude dwelling, the diplomats were bound hand and feet with some expertise. Abdul found some filthy rags in the pickup truck to use for gags, but they smelled so strongly of motor oil that Yusef feared they might injure the captives. So Meghan and the President were advised by gestures that these gags would be applied if they were needed. Then they were left in a small room with no window.

Abdul instructed Yusef on the use the AK-47, an ingenious killing device that is simple to operate. Then he left to find duct tape and a video camera. The duct tape would demonstrate technical sophistication. The video camera was for filming the death of the infidels.

Yusef studied his captive's passports. He knew what irregularities to look for, but found none. Nor had he expected to find any. They were clearly what he had been told to expect: low-level diplomats. But still American diplomats.

In the meantime, the driver of the Crown Victoria had been dragged from his car in the mistaken belief that he was responsible for the wreckage. He was roughed up by the crowd just enough to push one of his broken ribs through his lung. They stopped pummeling him when blood began to spurt from his mouth. As soon as his attackers dispersed, some teenagers began to jump up and down on him like he was a bull being sacrificed for a festival.

He had no last thoughts, just a dream of pain.

CHAPTER 24

Camp David, Maryland
Thursday, January 24, 4:53 AM EST

The Vice President picked up the telephone on the second ring. His reflexes were that good even in a strange setting. If bad news travels fast, then terrible news is supersonic. Major Fox was on the phone. He omitted the greeting. "They never made it to Bethlehem, Marco."

"What?"

"Just listen, *amigo*. They were stuck in traffic in East Jerusalem when at least two bombs exploded near them. They were probably the target, but that's not confirmed yet. Their driver tried to get the car out of there, but was unsuccessful. He's dead. So is their Marine escort. Matt and Meghan escaped on foot with someone believed to be an Arab. He was wearing a uniform which might be from the local power company. Several witnesses reported that he was blowing a police whistle. They vanished. Some witnesses say they drove away in a white pick-up truck, which doesn't narrow the field all that much. Mossad is involved. We'll probably know more soon."

"Does the press have it?"

"Nothing on the news about it yet, but that will change. We have to hope that no one got a picture."

"Do the Israelis know who they're looking for?"

"Not yet. Do we tell 'em?"

"Depends. Will it help?"

"As I understand it, the full resources of the State of Israel are already involved."

"Then let's wait a while. Any ideas?"

"About the only thing you can do up there is to be seen in public. Is there anyone you owe an exclusive interview to?"

"You mean the kind where I'm seen leaving the Aspen Lodge with the President waving good-bye and my wife shows up at the end for a minute?"

"Hmmm. That should do it."

"I'll set it up for this afternoon. Keep me posted."

"As soon as it comes in, you'll know."

"Thanks, Zorro."

"It's too soon to worry. They may show up any minute."

"They're both survivors."

Marco terminated the call, then made another call before announcing "Meghan, we're expected at the lodge."

"I'll be ready in a moment."

"We need to talk first."

CHAPTER 25

Jerusalem, Israel
Thursday, January 24, 10:57 Bravo (local)

The discussion became heated. Meghan heard most of it. Their captors were clearly not aware of their true identities.

"Didn't you plan to kill them both?" Abdul asked.

"That was the original plan," Yusef admitted.

"What has changed?"

"A bomb does not discriminate. To kill one you must also kill others. This is different. We must select each one we intend to kill."

Abdul was impressed by the truth of his brother's observation, but continued. "So we select them both."

"But the Koran does not teach us to select women to be killed. She is not a soldier." Yusef did not want to kill the woman, although he had considered ravishing her.

"She is an American! She works for the government!"

Yusef tried a different approach. "Never have you seen a woman captive being executed on *Al-Jazeera*. We want to show the world that we will kill our enemies. For that we choose a man!"

"God bless male chauvinism," Meghan said to herself.

Abdul took a moment to review in his mind the killings

that had aired on Arab television. His brother was right. "Agreed. We behead the man and then shoot the woman. We can record her death separately."

"All I have agreed to, my brother, is that we behead the man on camera. We may find another use for the woman." Yusef attempted to hide his desperation to have the attractive American woman.

Abdul dismissed further discussion of her. "Let's not waste time on her now, then. We can decide her fate later. We must prepare for the execution of the American man."

With the woman safe for now, Yusef was eager to proceed. "We need a sword! And a block to put his neck on."

"The others just used knives," Abdul reminded him.

"Knives are tools. Women use knives in kitchens. Swords are weapons. Soldiers use weapons. We will surpass the others!"

Practical person though he was, Abdul found it impossible to argue with that. "The relics dealer, Usama, has one in his shop. I will obtain it." With that he left.

Yusef called a local radio station to announce that two American diplomats had been captured in Jerusalem by the Defenders of the Sacred Faith. He had been waiting years to use that name. He disconnected quickly to avoid any possibility of a trace. Caller I.D. was not available in the Arab Quarter.

CHAPTER 26

Camp David, Maryland
Thursday, January 24, 6:13 AM EST

The voice of Major Fox delivered the news he had been dreading. "Some outfit called the Defenders of the Sacred Faith has reported holding two American diplomats captive. No one knows who these clowns are. It's a new name. The good news is that the captives seem to be alive."

"They don't know who they've got!"

"You'd think they'd mention it," the Major agreed.

"I've got to have the President issue a statement right away."

"Good idea."

"Anything else?"

"East Jerusalem Electric can't account for one of its vehicles. Who knows where that may lead."

"Stay on it."

"I will. By the way, I saw you on television this morning, leaving the Aspen Lodge with your missus."

"Network?"

"Fox and CNN, maybe others. Not exactly my department, but I thought you'd want to know. The networks should have it for their morning news."

When he disconnected, Marco announced "Honey, we're going out."

The agent who was posing as his wife put down her book and asked "Kidnapped?"

He thought a moment about whether he should tell her, then decided that the Secret Service would soon know anyway. "Allegedly, but the fake passports seem to be working."

"Maybe we can ransom them, do a prisoner exchange. Who has them?" Agent Meghan was putting herself in the loop.

"Could be a problem. The people holding them are off the radar."

"Use the media to contact them, then."

Marco considered the situation. Agent Meghan was well trained and perceptive. She would become bored if she did not have an active role. Her continuing cooperation was critical. She was already involved anyway. "I want you to help draft the President's statement."

"Let's do it." She put on her overcoat and strode to the front door.

"Sometimes you are so much like Meghan it amazes me."

"I'll take that as a compliment. But we're still sleeping in separate bedrooms, cowboy."

"That's what she would have said. You're not her long-lost twin sister, are you?"

"The evil twin the family never mentions?"

"That would be interesting...."

"Get over it."

"No," he said gravely. "We may have to get used to it."

That hit home. "This assignment is scheduled to end in a few days when your wife returns. What if she doesn't return?"

"Don't go there."

CHAPTER 27

Jerusalem, Israel
Thursday, January 24, 11:08 Bravo (local)

Meghan had related the overheard conversation between their captors to the President. They silently agreed that he was doomed unless the Mounties arrived unexpectedly. Her future was less specific, but by no means promising. Knowing that you have nothing to lose inspires boldness.

"I'm going to talk to him in Arabic," Meghan announced in a whisper.

"What will you say?"

"I'm going to wing it, I'm afraid. Feminine wiles may come into play."

"You're going to stick with the passport identities?"

"Absolutely. That's about all we have going for us."

"Go for it," the President whispered. "If you can save yourself, do it!"

Yusef couldn't believe his ears. The American woman was calling to him in Arabic. "*Minfadlek!* Please!"

Curiosity and desire overcame his fears. He opened the door and approached her.

"*Maya!* Water!" she pleaded.

He nodded and left, but returned with a glass jar of

brownish water. Grateful that she had been taking Bactrim as a prophylaxis, she eagerly sipped the fluid from the glass he held for her. Suddenly she fell forward into his arms as though in a faint. This caused him to drop the glass, spilling water all over her. As he checked her vital signs, she opened her eyes and smiled at him sweetly. Yusef had taken the bait. It was time to set the hook.

In Arabic, she requested that she be untied so she could remove her wet clothing. While Yusef worked at the knots his brother had tied, she explained that she was just a clerk who had been sent to help in place of a diplomat who had influenza. She had been selected, she told him, because her Lebanese step-father had taught her to speak Arabic. She was not, she pointed out, a career diplomat. She had merely been placed with the State Department by an employment agency to do filing. The clear implication was that there was no reason to harm her. Then she began to sob softly. Yusef would spare her if he could. They both knew it. She felt her wrists freed from the rope.

Meghan also knew she should say nothing to save the life of the President. To make an attempt would merely jeopardize her own reprieve. Maybe an opportunity would arise later.

Now her ankles had been untied. Yusef was looking at her expectantly. The President had question marks in his eyes. "Showtime," she announced in English to no one in particular. Turning to the President, she explained "Mr. Maarten, I asked him to untie me so I could remove my wet clothes. Kindly look the other way."

Meghan proceeded to unfasten her slacks and drop them to the floor, quickly adjusting her blouse to cover her thighs.

Then she bent over to remove her shoes. Yusef tried to watch the removal of her footwear, but his eyes succumbed to his divided agenda and drifted up her legs momentarily. That was enough. She pretended to trip over her pant leg and fell forward on Yusef with a shoe in one hand. If it had been a high-heeled shoe, it might have worked. As it was, the soft sole of the running shoe merely produced a stinging sensation as it collided with Yusef's left ear. It also deafened him on one side for several hours.

Yusef put his hands on her throat, but did not squeeze. She went limp and began apologizing for her clumsiness, inquiring whether he had been injured. Yusef was confused and suspicious, but she thought she could pass it off as an accident. She asked him to pull off the slacks. If that didn't distract him, there was always the blouse.

Yusef removed his hands from her neck and used them to pull her slacks over her feet. Her eyes searched the room in vain for a weapon.

Then Yusef left the room without a word, locking the door behind him. He took the slacks. Perhaps he felt he'd earned them.

Meghan loosened the President's bindings; so that he could escape if the opportunity arose.

Then she knocked softly on the door to their cell. Yusef opened it warily and admitted himself after she moved to the far wall. Then he locked it again. She knew this might be her last chance to regain her freedom. She spoke softly with her eyes lowered as a sign of subservience. "*Shucran.* Thank you."

"*Afwan,*" Yusef replied, saying she was welcome because he could think of nothing else to say. He had been awkward around women his entire life. Today would not be any different.

She continued in Arabic. "We are not important people. We mean you no harm. We are here to contact the representatives of the Palestinian people on behalf of our new President--- just to show his desire to continue the peace process."

"There is no peace, only talk," Yusef interrupted.

"Our new President intends to change that."

"We will speak no more of politics."

"Whether you believe there can be change or not, please understand that we were sent here to deliver that message. Nothing more."

Yusef stared at her impassively. She had to change her approach.

"Our government may be willing to exchange us for someone it holds...," she suggested.

"Your government does not bargain with terrorists," he pointed out sullenly.

"But it does reward those who rescue captives. That's what you did." To herself she added "That's putting a spin on it! God bless poly sci."

Yusef suddenly realized that they did not know that he was responsible for the bombs. Could he recast himself as a hero at this late date? Could he behead the man and still be a hero for saving the woman? Even after the kidnapping had been announced? He gazed at her exposed long legs. His mind went into deep boggle mode. Yusef fled the room.

Once the door was locked again, Yusef prayed. If this continued much longer, he noted wryly, he would become devout. Nevertheless, the assurance that Allah would provide restored his calm. That led to the belief that it might be possible to spare the woman from his bloodthirsty brother without losing face. She had provided the seed by suggesting he could profit from her release.

The attractive wife of the Vice President of the United States had unwittingly turned herself into a commodity.

CHAPTER 28

Jerusalem, Israel
Thursday, January 24, 12:48 Bravo (local)

Abdul returned, brandishing the sword triumphantly in his remaining hand. It was truly a thing of beauty, with Koranic verses inscribed into its curved, gleaming blade. Yusef had been right. This would impress the infidels more than any mere knife. After swinging it around his head a few times and taking some practice swings at an imaginary chopping block, he presented it to Yusef for inspection.

"Never have I seen such a magnificent instrument!" he exclaimed. "We must be sure to get a close-up of it before the beheading."

"And afterward," Abdul added. "Oh, and we are in the news!"

"Us?" Yusef was not sure this was good.

"The Defenders of the Sacred Faith. The President of the United States has issued a proclamation condemning the bombings and the kidnapping of its citizens. He said that it would be in the best interests of the captors to free the diplomats; so the Palestinian statehood negotiations could continue." He spat on the floor. "What negotiations? We shall kill them both!"

Yusef smiled at his brother and said "No. We will kill the man, but I have another idea for the woman."

Abdul started to protest, but he noticed that his brother had a confidence which he'd not seen earlier. He decided to listen.

"I've called Hassim," he explained. "He will know how to handle the matter."

Abdul grinned. Not for the first time that day, Abdul was impressed by his older brother's ability to adapt to a changing situation. Abdul had been the first bomber on the road to Bethlehem.

Yusef confidently moved to the next subject. "What about the video camera?"

"I shall obtain it now. We need to finish this business before the police find us." Then he added "Do you trust Hassim?"

"Hassim is a jackal, but he is our jackal."

"Exactly. Don't shake his hand," Abdul warned, displaying his stump by way of illustration. Then he left.

Yusef had seen this display before, but it still unnerved him.

CHAPTER 29

Camp David, Maryland
Thursday, January 24, 7:05 AM EST

The coffee was hot and strong, but the conversation had ebbed. It was Agent Meghan who broke the silence in Aspen Lodge. "Let's ransom them."

"You know we don't negotiate with terrorists," replied Marco.

The actor who was playing the role of President nodded in agreement, but he said nothing. His was a non-speaking role.

"In Iraq we offered rewards for information," she countered.

"That's already being done."

She returned to thought. Then "We don't know that the bombers and the kidnappers are connected, right?"

"Right. Where is this leading?"

"What if the kidnappers actually rescued the President and your wife from the car after the bombing? Wouldn't that qualify for a reward?"

"Until they announced the kidnapping."

"But maybe they didn't. That's my point. There is always some group that claims credit for these acts. What if it's not the same people who are holding them?" Then she drove it home.

"What if the kidnappers are waiting until it's safe to free them?"

She had him. "Even if that weren't true, it could work...."

"Then how do we offer the reward?"

Marco looked at Meghan's substitute with admiration. Neither could have known that this was the very path Meghan had just trod six time zones to the East.

"Excuse me." The actor raised his hand timidly, as if asking permission to address his grade school teacher. They looked at him expectantly. Thus encouraged, he proceeded. "Lie." Neither reacted, so he explained. "Create a deception with which to deliver your message. That's what theater is." Then he fell silent, as if he might never speak again.

She picked up the ball and ran with it. "He's right! We announce that we have received word that the captive diplomats have been rescued and that the rescuers are to be rewarded without revealing their identities."

"In order to protect them," Marco added.

"As they requested," she confirmed.

CHAPTER 30

Jerusalem, Israel
Thursday, January 24, 13:38 Bravo (local)

Hassim rapped once, then entered unbidden. He was always welcome. He was the consummate middle man, who brought everyone what he needed, and kept plenty for himself in the bargain. Yusef looked up expectantly.

"*Salaam, effendi*," Hassim greeted him.

"May Allah be with you."

"Where is the woman?"

"I will bring her." Yusef slid into the adjoining room without fully opening the door. To Meghan he hissed "If you mention your companion or your employment, I will be unable to save you."

Meghan resolved to hold her tongue --- to the extent possible for her. She was pushed by Yusef to about six feet from the strange man. From this distance they appraised each other. He was tall, thin and well dressed in a black blazer over a white shirt and light khaki trousers. He had a meticulously trimmed beard. His eyes were sharp and piercing. His fingernails were manicured. He couldn't have been much more than thirty years old. "An Arab preppie," Meghan thought. She took him to be a trader, or an arranger. This trader saw an attractive Caucasian woman with smooth skin, wearing only a blouse. He liked what he saw. He smiled at her. She did not smile back.

"Leave us!" he ordered Yusef, who looked at the front door before deciding to join the other captive. He was sure that Hassim had not seen the American man. He wished to keep it that way.

In British-accented English, Hassim addressed Meghan. "Just listen for now, Miss Hill. My name is unimportant, but it is Hassim. I represent a Palestinian relief organization. You are a lower level American diplomat who has been caught in a snare intended for other prey. Through no fault of your own, you have created a deadly dilemma for poor Yusef. He tells me that you were attacked in your car and that you saved you from the attackers. It may not have been that dramatic. Palestinians exaggerate." Hassim shrugged at this. The gesture struck her as rather French. She filed this information away as he continued. "There is a saying that danger invites rescue...."

"Aha!" she thought. "It's not a saying, it's a legal doctrine." Another tidbit filed away. She was an active listener.

"So, when poor Yusef observed your situation, he sprang into action without a thought for himself. Or so he would have me believe." He paused to make sure she knew that he might not be buying Yusef's version of the facts. "Whatever his motives, his actions put him in danger from the attackers. When he realized his situation, he knew that your attackers would kill him to get to you. He also realized that you might be killed if he simply released you. So he brought you to these humble surroundings whilst he sorted matters out. Unable to resolve matters satisfactorily himself, he called upon our organization to assist in your return. It was a wise move --- and beneficial to you." He stopped speaking.

"The facts as you have related them are correct, except that I am not a diplomat. I am a clerk who happens to work at the present time for the State Department. I was a last-minute replacement for someone more qualified and informed than I."

Hassim raised an eyebrow. "You would have me believe that you are a temp?"

"No. But neither am I a career government employee. I was placed by an employment agency. I have since come to regret that."

"That I truly believe."

"I am grateful to Mr. Yusef and to your organization. I would like to go home."

"We will arrange that for you. However, we are a bureaucracy. It will not be instantaneous." He glanced around the room. "You will have better accommodations during the process. Please bear with us whilst we work out the arrangements."

"I understand. Remember, I work for a bureaucracy myself."

"That brings up a point I planned to raise later. It is crucial to the effectiveness of our organization in this type of matter that our participation remain unknown. If anyone learns of our activities in this field, we will no longer be able to engage in them. You must never disclose anything that has happened to you today, to anyone."

"That makes sense," she lied. "When do we leave?"

"There is one more bit of bureaucracy to be satisfied before we go. Under ideal circumstances, I would be accompanied by a woman from the organization...."

She became wary. What was the price of freedom? "But what?"

He embodied embarrassment. "We must examine you for injuries before taking custody."

"Or you don't get your deposit back?" The sarcasm slipped out.

A smile flickered and died. "Something like that," he muttered. He stared at her blouse.

"Then we leave?"

"Yes. Then we leave."

Meghan sighed as she began to unbutton her blouse. It was all she could do to avoid glaring at him as she disrobed, but she was playing the role of Erin Hill.

The examination was cursory and did not involve removal of her undergarments. Thankfully, there was no groping. She had apparently passed muster, for she now sat in a nearly new black Nissan Maxima on her way to freedom. She even had her passport and her blouse. Yusef apparently couldn't bring himself to part with her slacks. Maybe they were a trophy. Meghan didn't need them now. She was wearing a grey *burqa* which was a great deal more than mere modesty required. So was the blindfold.

In about an hour they passed through the gates of an old rural mansion. "We work from a private residence to avoid inquiry. We are an unofficial organization. It works best in this part of the world." Meghan doubted him, but felt that she had improved her lot. After all, Yusef's brother had been intent upon killing her. And Yusef.... She didn't want to dwell on what he wanted to do to her.

The car stopped and the door opened. Her blindfold was removed. Looking down, away from the light until her eyes adjusted, the first thing she noticed was the expensive tassel loafers worn by her captor. He was obviously in a different class of person than her previous captors. The mere thought that she was adjusting to think this way amused her; yet she seized upon this faint ray of hope like a thirsty man on a stein of cold beer.

They were let out before a broad stone staircase which led to a porch that ran the length of the front of the building. Across that was a grand front door, through which they passed at the invitation of the smiling man who had opened it --- the same man who then grabbed her from behind, pinning her arms to her sides. He was still smiling.

Another man handed Hassim a syringe, which he promptly plunged through the fabric and emptied into her bicep.

CHAPTER 31

Camp David, Maryland
Thursday, January 24, 8:25 AM EST

"Turn on the news, now!" That was all Major Fox had said. Actually, CNN had been running in the Aspen Lodge all morning, with the volume turned down. Marco grabbed the remote and raised it high. Agent Meghan and the other actor promptly turned their attention to the monitor.

"The Arab television network *Al-Jazeera* has just announced that one of the U.S. diplomats kidnapped yesterday has been executed. The following footage has been provided by *Al-Jazeera* and has been running for about fifteen minutes in a continuous loop. We will come in at the beginning and run it twice at this time. Because of specifications for broadcast television vary in different regions of the world, the picture you see will be grainy. You will not be able to improve it by adjusting your set. As soon as we can, we will provide you with an enhanced picture. The commentary portion has been translated from the Arabic. Any other sounds you may hear are original. We warn you that the raw footage you are about to view is shockingly violent and not suitable for children. We will have an edited version later. This is your opportunity to change channels or leave the room."

There was a pause of some ten seconds before the anchorperson was replaced by a picture of three men standing next to each other in a small, plain room. The middle of the three had a cloth bag over his head and appeared to have his hands bound behind his back. The other two men made no effort to conceal their faces. It soon became clear that the camera was mounted, for it did not move.

An unimpressive young man limped forward from camera left and produced a United States passport, which he opened to display the identity of Per Maarten. According to the commentary, the same man proclaimed that he was the Chairman of the Supreme Council of the Defenders of the Sacred Faith. The other unassuming Arab man was then introduced as the Official Executioner of the Defenders of the Sacred Faith. His right hand was missing.

He recognized it as an unworthy thought, but Marco briefly wondered "Where's Curly?"

As he discarded the question, the Official Executioner brought a magnificent ceremonial sword forward for display. He held it in his left hand and twisted it for the camera to examine. Loathsome as the situation was, every man watching could not resist admiring the craftsmanship of the weapon. Even before the sword and its bearer returned to their places at the right field of the camera, the self-styled Chairman continued.

According to the commentary he said "Per Maarten is an agent of the United States of America and an enemy of Islam. He was captured while on a mission to undermine the Palestinian government. He has been prevented from achieving this objective by the swift action of the Defenders of the Sacred

Faith. Now his threat to Islam will be removed forever." The narration had been halting and broken, as if the speaker were reciting memorized lines. Marco had determined that it was not the fault of the commentator.

With a look of relief at having gotten his lines out straight, the Chairman returned to his original place and removed the cloth sack from the head of the captive. It was Matthew Chambers, the President of the United States of America. Even with the grainy picture, it was Matt. The enhanced pictures would make it obvious later. Of course, viewers of *Al Jazeera* were already seeing a clear picture. Marco was thinking of ways to counter these images when the Official Executioner raised his sword.

"*Allahu akbar!*" the Official Executioner screamed as he swung the sword with his left hand. The captive had just enough time to duck, but he remained rigid. Marco thought he saw him flinch before the blade reached his throat. The sword penetrated to the spine. Blood erupted from the wound. The captive was knocked backward by the blow. The efforts of Chairman Yusef were insufficient to prevent the captive from crumbling to the floor --- out of camera range. The Chairman went down with him. Official Executioner Abdul, covered in his victim's blood stepped forward again to display the sword. Chairman Yusef, unable to lift the inert body of the captive, scrambled to his feet with the intention of altering the camera angle. Abdul continued to shout "*Allahu akbar!*" in the general direction of the video camera. After a few jerky adjustments, the camera focused again on the captive. Abdul took this opportunity to bend his victim's head back to demonstrate that it had been all but severed in a single blow. He was proud of his work and looked forward to a new career of ever more beheadings. "*Allahu akbar!*"

The screen went dark, then started to replay the scene. Marco turned the television off. No one complained.

To Agent Meghan he said "Start drafting a response. Be sure to include that, despite our disappointment, we are still expecting the release of the woman captive." Marco picked up the telephone receiver. "Get me the Chief Justice of the Supreme Court."

CHAPTER 32

The West Bank, Palestine
Thursday, January 24, 15:14 Bravo (local)

Meghan awoke slowly. She was lying on her face in some furniture contraption. After some thought, she guessed it might be a massage chair folded flat. That, she reflected, wouldn't be any stranger than what had already happened to her. She took inventory. Her hands were tied to the frame of the chair. Her back was bare and hurt like Hell. Her arm was sore from the injection. She still wore her panties, which she considered to be a favorable situation. Her head throbbed. She didn't know what fate awaited her. Nothing was beyond belief anymore. "Other than that, it's a wonderful day in the neighborhood," she mumbled to herself. Then she remembered. "Oh yeah, what is the neighborhood?" she asked herself. She heard someone moving behind her, leaving the room.

In a few minutes, another person entered. "I trust you had a pleasant rest," Hassim said in a disinterested manner.

"What was that?" she asked.

"Oh. A tranquilizer."

"Works fast."

"It's for horses," he explained.

"Why does my back hurt?"

"Does it hurt?"

"I wouldn't have asked if it didn't."

"No. I guess not." He clearly was not interested in her questions. "Anything else?"

"Where's Mr. Maarten?"

"According to the television, he's dead," he advised with the same degree of emotion as if telling her the time of day. "I'm not political. I'm a businessman, a broker of commodities."

Meghan groaned.

"Were you close?"

"I only met him a few days ago. I don't normally work in his department."

"Just pretend you never met, then."

"Can I turn over? This position is very uncomfortable after a while."

"'Afraid not. Might spoil the artwork. One hour more."

She wasn't sure she had heard him correctly. Her head was still a bit foggy. "Artwork?"

"Actually, Islam doesn't hold art in the same esteem as Christianity...."

"Just tell me," she moaned.

"It's writing. Calligraphy. Arabic is so poignant when rendered in calligraphy. Not like Western alphabets. Because your skin is so light, the artist was able to use a complete palette. It's really quite striking. I'll have someone take a digital photo for you."

"Thank you," she said with exasperation. "Until that sublime moment arrives, could you please tell me what it says?"

"The message is always the same. It's the *Takbir*: *Allahu akbar min kulli shay*. It means Allah is greater than everything.

The Sheik never deviates."

"What sheik?" she shouted.

"You should watch your tongue. If it brings more displeasure than pleasure to him, the Sheik will cut it out. I've seen him do it. He's really quite proficient at it."

"Every man needs a hobby, I guess."

Hassim laughed. "Now that's witty. If you play your cards right, you can keep your tongue. Maybe even become a favored concubine."

"Now there's the future every girl dreams about...."

"The Sheik speaks English, by the way. You'll get on famously with him. He attended Columbia."

Although she found it incredible, that particular revelation almost put her over the edge. He might recognize her. He might have a yearbook with her picture. She needed to respond before Hassim became curious. "The university or the motion picture studio?"

"Why? Do you want to be a movie star?"

"It crossed my mind."

"A terrible waste it would be. I fear you would not enjoy speaking lines written by others."

"You've got me," she admitted.

"Yes, but the question is what do I do with you?"

"Did the Sheik's check bounce?" she asked with mock hopefulness.

"No. It never does."

"It's probably a wire transfer," Meghan probed.

"That's how commerce is conducted now," he admitted.

"What's he paying you?"

"Significantly more than you're worth, I'm afraid."

"I had a student loan. That means I'm worth something," she volunteered to keep the conversation alive.

"One hundred thousand euros."

"Is that all?" she replied with indignation.

"Concubines are depreciating assets. It affects the price, but it makes for repeat business."

Once you accepted the notion that women were commodities, he made sense. She shook her head to clear it. It banged against the padded sides of the massage chair. That seemed to help. "I can raise that."

"Nice try, but ransom is a lot riskier than a straight sale to an established customer."

"I see what you mean."

"I don't fancy spending the prime of my life in a prison."

"Don't see why that should happen. The money gets sent to a numbered account at a small bank in the Caribbean. You've probably got that set up already."

"Are you a spy?"

"No. I just read too many novels."

"It's still riskier," he reiterated without admitting anything.

"Then suppose I double it?"

She had his attention. "You can raise two hundred thousand euros? That's nearly three hundred thousand dollars."

"I think I can. Might take a week. What have you got to lose?"

"You've got three days."

"Three business days," she countered.

"Of course. And one telephone call."

"That's going to be some call."

"It had better be," he agreed.

"When do we start?"

"When the ink dries." As he walked away, he casually added "By the way, your hair is blonde now. The Sheik likes blondes."

"Oh no," she thought. "I'm sure to be recognized now."

CHAPTER 33

Camp David, Maryland
Thursday, January 24, 11:44 AM EST

"Tell me what you need. I've played Hamlet. I can do a convincing death scene, but I can't lie in state for three days." The actor was anticipating his final scene. "I could use the practice."

Agent Meghan inquired. "For your next gig, or are you planning to die soon?"

The actor sighed. "A bit of both, I guess. I have an inoperable tumor, but the timeline is unpredictable. Three more years tops is what they tell me. But nobody really knows."

She looked him squarely in the eyes. "I'm sorry to hear that. Let's hope they're wrong."

"I shouldn't have mentioned it. Poor choice for an actor."

"Most actors get to go home every night," she pointed out. "This must be exhausting for you."

"Well, I don't have to get into character before each performance. But after a while, I relax and it becomes harder to suppress my own life."

Acting President Marco Redondo spoke. "I'm thinking a massive heart attack, right after you return to the White House."

"Why not here. It's less risky," observed Agent Meghan.

"That's why. If the President isn't seen returning to the White House after the execution, it will tie the two events together. That plus the enhanced video of the victim will create too much doubt."

"And I have to accompany you back?"

"As my wife, until Meghan returns."

"I should get a promotion."

"You have. You're now impersonating the acting First Lady."

"But nobody knows you're the acting President."

"You do. After all, it's your promotion."

"Politicians," she moaned.

"There's more. We can't go back to the Admiral's House."

Confused, she replied "I wasn't planning to...."

"The Admiral's House is the residence provided by the government for the Vice President and his family."

"Of course it is. I had thought I might return to my own lodgings some day."

"Not yet, agent. We need to invent a problem which would require my 'round-the-clock presence at the White House."

"But not mine," she protested. "Too risky."

"You're right. We'll both accompany the President here back to the White House. Then you'll return to the Admiral's House...."

"Because we didn't bring appropriate clothes for the White House...."

"And you're still settling in...."

"So it's a photo-op kiss on the cheek by the helipad and off I go in a limo," she finished. "I'll need a floor plan. You'll need something too."

"You can send over some clothes."

"I mean a plausible reason for staying at the White House."

"The President and I are still dealing with the West Bank events."

"Besides," she added, "the President has the flu."

"Hmmm. That could set him up for an unexpected death."

"Exactly."

From across the room, the actor coughed. Neither of them knew if it was intentional, but at that moment, Marco and the agent were sure it could work. "So what could go wrong?" She smiled as she uttered the jinx.

"You're not supposed to say that --- ever!" Then it hit him. "Paul! Meghan's father."

"You're right. Maybe I should contract the flu too...."

"Send him an e-mail. Tell him you think you have the 24-hour virus that's been going around...."

"And I plan to hibernate until it passes. He should keep his distance until then...."

"You'll contact him the next day, no matter what."

"Is that necessary?" she wondered.

"I'm afraid it is. He dotes on you."

"Gee. I've never been doted on."

"It probably looks better than it is." He cautioned.

"My love, I do believe you're a spoil sport."

CHAPTER 34

The West Bank, Palestine
Thursday, January 24, 17:51 Bravo (local)

Meghan had been released from the massage chair and permitted to shower. Dressed in a sweater and skirt, she sat in a magnificent bedroom awaiting Hassim. Her hair was wrapped in a towel, ostensibly because it was wet, but actually to hide it. When Hassim arrived, he appeared puzzled.

"Are you aware of any negotiations for your release?" he asked her without preamble.

"No. Are there any?"

"Your government issued a statement earlier claiming that you had been rescued and a reward was to be paid anonymously. That was before your companion was beheaded, of course."

"If you want the reward, I'll try to get it for you."

Hassim looked at her skeptically.

"Look, all I want is my life back. It wasn't much, but at least it was mine. I don't have any interest in bringing anyone to justice. All I've lost so far is a few days --- probably the most interesting days of my life. I have nothing to avenge. Hell, I'll probably be a hero! You can watch me on television describing my rescue by this Palestinian relief organization which prefers to remain anonymous."

"The same line I fed you?"

"Why not? It worked."

He considered this a moment. "It must be at least two hundred thousand euros," he said flatly.

"But you'll accept the equivalent in dollars?"

"Of course," he proclaimed magnanimously. "And make that a Muslim relief organization."

"Spread the good will around?" Meghan suggested.

"I may miss you, little temp," Hassim confessed. "You amuse me at times."

"But for two hundred thousand euros...."

"I can afford other amusements to distract me from your absence." he concluded. "Let's make that telephone call to freedom now."

He handed her a prepaid cell phone.

"Untraceable?"

"Absolutely. And after your call it will cease to exist."

"And it will work?"

"Digital auto-scan GSM, fourth generation," he bragged. "You won't have these in America for two more years."

"Can I speak in private?"

"Don't waste my time."

"What is the local code for international calls?"

Hassim told her and Meghan entered it, followed by 1, then a cell phone number with a Virginia area code. Paul Carnegie answered in three rings. "I'm listening." He didn't want people with the wrong number to know whom they'd reached.

"Daddy, don't say a word. Just listen. This is Erin, daddy.

I've been kidnapped. I'm being held for ransom in another country. They want 200,000 euros. If they don't get it by tomorrow, they will torture me. I know you don't have that kind of money, but talk to my boss at the State Department, Mr. Pecos. It's the same number as mine. I don't know the extension. Don't talk to anyone else. I know I'll be freed if you can do this. Here are the wiring instructions." She read from the paper Hassim handed her, then added "I won't be able to call you again until I'm free; so repeat the instructions to me now. I love you, daddy."

Hassim snatched the phone from her hand to listen to the confirmation of the instructions. Satisfied, he ended the call.

"Good luck, Miss Hill," he called as he left the room. He always had somewhere else more important to be.

"*In'shallah*," she whispered to herself.

An intelligent young man awaited Hassim in the hallway. Hassim handed him a miniature digital recorder. "Determine the number from the tones and tell me who answers that phone."

"To hear is to obey, master."

"And cut the crap, Khalid."

CHAPTER 35

The White House, Washington, D.C.
Thursday, January 24, 1:26 PM EST

The moment Marco stepped out onto the helipad, his cell phone went off. Since only half a dozen important people had this number, he reached for it. The display read "LAW," which was his abbreviation for his father-in-law. He sighed and stepped away.

"What the Hell's going on?" was the greeting. Marco couldn't blame him, but how had he found out?

"We need to talk, privately. Are you in town?"

"You bet!" Carnegie yelled.

"Meet me at the Admiral's House in thirty minutes. We have a lot to catch up on."

"I'll be there in twenty."

"I won't; so take your time. Observe the speed limit for a change."

Paul Carnegie disconnected.

Marco approached the actor President and Agent Meghan, who had lingered nearby, as if awaiting instructions.

"Change of plans. I have to go home. Meghan, let's escort the President to his quarters before we leave."

The three of them walked briskly through the bleak

winter afternoon toward the White House, apparently engaged in pleasant conversation. "Try not to start a thermonuclear war while I'm gone," Marco was saying to the actor.

"Not with this terrible flu," the actor said convincingly.

"You need to rest," added Agent Meghan.

CHAPTER 36

The Admiral's House, Washington, D.C.
Thursday, January 24, 2:03 PM EST

Paul Carnegie was pacing in the portico of the great house. He was relieved to see his daughter arrive with his son-in-law. However, relief turned to confusion when he approached her. "What?"

"Like my new look, daddy?" Agent Meghan tried gamely, but it was no use. A father knows his only daughter.

Marco quickly intervened, putting his arm around Carnegie as if slapping him on the back. He whispered "Lots to talk about. Play along."

As it became clear to him that the ransom call was probably genuine, Carnegie joined the charade. He gave Agent Meghan a fast hug and allowed himself to be led into the foyer, then up the stairs to the informal office where previous Vice Presidents had changed the course of history while working in their pajamas late into the night.

All three seated themselves. Marco summarized the plans for the visit to Bethlehem and the outcome so far, then asked Carnegie how he had found out.

"She called me on my cell phone. Just called me. Simple as that. Called me daddy and said she was my daughter Erin. It did sound like her, but you never can be sure with cell phones. Then she told me she'd been kidnapped and needed 200,000 euros. I thought it was a prank, or a hoax, but I kept listening. Then she said I should contact her boss, Mr. Pecos. That's when I knew it was her."

"She called herself Erin?" Marco asked.

"Yes."

"Erin was her undercover identity. That means they still don't know who she is. We've got a chance to save her as long as she's just Erin from the State Department."

Paul Carnegie brightened, then seemed to remember something. "I have wiring instructions." He pulled a folded sheet of paper from his breast shirt pocket and handed it to Marco. "Don't lose that. I haven't made a copy."

Marco went straight to the copier and made three copies. He handed one back to Carnegie, who folded it with care, and put one in the desk drawer. He obviously intended to keep the original with him. The third was for the wire department, he explained. "Let's go."

"Wait! Aren't we going to set up an exchange? What assurance do we have that they'll release her after we've sent the money?"

"None at all," said Marco, "but time is running against us. Once they find out her identity, it could be too late to ransom her. We have to do it now."

Carnegie nodded in agreement.

Marco wished he had some idea how to go about authorizing the wire transfer. He would have to find out.

"There is one thing I need to do first. It won't take long." Marco pressed the intercom button. "Send him in now."

Carnegie and Agent Meghan turned their eyes to the door. A moment later, the Chief Justice of the Supreme Court entered and introduced himself.

"I believe you specified quick and dirty...."

Marco blushed a bit. "Well, mostly quick, your Honor. We have a crisis right now. We can do it right next time."

"I understand." Then he swore in Marco Redondo as the President of the United States, but it was to remain a secret. It was a bit like boxing with one hand tied behind your back, Marco reflected. Maybe both hands.

Marco thanked him for his discretion, and walked him out the door. Ignoring the others, he called Major Fox to alert the wire room and locate a slush fund to deplete. "I'm going to the White House. You stay here and chat with your...." He'd almost said "your daughter."

Agent Meghan spoke for the first time. "It's probably best that we become acquainted, Mr. Carnegie."

"Yes. Maintain appearances. Be seen together." With that Marco left the room. Carnegie and his purported daughter sat silently until Agent Meghan finally broke the ice. "I'm not going to tell you my name. Just call me Meghan."

Paul Carnegie sighed deeply and looked into the intelligent eyes of the woman who was sitting where his daughter should be.

"Call me daddy from now on."

"Your voice sounds familiar."

"It should. You've heard it on television," he explained. "Political talk shows, not advertisements."

"You never pitched hemorrhoid treatments? I could have sworn...."

Carnegie smiled. "Keep it up. Now you sound like my daughter."

"Oh dear. She's a...."

"Regular smart ass is the term you're looking for. Accent on the smart."

"I should probably come out to visit, see where she grew up."

"Have to be the maid's night off, which is usually Friday. After you get settled in here, we'll set it up."

"Tomorrow's Friday. See if that works. I need to get up to speed fast."

"And I need to have a private talk with my son-in-law --- the sooner the better."

CHAPTER 37

The West Bank, Palestine
Thursday, January 24, 20:34 Bravo (local)

Something wasn't right. Hassim knew it, but it would not reveal itself to him. He had reviewed her passport many times. It was flawless. She had not deviated in her story. Her presence as a clerk in a low-level diplomatic mission did not raise any red flags. The story fit together. The problem was that she didn't fit the part all that well. "Why would such a remarkable woman be holding a clerical position?" he asked himself, not for the first time. She had explained that policy dictated that no new hires enter the Department above GS-9 grade. This was to learn the ropes--- a strange expression for a modern society.

Perhaps the United States was full of attractive, intelligent women who competed for such jobs. He doubted it. Maybe it was her attitude. She was so confident and unafraid. What could cause that? "She must be privileged!" he deduced aloud.

After knocking, Khalid entered. "I have traced the number."

He acknowledged Khalid's presence by asking "A wealthy man?"

"Paul Carnegie."

"Why is that name familiar?"

"Paul Carnegie was the campaign manager for Vice President Marco Redondo in the last election, sir."

"She called him daddy," Hassim mused aloud. "If true, she is wealthy and highly educated." A rage was building. "She is not a temporary government clerk! Do you have a photograph?"

"No, but I can certainly obtain a recent one in a few minutes," Khalid offered.

"Then do so." As Khalid approached the door, Hassim called to him. "A minute, young Khalid."

Khalid stopped and turned back to face Hassim.

"How can you be sure that you will obtain this photograph so quickly?"

"If she is the daughter of Paul Carnegie, then she is also the wife of the Vice President."

"Her real name?"

"It would be Meghan. Meghan Carnegie Redondo."

"Bring me photographs of her with her father and with her husband. At once!"

Khalid bowed slightly, then ran out the door to do his master's bidding. He knew he would be well rewarded for his efforts. The upward mobility of a computer geek in a primitive society was astounding. He was saving up for a BMW.

"What would cause one of the most important persons in America to come to Palestine disguised as a clerk?" Hassim wondered. Curiosity replaced his rage. He began to pace aimlessly.

CHAPTER 38

The White House, Washington, D.C.
Thursday, January 24, 2:46 PM EST

The wire transfer was initiated from a clandestine account maintained at a bank in Douglas, the quaint capital of the Isle of Man. It would arrive at the target bank in Dubai within minutes.

"Now what?" Marco said, with some relief.

Major Fox rubbed his chin, as though there was some stubble to be detected on his clean-shaven face. "Can we approach this as a military operation?"

"We can try. So far, we've just been reacting to events. What does the military do when it can't take control of the situation?"

There was a slight hesitation as the Major framed his response. "We create a situation we can control."

"Counter-attack?"

"Yes, but we're already trying to find a way to do that. However, a diversion might be helpful."

"Take the public's mind off the beheading...."

"And keep the kidnappers off balance, if we can."

"Tricky business. If we go in strong, we reveal her true value."

"I was thinking we should try something that would grab their attention without being tied directly to Meghan," Major Fox offered.

"Great! What's the plan?"

"Hadn't gotten that far yet, but it has occurred to me that Matt Chambers will be held responsible for anything that happens as long as he's supposed to be alive."

"He favored bold moves and freedom. For instance, he told me it was a travesty that the United States forbade its citizens to travel in certain countries."

"Let's give him a legacy then."

"I'll have a press release sent out to that effect immediately. We'll schedule a press conference to discuss it for later."

"A press conference that will never be held...." Major Fox stopped, lost in thought. "Then again, why not?"

Marco prepared to list the numerous obvious reasons why the actor could not give a press conference, but decided otherwise. "What's going on in that cranium of yours, Zorro?"

"We want to firmly establish that the President is still with us, right?"

Marco nodded.

"What if he schedules a press conference, outside, in the open, but never speaks?"

"But why doesn't he speak?"

Major Fox put his hands over his eyes and thought. After about a minute he said "Laryngitis. Remember, he's already supposed to have the flu."

"So he appears, but has someone else read the statement for him while he stands nearby. No questions, of course."

"He could walk up to the lectern, wave and step back." Marco could picture the actor in this part. "Have him shrug. Put a little humor into it. That's how Matt would have done it."

"Good. It will focus the public's attention on their living President."

"Who's about to succumb to complications of influenza."

"Then he dies in his sleep that night?" asked Major Fox.

"The sooner, the better. Every minute he plays the President is another risk of exposure."

"Is the President scheduled to be out of the White House in the next few days?"

"We canceled all appearances, citing the diplomats' abductions. It's probably better to do it at the White House. We'd have more control. We could bill it as a brief presidential announcement from the Rose Garden. In the meantime, I'll see that the press release is distributed."

"What about the President's physician? Is he going to insist on an autopsy?" the Major inquired. "He won't be too happy to have the President die on his watch."

"Who would he autopsy?"

"This scenario is so convincing that I forgot there won't be a real dead person. Maybe he wanted to be cremated...."

"That would certainly be a big logistical help. Maybe I can find out."

"Permission to discuss this with my staff?"

"You mean Yolanda?"

"That's my staff."

"If you think she can keep it secret, go ahead. She knows about the President already."

"I'll check with you later then, Mr. --- Vice President."

CHAPTER 39

The West Bank, Palestine
Thursday, January 24, 20:58 Bravo (local)

The door was opened from the outside. Meghan watched in silence as Hassim approached her. "Have the funds arrived already?"

"When they do, they will be insufficient."

"What? We had a deal."

"I made a bargain with Erin Hill," he replied gruffly. "Now I am negotiating with Meghan Redondo."

"What are you...." Before she could finish he placed a dagger on her throat.

"I don't have time for your denials. Neither do you. These are your choices. Delivery to *Al Qaeda*, where you will be humiliated and tortured, then exposed to the world as the wife of the Vice President, then publicly executed in a slow and photogenic manner --- perhaps impalement, which would provide hours of entertainment for *Al Jazeera*. When you become too weak to scream, they will play that martial music they're so fond of. Did you know that most victims survive several hours --- until the stake finally pierces the heart?"

She had been determined to be stoic, but that made her shudder involuntarily. She made no other response.

"You see, they will find out about you, just as I have. When they do, you need to be home in America. Otherwise, the brief remainder of your life will be devoted exclusively to excruciating pain." He paused to see if she understood. Despite her resolve, she had wrapped her arms around herself. It was an unconscious defensive posture. He had her attention.

Meghan nodded, eyes wide. "I can get more money."

"Ah. The American solution for everything. Unfortunately, I could never spend it. My failure to turn you over would be an act of suicide. Do you understand?"

She nodded again. "So?"

"I need full United States citizenship, with a passport, of course. There must be complete amnesty for whatever I may be accused of in relation to your abduction. I need safe passage, accompanied by you, to the United States. I must be received as the man who saved you and be rewarded for this heroic act."

The astonishment faded from her face quickly, as she realized his position. "How much reward?"

"I'm surprised at you, Meghan. I thought you knew me by now. I'm not cut out for an idle lifestyle. I wish to work."

"To work...."

"Yes. Your administration obviously needs an advisor who understands the people who inhabit this region. I was born in Marseilles, raised in France and Lebanon, attended the London School of Economics, speak three languages fluently, and am brilliant.

"You're too modest."

He ignored her. "I'm overqualified, but I'll take the position for a token $100,000 a year, guaranteed employment for one year. After that, I can be let go --- with a good reference, of course. I had planned to return to the West as soon as I had enough saved to live comfortably. This arrangement would permit me to advance my schedule."

"And you would never reveal what you know?"

"I don't want to die, Mrs. Redondo. Of course, I won't."

It was audacious, but made perfect sense from Hassim's perspective. "Hassim, if you apply that devious brain of yours on behalf of the United States, you could become invaluable."

"Thank you." He bowed. Then he handed her another disposable cell phone.

"But what about the 200,000 euros?" she asked.

"It was an expensive tattoo."

CHAPTER 40

The White House, Washington, D.C.
Thursday, January 24, 3:17 PM EST

The new ransom proposal was related to Marco by Paul Carnegie over a secure line from the Admiral's House. Carnegie was trying to make a case for accepting it, repeating Meghan's praise of her treatment by Hassim.

But Marco was miles ahead of him. "I wanted to get him out of the region anyway --- especially since he's discovered her identity. I certainly didn't expect him to demand to leave."

"He still doesn't know that she's now the wife of the new President," observed Carnegie.

"Let's keep it a surprise. In the meantime I'll have the CIA produce a passport for him at the Embassy in Tel Aviv. Did you remind her they'd need photos?"

"Didn't need to. He already has them."

"This Hassim sounds like an efficient individual."

"He could be a plant," Carnegie cautioned.

"Yes. We'll have to treat him as a potential spy. That could diminish the value of the advice he provides."

"What's the timetable?"

"I want them on a commercial flight to JFK tomorrow."

"Not Dulles?"

"Too obvious."

"Let me know when."

"I will, but you can't be there."

Paul Carnegie took a moment to digest that. "I guess I can wait a bit longer."

"Sorry, Paul."

"No. Don't be. I can see that my presence couldn't be explained. How do you plan to switch the agent with Meghan?"

"Can't be at the airport. We don't even know what she'll look like when she lands. She was a brunette when she left."

"And a member of the press could be there."

"We'll avoid any reporters, Paul."

"At some time you will have to account for this Erin Hill. Everyone will want to interview her."

"We'll have to provide a ringer if and when the time comes," Marco replied. He already had a candidate. "Paul, if you don't want me to ransom your daughter, just say so."

"I'm not trying to throw up road blocks. Just want to be prepared. Maybe you can have the Secret Service meet Erin Hill's plane on the runway, before it gets to the gate, and remove her."

"Spirit her away? Why would we do that?"

"Debriefing. The cover story could be that Erin Hill is not her real name. She's a CIA agent operating under cover."

"She'll never talk to the press then." Marco liked this.

"But she could write a book about her experiences later."

"Cement the whole episode in history as we want it to be presented."

"I think we're on to something, Marco."

"You're quite the father-in-law, Paul."

"I'll take that as a compliment, Mr. President."

"Shhhh. Not yet."

"By the way, you and Meghan are invited over tomorrow evening for dinner. I'll have Jeannie prepare something before she leaves."

"How will that look?"

"Since you're the Vice President and Meghan is my only daughter, I'd say it would look normal. It would also tend to confirm that Meghan is here."

"Reality got in the way of perception for a minute. You're right, Paul."

"And I'm still your political advisor. We have much to discuss."

CHAPTER 41

Tel Aviv, Israel
Friday, January 25, 8:30 Bravo (local)

The Marines from the Embassy detachment had met their car on the highway from Ramullah. One had taken Meghan aside and inquired about her health, offering to "beat the livin' daylights out of" her male companion if she requested. She had indicated that her health was fine and declined the tempting offer, citing a continuing need for his cooperation. Too bad they didn't have time to tattoo Hassim, though.

Hassim's new passport proclaimed him to be a naturalized citizen. According to the cover story, he was a native of Tikrit who had been fast-tracked for U.S. citizenship after leading the Marines to an *Al Qaeda* safe house. He was employed as a business consultant specializing in dealing with Arab customers.

At Ben Gurion International Airport, her lack of luggage presented no problem. Nobody noticed because Hassim had five suitcases. He obviously didn't intend to return to the Middle East.

So they sat in first class on British Air flight 1106, bound for New York with an "equipment change" at Heathrow. Normally the first class cabin was filled with tourists, since the businessmen preferred the El Al nonstop flight to New York. Today, the remainder of the first class compartment was empty, save for two large CIA agents sent to protect the released hostage. They had been instructed not to talk to Ms. Hill or her companion; so they sat in the next row on opposite sides of the single aisle to maximize their field of vision. After futile attempts at chatting up the flight attendants, the agents agreed to take turns dozing.

Meghan had insisted upon the right front aisle seat. In the window seat next to her, Hassim discussed his beloved France with Meghan, expressing his dream of living in a fine apartment in the *premiere arrondissement*, where the heartbeat of the city could be felt. Let those with inherited wealth have the *Avenue Foch*, with its fine residences, Mercedes-Benz automobiles and expensive *belles du nuit*. Speaking of Paris, they had lapsed into French without realizing it.

It didn't appear to have occurred to Hassim that the tables had turned --- that he was now the captive. Either that, or he had accepted this risk and was proceeding with his colorful life. On the other hand, wariness was a part of his personality that would never completely recede. He insisted that his glass be poured only halfway, explaining that the champagne would lose its chill before he could consume an entire flute. In reality, he drank very little under any circumstances and did not wish to become even slightly intoxicated.

Meghan had thoroughly enjoyed her champagne at first, feeling the accumulated tension melt away. She relaxed for the first time since Camp David. Enough so that she playfully asked

Hassim "Why didn't you ravish me when you could have?"

"I never mix business with pleasure."

"At least I fall into the pleasure category," she mused.

"You are a stimulating woman. That is what the mind craves. The body will settle for less. Why? Did you want to be ravished?"

"No. But I confess to wanting to be desired. I was afraid I'd lost my allure."

"You need not worry on that account, but I fear I've missed my chance."

"Life is full of surprises," she replied enigmatically. Then she excused herself for a nap. They had arisen long before sunrise, and even she wasn't accustomed to champagne before Noon.

CHAPTER 42

The White House, Washington, D.C.
Friday, January 25, 8:58 AM EST

The actor portraying President Chambers entered the Rose Garden at the brisk pace for which Matthew Chambers was renown. There was barely enough sunlight to find the path, but he could see his breath. He could also feel the fledgling arthritis in his knees. "Ah, Washington in winter!" he thought. The early hour had been chosen to limit the turnout. The weather wouldn't hurt either. His press secretary walked at his side. She trotted to keep up.

He held his head high as if enjoying the elements. It was his first big scene in this part and he had worked hard to get it right --- even though he had no lines to speak. He strode up to the outdoor lectern waving to the dozen or so assembled. He smiled and opened his mouth. There was no sound. The press corps was puzzled. He closed his mouth and shrugged, holding his palms upward. Then he stepped back to let his press secretary approach the lectern.

"President Chambers regrets to inform you that he has laryngitis. In the event he can't speak, which is evidently the case this morning, he has requested that I read you the following brief statement." She announced "It is no longer the policy of the United States to prohibit its citizens from traveling anywhere in the world. The restrictions which had previously existed were part of a plan to isolate certain hostile regimes; however, there was scant evidence that any benefits had been achieved under this program. Therefore, these restrictions which were contrary to the American spirit of freedom are being lifted today. This is the first installment of the administration's new policy of openness." She looked to the President, who nodded encouragement. "Since the President will not be taking questions this morning, he has anticipated the obvious one. Yes, this does mean that we will open a dialogue with Cuba and other states that have firmly established governments which we have shunned in the past. As the President puts it, 'Fifty years is too long not to talk to your neighbor.' That does not mean we will condone the activities of these states or support their leaders. But it was commerce and the exchange of ideas that paved the way to the new Russia. After decades of isolation, Cuba is the last bastion of Communism. The President believes this to be the case because of, not in spite of, our sanctions against it. Albert Einstein defined insanity as doing the same thing over and over --- and expecting different results. This administration intends to replace all failed policies. This is simply the first." She paused to clear her throat.

The press corps was silent. Not a hand was raised.

"Thank you for coming out on this chilly morning. Now get inside before you freeze."

That brought them around. There were some chuckles and a few "Amens" as they waited for the President to leave. Stepping back to the lectern the President joined his press secretary with a smile, and waved a hearty good-bye to the press corps. He leaned over and playfully pointed his finger at Fred Sonner, who had covered the campaign. It was a gesture they had all come to know. It was the signal that the President was through.

As the President turned to go, his head disappeared in a fine pink mist.

CHAPTER 43

Above France
Friday, January 25, 15:07 Western European Time

The 9/11 hijackers had made a number of errors. They failed to disguise their preparations by refusing to learn how to take-off or land. The FBI agent who reported this months before was told it was unimportant. Their outward behavior was so suspicious that Mohammed Atta was refused boarding by airline personnel at Boston Logan airport the day before the World Trade Center and Pentagon were attacked. The hijackers waited too long to crash the aircraft after seizing control. At Newark, they hijacked a flight that was famous for its late departures. They allowed passengers to make phone calls which revealed their intentions, presumably causing the passenger revolt on United Flight 93. Incredibly, not one United States government agency was able to turn any of these serious mistakes against the hijackers. It was a failure of communications as well as imagination. But such mistakes made today would inevitably lead to failure.

Mustapha was determined to succeed. He was sitting two rows behind Meghan, in a bulkhead seat. He had no idea that the former American captive was on the plane. It was random. He did know for a fact that this particular Airbus 318 had two rows of first class seats (two on each side of the aisle) and ninety-nine coach seats (three on each side of the aisle). Only four seats in first class were occupied, by three men and a woman. In coach, all the aisle seats back through the exit row and the rearmost aisle seat were occupied by terrorists. According to his observations, there would be fewer than forty male passengers to contend with in coach. Each of Mustapha's men was skilled in hand-to-hand combat. Several carried eight-inch hinged stilettos concealed inside ballpoint pens. In addition, three were experienced pilots. Mustapha was a big fan of overkill.

The challenge would be to enter the cockpit quickly. Threatening to harm the crew could not be expected to accomplish this. Experimenting on an older but similar Airbus, they had soon discovered that the locking mechanism was the strongest part of the door. There was no access to the sturdy piano hinge mounted inside the cockpit door. It had taken five days to find the weakness, even though it was right before their eyes the whole time. Above the cockpit door was a lamp. This indicated the presence of a small electrical junction box recessed into the bulkhead wall. To their amazement, they found a matching lamp on the other side of the wall. The installation of this junction box had compromised the structural integrity of the upper wall. They could simply remove the junction box and reach in to unlock the door from the inside. Unfortunately, the junction box was too far from the locking device to reach it by hand. Mustapha had solved this problem by making the handles of their roll-on bags detachable.

And, in the spirit of overkill, another team could be sent into the baggage compartment to seek access to the cockpit from below. A third team could torture a flight attendant over the intercom. Even if it didn't get the pilots to open the door, it would stress the pilots and persuade the passengers to remain in their seats.

Mustapha's teams had rehearsed relentlessly. They would perform flawlessly. Each man knew every detail --- except one. Only Mustapha knew what the target was. His teams believed they would be in a Heathrow transit lounge before long, waiting for a plane to Dulles International --- which they would fly into the White House. The White House had been selected for two reasons. It was the symbol of the American government, and there would not be enough fuel left to blow up anything bigger.

But Mustapha had realized that changing planes and waiting in transit lounges would multiply the opportunities for discovery. That was unacceptable.

It had not taken long to find a similar target on the East side of the Atlantic. One of Mustapha's heros had identified it over seventy years before. In 1941, Adolf Hitler had ordered the *Luftwaffe* to destroy St. Paul's Cathedral during the London blitz. Not only was it a symbol of Great Britain, it was a cherished site of the infidel Christian religion. How sweet it would be to finally complete that most necessary task at last --- with a British Airways aircraft, no less.

CHAPTER 44

The White House, Washington, D.C.
Friday, January 25, 9:14 AM EST

The mind has the capacity to recognize patterns. This is basic to communications and other survival functions. The more patterns that it encounters, the easier it becomes to recognize a pattern from several of its parts. This is alleged to be the basis of abstract art. It explains how people can find reindeer and ships in cloud formations. Nevertheless, the pattern derived at first sight is often not the correct one.

"Cotton candy," Marco thought. "Why does the President's head look like cotton candy?"

The actor portraying the President crumpled in place, settling on the grass in a pile. Other than the blood spurting into the air from his severed neck, there was no movement.

Horror replaced shock. The press secretary fell to her knees beside the body, shrieking. And she was one of the few persons who knew he wasn't really the President. That detail was lost in the moment.

Marco was pulled inside, away from the door, away from any windows. His presidency was no longer a secret. The Secret Service quickly sealed the area, to the groans of the press corps who began filing their reports via cell phones and PDAs. There would be no speculation about survival, no vigil. The President's head had exploded. In an instant, he had ceased to exist as a life form. And the Washington press corps had witnessed it live.

Matthew Chambers' term had ended officially in the nation's capital just one day after he had been beheaded in Jerusalem.

"Take me to Major Fox," Marco ordered. "And don't release anyone until I've made a statement."

"Over here, Mr. President!" Major Fox shouted as he approached him through the crowded corridor. There was a noticeable pause in the hall for mental adjustment as it sank in. Marco Redondo was the President of the United States now.

"Detain everyone in range who could have shot President Chambers! And keep them in custody! We won't have another Dallas fiasco here!" Marco was angry, but firmly in control. As they entered the Major's office, he instructed "Contact the Chief Justice. We're not going to wait for a public ceremony when we're under attack. And give us ten minutes --- uninterrupted."

When they were seated, Major Fox softly said "*Cálmate,* Marco. Let it all bounce off the inside of your cranium for a minute. Let your thoughts organize themselves without interference from your reactions."

Marco smiled briefly. "You should have been a monk, Zorro."

"Piloting a jet aircraft at Mach 3 works for me."

"So advise me, *amigo.*"

"President Chambers is now officially dead. We have a body to bury now. There can be no doubt as to the time and place. The White House press corps will take care of that. I'm sure we will have a suspect soon. It's not as tricky as the other plan."

"No one is going to ask why the doctors couldn't save him...."

"Not after they see the video."

"Was someone taping?"

"Someone's always taping these days."

"But what about an autopsy? DNA?"

"Since the cause of death is so obvious, the autopsy will be strictly limited to avoid further desecration of the President's body. That's a big advantage over him dying in his sleep."

"Makes sense," Marco admitted. He thought for a minute, looking at the ceiling. "You need a new office, Luís."

"Don't I know it. Yolanda would agree."

"And where is she this morning?"

"She's around here somewhere. Came in before I did. Probably looking for me now."

Marco rose. "I think I should address the members of the press, before they riot."

"With a sniper out there?"

"I doubt that he's still in firing position. I don't want to be described as cowering in the White House."

"Hmm. You're right. Let's go, Mr. President."

"Thanks for the perspective, Major."

CHAPTER 45

Above France
Friday, January 25, 15:18 Western European Time

Mustapha arose from his seat calmly and strolled into the first class cabin. That was the signal. Two of his men on the exit aisles headed back, towards the two flight attendants in the rear.

Mustapha continued to the front galley, where the startled flight attendant asked him to please return to his seat. He held his stomach and whispered hoarsely *"Toilette, s'il vous plait."*

She frowned as she switched languages to tell him he couldn't use the first class loo. *"Je suis désolé, monsieur, mais...."* Her eyes went wide as he crushed her windpipe with a single chop.

"Merci beaucoup," he said to the choking attendant as he backed out of the galley. He tried the cockpit door. It was locked, as expected. But now he knew for sure. By now both CIA agents were monitoring his moves. Mustapha then appeared to see the toilet door for the first time and entered hastily, locking it behind him.

One of the CIA agents advanced to position himself between it and the cockpit. It was a reflex action. He had no idea anything was amiss until he reached the galley. What he saw put him on full alert. The flight attendant was trying to stab a hole in her trachea with a plastic knife. "Trouble!" he called to the other agent before he went to the aid of the frantic flight attendant. In the dim light, he accomplished a crude tracheotomy that covered them both in blood. Then he jammed a cardboard cylinder into the hole to prevent her lungs from filing with blood. Not understanding this portion of the procedure, she fought him with her remaining strength, landing a high knee to his groin. At this moment, Mustapha emerged from the toilet with a stiletto in his hand. Concerned with fending off the blows of the flight attendant without harming her, the agent barely noticed the blade that punctured his heart. He was completely surprised to realize he was dying. His last glance was toward the other agent, who had remained seated throughout thanks to a stiletto of his own which protruded from his right ear.

Mustapha checked the agent he had felled. Finding a weak pulse, he placed his foot on the agent's neck and pulled his head back until the cervical verte brae popped. The flight attendant was lying on her back, covered with her own blood. Her lungs emitted a gurgling noise. He dragged the body of the agent out of the way and dumped it on her. She would be dead soon enough, one way or the other.

Meghan and Hassim both just looked at Mustapha, who winked and whispered "*Allahu akbar*" as if sharing a secret with them.

"I don't suppose you saw any champagne," Meghan replied in Arabic.

Hassim caught on quickly. "It will just make you sleepy,"

he said to Meghan as if peeved by her request.

Surprised by the Arabic and the audacity of the request, Mustapha chose to be amused. He reached back into the galley and retrieved an unopened bottle for them.

"*Shucran*," Meghan thanked him as she accepted it. Now she had a weapon. And it could be used more than once. She pretended to be opening it, removing the foil.

Mustapha turned his attention to the cockpit door. Meghan shook the bottle. Mustapha appeared to be examining the light above it. "He's got a way in," she said to Hassim. "We've got to warn the pilot."

"There's an intercom in the galley. Can you use it?"

"If I can get there."

"I'll engage our terrorist, offer to help."

"I'll pretend to be looking for a glass for the champagne."

Hassim cleared his throat to get Mustapha's attention. He didn't want to surprise him, not yet. Mustapha turned around, clearly annoyed.

"I offer my services, *effendi*."

Mustapha looked skeptical until Meghan turned to Hassim in shock, saying "You're one of them, you son of a bitch!"

"Shut up or I'll kill you now, American whore!" Hassim shot back.

"I was O.K. a few minutes ago when you were trying to talk me into having sex."

"You disgust me. You are a skinny pig."

She had to admit he was good at this. She was beginning to hate him for his remarks. "Then we only need one glass, since you *jihadis* can't touch alcohol."

"Get it yourself," he replied sulkily.

As she rose from her aisle seat, it was two steps to the galley. Mustapha moved to stop her, but decided she posed no real threat. As she stepped around the bodies, she pretended to search for a glass.

Hassim introduced himself to Mustapha as the mastermind behind the recent capture of the American diplomats. He knew enough facts to give a credible account. Mustapha was impressed. Another embellishment was that he had been apprenticed to a carpenter as a boy, and could put that knowledge to use for the hijackers if they wished. He said "You know, that door is the strongest part of the aircraft" which sealed the deal. Hassim had officially joined the team.

The pilots were discussing the football rankings when the intercom boomed out. "Just listen. Hijackers have control of the cabins. They plan to enter the cockpit. Land now!"

"Did you hear that?" asked the co-pilot.

"Take her down!"

"I'll find a runway." He flipped a switch. "This is BA 1106 declaring an emergency. We need to land now. Hijackers reported on board."

"BA 1106. Scrambling military escort. Land at French Air Force base near Le Mans. Follow the jets in. Airspace is being cleared. Begin your descent now. Use the word "capacity" to indicate terrorists are in control of the cockpit. *Bonne chance,* BA 1106."

"Oops!" Meghan tumbled into the aisle, grabbing Mustapha's leg as she went down. As he moved to dislodge her, Hassim planted the champagne bottle firmly against the side of his head. Immediately unconscious, Mustapha fell on top of

Meghan. Five terrorists headed up the aisle towards Hassim. The popping cork hit the first one in the eye, but it was the spray of champagne that blinded him long enough for Hassim to soccer kick him under the chin. The second hijacker ran into the first, spilling both onto the seats.

Just then the Airbus banked sharply and began to dive. Only those with seat belts fastened avoided colliding with the left wall. It came just in time. Hassim was out of ideas.

CHAPTER 46

The White House, Washington, D.C.
Friday, January 25, 9:31 AM EST

The Secret Service had declared the Oval Office off limits until the sniper was found. It made sense to Marco. He was in no hurry. Although he was better prepared to take over the office during a term than anyone since Gerald Ford, he already had a full plate. The Chief Justice administered the oath of office in the Strategic Planning Office in the fortified basement. Everyone called it the bunker. Marco had remained there with Major Fox and a Secret Service agent, who stood by the door.

The head of Secret Service entered. "Excuse me, Mr. President. We think we've located the sniper's nest. It's the roof of the West Colonnade, sir."

"The shot came from the White House?"

"Yes sir. We've found residue from the shooting. There's no spent cartridge, but that's not surprising. A professional shooter would have policed his brass. They're dusting for fingerprints now."

"Keep me informed."

"Yes, Mr. President."

"An inside job?" Major Fox speculated. "That would make it possible that the shooter knew about the impersonation."

"And was just trying to help out?"

"It could explain the head shot...."

"That bothers me too. If someone has a clear body shot, even just one, that is all you need to kill a man.

"And the target area is twice the size."

"So why take the head shot?"

"There's confidence. The shooter had to be sure he wouldn't miss. Even over the relatively short distance, that means the shooter is damn good."

"A marksman?" asked Marco.

"Not necessarily. Let's just leave it at real good for now. Could be somebody who never competed."

"I'll buy that. But do you take the head shot just to show you can?"

"No. Too risky. He had to take the head shot for some reason."

"Like obliterating the face?"

"Damn good reason, but it presumes knowledge of the impersonation."

"Limits the suspects, at least," Marco observed. "Any other reasons --- like to avoid hitting a Kevlar vest?"

Major Fox thought a moment, then dismissed the idea. "A vest wouldn't have stopped that bullet. The shooter would have known that."

"But he might have survived...."

"Unlikely, but his death wouldn't have been so shocking if there had been any doubt about survival."

Marco pondered that. "So we have at least two reasons for the head shot: to prevent identification and to clearly mark the time and place of death."

"I don't like where this leads. Could our knowledge of the President's stand-in be obscuring our reasoning?"

"No doubt, but we're stuck with it. That's one reason to keep that to ourselves." Marco thought about it, then asked "If you had been the assassin, why would you have taken the head shot?"

"You might be on to something. Unless I was acting on my own, I would follow the orders."

"So a head shot may have been specified?"

Major Fox looked at him thoughtfully. "Thanks for throwing out the first conspiracy theory. I always wondered how they started."

"But?"

"Yes. It's certainly possible."

"I'm troubled by the convenience of it. We needed to have Matt Chambers officially dead, in a way that would not make anyone wonder whether he was beheaded in the West Bank. And we needed it *pronto.*"

"You don't believe in fortunate coincidences?"

"We're way past coincidence here. This might be a miracle."

"It could qualify," Major Fox admitted. "Let's start with all the people who knew about the actor."

"We can eliminate ourselves, the press secretary and my Secret Service *ersatz* wife, who was at the Admiral's House." There was something in the back of the President's mind. Major Fox knew what it was.

"It wasn't Yolanda, Marco."

"I sure hope you're right."

"I know I'm right. She didn't have anything to do with it."

"O.K. Subject's closed. Who did it then?"

"We'll know more soon. Let the investigators do their jobs."

"Just when I thought we had everything under control...."

"Control is an illusion," Major Fox reminded him. "You told me that."

"I was referring to bull riding at the time."

"There's a difference?"

Marco huffed a laugh. "Maybe I've been applying it too narrowly."

"That's the spirit, *amigo*. Don't let your first day in office get you down."

A Secret Service agent entered and waited to be recognized.

"Is there any news?" the President asked.

"Yes, sir. British Airways Flight 1106 reports hijackers aboard."

This was not the kind of news he had expected. It took a moment to sink in. "Not the flight Miss Hill is on?"

"Yes, sir. It is. The pilot is trying to land before they breach the cockpit door. We don't have any further reports yet. The French Air Force is intercepting the plane to make sure it doesn't turn toward Paris."

"Keep me advised as soon as you have any further information."

"Yes, sir, Mr. President."

Marco looked back at Major Fox, who replied to his gaze

with "Don't some days just start off nasty?"

CHAPTER 47

Above France
Friday, January 25, 15:33 Western European Time

The former Royal Air Force pilot was testing the structural limits of the Airbus 318 as it dived toward the rolling French countryside. He wasn't worried about the dive itself, but pulling out of it could shear the wings off. It would require a delicate touch to a machine that weighed tons. He wasn't sure he had time to be delicate. There were frantic noises at the cockpit door. The co-pilot was watching the mirror for signs of entry.

The terrorists controlled both cabins now, but mobility was compromised by the steep angle of descent. Mustapha had not regained consciousness, leaving the hijackers leaderless. Hassim was stretched out in the aisle with a terrorist sitting on top of him. Meghan had managed to lock herself in the first class bathroom.

Amid the confusion, two determined terrorists attacked the lamp above the cockpit door, pulling off the fixture and wrenching the junction box free. This produced sounds of satisfaction from them, which in turn inspired Meghan to open the lavatory door as wide and hard as possible. The door struck the nearest one, who groaned but kept working. She leapt into the aisle and jumped on the startled terrorist who was holding Hassim.

Suddenly freed, Hassim pulled the terrorist from the hole above the door down onto the floor. Hassim knew he was no fighter, but the longer he could keep them from the cockpit, the better the chances were for survival. For that, he would take some punishment. Just then, a terrorist pushed out the lamp that was inside the cockpit. It crashed to the deck. The co-pilot scrambled to the cockpit door and struck the hand emerging through the resulting hole. The hand retreated briefly, then reappeared as the terrorist attempted to shove his arm through the opening. Seeing that the hand was reaching for the door's unlocking mechanism, the co-pilot grabbed the hand and bit into it like a bulldog. There was a howl on the cabin side of the door. The co-pilot willed himself to bite through the hand if possible, but the arm managed to jerk it away from him. The co-pilot tasted blood in his mouth as he waited for the next attempt.

"Hold 'em off!" the pilot shouted. The altitude continued to fall rapidly as he followed the F-16 towards earth.

A metal bar shot through the opening. It caught the co-pilot in the ear. Dazed, he released his grip on the door handle and fell forward. Unable to reach it, he watched the metal rod swing toward the unlocking mechanism. The contact was perfect. The door was unlocked, but the terrorist didn't know it yet. He hadn't expected to be so fortunate. The piece of metal swung again. The co-pilot lunged for it, trying to pull it free. As he did so he quickly relocked the door. "Captain, I can't hold them off forever."

The plane began to level off. Everyone was aware that

the hijackers were running out of time.

Unable to dislodge the co-pilot's grip, the hijacker suddenly released the metal rod. The co-pilot went backward into his seat back, striking his back with sufficient force to knock the wind out of him. The hand reappeared with another metal bar like the first. All the co-pilot could do was watch.

The flight attendant awoke in a fog. Someone huge was lying across her. Her lungs rattled. There was no place that didn't hurt, but whatever was stuck in her neck was easily the worst of it. She crawled from under the dead CIA agent and used the galley drawer handles to pull herself upright with as much stealth as she could muster. She saw a tall man with his arm in the wall above the cockpit. The vibrations told her the plane was still in the air; so the man couldn't be up to any good. With his shoulder against the bulkhead wall, his back was to her. She had the element of surprise, but not much else.

She found a corkscrew. It would have to be enough. Holding it in both hands, she brought the corkscrew down on his back with all her weight behind it. He screamed, dropping the metal rod inside the cockpit. She began to screw it into him. He attempted to pull his arm from the hole, but she was leaning against him. The terrorist who had been pummeling Hassim grabbed the flight attendant's arm and flung her onto the seats.

Another metal rod was produced and the wounded terrorist gave it another try. He succeeded in unlocking the door on the third attempt. Two of his comrades opened it and charged inside.

The co-pilot tackled the first through the door. Hassim jumped on the back of the other. As they struggled, the pilot shouted over the intercom "Brace for emergency landing!"

CHAPTER 48

Blois, France
Friday, January 25, 15:42 Western European Time

Flight 1106 barely cleared the hilltop chateau where Mary, Queen of Scots had been raised on its way to destiny. The pilot spotted the *Autoroute L'Aquitaine* and decided he couldn't wait for an airfield. He could only hope to avoid the traffic. Without confirming that the landing gear had deployed, he smashed the Airbus 318 into the asphalt and stood on the brakes as the various combatants ricocheted around the cockpit. He also prayed for his soul. He didn't hold out much hope for his body.

Before him was his nightmare --- a huge lorry entering the highway, completely oblivious to the exceptional traffic approaching him from behind. If the driver stayed in the right lane, the right wing might clear --- provided he could keep the plane far enough to the left. The problem was that aircraft are not that maneuverable over short distances. The right engine made contact with the vehicle and, before it sheared off, imparted a clockwise spin to the fuselage. There was nothing the pilot could do now but watch, as Flight 1106 shot off the road at ninety-eight miles per hour.

Without the friction of the road surface, the spin

intensified. The tail section was first to hit the massive elms that lined the highway. The fuselage cracked apart just forward of the rear galley. The rear portion crumpled at the base of the trees. No one in there survived. The forward part landed across the swale, breaking off both wings on impact. Aviation fuel began to fill the swale. There was an eerie silence as those who could still breathe became acquainted with their unexpected deliverance. Then all Hell broke loose as the passengers realized they were about to be incinerated.

The pilot was surprised to find himself not only alive, but relatively unharmed. If his blood pressure didn't take him out in the next few minutes, he would probably survive. He unbuckled from the seat and opened the emergency door. The drop to the ground was less than ten feet. He then checked his co-pilot, who was moaning. Unable to make him alert, he continued his inventory. There were two hijackers and another Arab, who was dressed in Western style. He poked him in the chest. "Who are you!"

"Hassim. I'm not with them."

"Help me get the co-pilot out!"

"My leg's broken. Where's the lady?"

Just then, Meghan rose from beneath the body of a hijacker and bashed his head with the heel of her shoe. "Right here. I'll help you with them."

The pilot jumped to the ground to receive the co-pilot. Then Meghan went for Hassim. "You know, you're my hero." She kissed him briefly.

"Don't make any promises you can't keep --- in case I live."

"Oh, you're going to live all right. It's just going to hurt for a while." She dragged him to the exit and pushed him through.

"What about the other hijackers?" cried the pilot.

"I hope they're dead, but I'll try to get them out. Promise you won't break their falls."

To his utter surprise, the pilot laughed as he stepped aside to express his intention to allow gravity to have its way with the hijackers. Both bodies emitted noises which indicated they were alive, but neither appeared to pose a threat. The pilot looked up to Meghan, who was preparing to drop from the cockpit emergency hatch.

Instead of falling, she flew.

The pilot did not have time to assimilate this. The blast knocked him to the ground. He rolled over reflexively to hide his face from the fireball.

CHAPTER 49

The White House, Washington, D.C.
Friday, January 25, 10:03 AM EST

The man in the grey suit introduced himself as Randall Murphy. He would lead the FBI investigation into the assassination of President Chambers. "It is a matter of protocol that the Secret Service cannot investigate an incident for which it provided security. Nevertheless, we understand that they were on the scene and have taken appropriate action to preserve the scene and detain potential suspects. It would be naive to assume that the Secret Service has not begun to investigate this crime. To avoid any question, the Director has requested that you confirm to the Secret Service that all information about the event in its possession should be turned over to us at this time; so we may not lose time catching up. To avoid any appearance of competition, I suggest that I not be present when you advise them, Mr. President."

"Well put, Agent Murphy. I'll speak to the Head of Secret Service immediately. By the way, there is an unrelated matter of lesser importance which the Secret Service is dealing with at this time. You are not to become involved in that matter. It would serve no purpose except to distract you. All I will tell you is that it does not involve the events of this morning at the

White House."

"Thank you, sir." Agent Murphy turned and left the room. He was clearly unhappy.

"Petulant when they don't get their way," Major Fox observed.

"He got what he came for, though."

"Did he?"

"Well, not quite. We'll let him think it was President Chambers. And I still want to know what the Secret Service comes up with."

"We've got the bullet, sir!" The Head of Secret Service was excited as he was shown in. While recovery of the bullet was a certainty, his team had achieved it before the FBI had arrived. That made it an accomplishment.

"What is it?" The President wasn't military, but he was a hunter.

"It hasn't been tested yet, but it appears to be some kind of big game hunting cartridge. Large caliber. Like for shooting elephants." He was confused. "Not a typical assassin's weapon."

"Keep me posted. If I'm not available, tell Major Fox what you've learned. In the meantime, you need to copy everything you have before turning it over to the FBI. This is your turf. I want you to concentrate on how the shooter gained access and exited. Also I want the location of everyone in the White House at the time of the shooting. If the FBI asks for anything, give it to them --- with two exceptions. There is to be no release of information regarding the West Bank hostages. Second, as far as the FBI is concerned, it was President Chambers who was shot today. If you have any news, bring it to me first."

"Thank you, Mr. President."

Marco turned to Major Fox again. "A big game rifle?"

"If that's true, our shooter just got more confident. Those don't reload themselves."

"Wouldn't it be too big to hide?"

"Not necessarily. Remington, Browning and some others make compact models. Barrels as short as 16½ inches; overall length less than three feet. And the stocks can be shortened further. In this weather, with overcoats, concealment would not be a big problem."

"What about caliber?"

"I've read that the Ruger M77 will fire a .458 Lott African cartridge. Of course, you have to get the right barrel. It's pretty exotic. If that's the type of cartridge, it could be traceable...."

"I gather you don't think it will be."

"No. On the other hand, the kick will certainly be enough to leave a mark on the shooter. Especially if it is a compact model. The advertising doesn't tell you that. People buy them for their teenagers and then get upset by the orthopedic surgeon's bills."

"So, since our shooter knows what he's doing, should we look for a large person?"

"Not necessarily. Could be what he expects us to do. But we should look for bruising on the shoulder."

"Get Secret Service to organize it. Start with the staff."

CHAPTER 50

Blois, France
Friday, January 25, 16:35 Western European Time

By now, cars had stopped along the *Autoroute* to render assistance, to take pictures, or to merely gawk at the spectacle. Most did not know their own motives at the times they first applied the brakes. It was an automatic response. To their credit, most called in the accident to the local police. Between the wrecked lorry, the explosion and the airplane crash, the dispatcher wasn't sure how many incidents he was dealing with, but they all seemed to be in the same area. So he sent everything he had there.

It wasn't enough. There were third degree burn victims. There were live people missing limbs. There were people whose bodies were shattered, but who still breathed. There were those in shock, who wandered into the traffic seeking help. Then there were the limp and the dismembered, some hanging from the fuselage, others in trees. In the center burned the residue of the aviation fuel, like an *al fresco* crematorium in the bright French countryside.

Meghan moaned. She saw the cold sky above, first with one eye, then the other. That gave her some comfort. She used her hands to make an inventory. Her long hair was singed short. What little remained was a tangle. Her face was blistered from the fireball. She was still dressed, but would require a wardrobe change at some point. She raised her head to look for her feet. They were both where she had predicted they would be, presumably attached to her legs. She had no shoes, but decided they were lost in the cockpit scuffle. Inventory completed, she willed herself to get up.

She raised up on both elbows, but nothing South of her belt was responding. "Nooooo," was the last sound she uttered before she passed out.

Hassim's face. That's what she saw. As it came into focus, so did the background. The harsh, invasive light told her she was in a hospital room. She tried to turn her head to take its measure, but her head seemed to be in a shiny steel cage. She looked into Hassim's eyes. His face was cut and bruised, presumably from the fighting.

"You were lucky. They saved the tattoo."

She didn't know whether to laugh or cry; so she tried a little of each. The crying won. "How bad?"

"You're broken, my little temp. They will try to repair you. It may take months. You have to help them, up here." He pointed to her head. "This part still works."

"My legs?"

"Your legs are scandalously long and sensuous. You didn't think I'd noticed?"

"I can't move them."

"That's because they are healing, and need to rest."

"Touch them."

"What?"

"Touch them. Make them tingle."

"I think you should know that I am not trained in this field of endeavor." Even so, he moved to the foot of the bed. "I will start with the toes. This is because they are the furthest point."

"Stop the clinical bull and touch me, Hassim!"

He wiggled her toes, then caressed her feet. She felt nothing. His hands moved onto her calves, but still she felt no sensation.

"Try pinching me." He complied, with no result. "Keep going. Tickle my inner thigh." He reached under the sheet without looking. His hand stopped just above her knee. There was no sensation.

"Now you are modest?"

"Ironic, isn't it?" he admitted.

"Okay. So I'm stuck here. What else is new?"

Hassim talked to her for two hours, until she fell asleep.

While Meghan slept, the doctors tried to locate a relative to contact. Hassim finally gave them the telephone number of Paul Carnegie without telling them who it was.

CHAPTER 51

The White House, Washington, D.C.
Friday, January 25, 1:14 PM EST

"I went first. It wasn't me," Major Fox announced as he entered the room.

"That's comforting," Marco admitted, "but you couldn't have made it down from the roof of the West Colonnade by the time I saw you by the entrance to the Rose Garden."

"Nice to know you'd vouch for me, but I did it to show them where to look. I also reminded them that some people are left-handed."

"Has Yolanda been screened?"

"She went with me. Cool customer. She simply took off her blouse and pointed to the places where there would be bruising, staring at the men defiantly. Said she didn't need to wait for the female screeners to show up."

"Sounds like quite a show."

"It was, but don't get the wrong idea. Yolanda appears to obtain her undergarments from Wal-Mart, not Victoria's Secret. Anyway, now you can let that wild idea loose."

"Good. It's a relief. I like Yolanda, you know."

"She likes you too. Try to leave it at that."

"I will. I seem to have enough problems to deal with."

"Like this Hassim character?"

"Yeah. My new advisor, if he made it"

"Made what?"

"I forgot you were away. Secret Service advised me that the plane crash-landed on a freeway in the Loire Valley, but then hit a truck. Quite a few passengers survived. The first class cabin was intact. The bodyguards were both dead. There was a dead woman dressed as a flight attendant; so it is presumed that Meghan got out. She may be in a local hospital. We have to wait for word of Erin Hill."

"Tangled in our own web of deceit," Major Fox observed. "Have you alerted the embassy?"

"Not yet. We're giving her the chance to contact us first."

"What about Hassim?"

"No word. There was at least one dead Arab in first class. This could account for Hassim."

"Maybe he was in on the hijacking."

"Let's see if he's alive before we pursue that."

The telephone rang. They looked at each other; then Major Fox answered it.

"It's your father-in-law," he announced as he handed the receiver to Marco. Paul Carnegie was agitated.

"She's alive, but she's injured. They're moving her to a hospital in Paris for treatment now."

"What's her injury?" Marco asked.

"She can't move her legs. They won't know any more until they run tests in Paris."

"You can't go there. You're too recognizable. We'll send someone else to monitor her progress."

"There's already someone named Hassim with her.

Who's that?"

Marco thought for a moment before responding. "He's the man from the organization that rescued her."

It didn't work. "Her kidnapper?"

"Calm down. He's a U.S. government agent. He's on our side. He's the logical person for the job, since he was on the plane too."

"Can't say I like this."

"No one's cheering here either, but this is what we have for now. Give it some time, Paul. In a day or two, we'll know her prognosis. Then we can arrange her return to the States."

Paul Carnegie grumbled a bit, but ultimately agreed to this short-term plan. "By the way, I assume dinner is off. But we need to talk as soon as possible."

"Yes. I doubt that the Secret Service wants me wandering around the countryside tonight."

When he had disconnected, Major Fox reminded the President to bring the Secret Service up to date about Meghan.

CHAPTER 52

Jerusalem, Israel
Friday, January 25, 20:02 Bravo (local)

Yusef was lying on his back in the rude dwelling where the Defenders of the Sacred Faith had so recently made their auspicious television debut. He was sure that the minor difficulties, such as him falling over as he tried to keep the victim upright, were lost in the glory of the capture and beheading of the infidel. He sipped peppermint tea from a silver and glass cup that his father had passed on to him. He was sure that his father was proud of his illustrious son, who had advanced the cause of Allah so dramatically.

Of course, Abdul had also performed well. Yusef fancied himself a fair leader. Being such, he could share the accolades his imagination was providing. There were enough to go around.

Word had quickly spread through the community that it was he who had masterminded the strike against the diplomats. He, Yusef, had brought the suffering of the Palestinians to the Americans. He was treated with awe and respect. Small boys followed him down the alleys, just to bask in his presence. Women now feared him, which he found to be a great improvement to their previous indifference.

At times he regretted selling the American woman to Hassim. He could have used her in a second telecast to continue to build his public persona, to remind the Americans that Yusef could strike at any minute, to remind the Palestinians that they had an avenger. But then he would remember how intoxicated he became in her presence and decided he was best rid of her. And with the Dollars exchanged for her, he could purchase more bomb-making materials and weapons for the further exploits of the Defenders of the Sacred Faith. He had already obtained his own DVD video camera to chronicle those very exploits.

The future beckoned to Chairman Yusef.

The wooden door to the street exploded inward, blowing the teacup from his hand and blinding him.

Yusef regained consciousness in unfamiliar surroundings. He appeared to be in a warehouse. A fire was burning in a 55-gallon oil drum. Smoke irritated his lungs. He was coughing. He was hanging by his feet directly over the fire. "Help me!" he implored.

The group of men milling around the fire found this amusing. To enhance their amusement, they added fuel to the fire. Then Yusef began to descend.

"I am Chairman Yusef of the Defenders of the Sacred Faith!" he exclaimed. "Why do you dishonor me?"

A stern voice replied. "We will ask the questions on this last night. Any answer we distrust or dislike will bring you closer to the fire until you are roasted like the brainless goat that you are."

"Allah be merciful!"

"If you speak the truth, Allah will grant you a quick death, nothing more. But you will embrace it as if it was a beautiful woman when the time comes."

"But why?"

"Tell us of your activities regarding the Americans. Leave nothing out." To encourage Yusef in this endeavor, he was lowered a meter. "Start now unless you wish to be even closer to the flames."

With tears streaming from both eyes, Yusef began his story. He was interrupted only to ask what he had done with the beheaded body. When he told them that he had burned it in the desert, he was lowered another half meter towards the fire. After that, they had to throw water on his head every few minutes to prevent his hair from igniting. Yusef took this as a good sign. He was desperate for encouragement.

When Yusef remembered that the girl spoke Arabic, they questioned him relentlessly about her. Her very presence on a diplomatic mission headed for Bethlehem had already indicated that she was not a low-level diplomatic employee.

The questioning was halted to discuss this revelation, then they questioned Yusef about Hassim and his plans for the girl.

Finally, the questioning ended. The rope was raised. With his remaining strength, Yusef cried "*Allahu akbar!*"

One of the men brought a ladder over, and cut the rope, sending Yusef plummeting head-first into the fire. His legs kicked the air for exactly one minute, fifty-two seconds, according to the stopwatch. After a few moments of calculations, the man who had guessed the closest time collected his winnings from the others.

CHAPTER 53

Paris, France
Friday, January 25, 21:44 Western European Time

Hassim was an out-patient. Since he was not a relative, he could not spend the night watching over Meghan.

He made his way a bit stiffly down the front steps into the cold night air, trying to favor every part of his body that ached. It was impossible. On top of that, he was exhausted. For the first time in his young life, he could feel the limits of his resources. He wondered if it were possible to deplete one's adrenalin supply. He suspected that it was. Vowing to obtain a warm coat in the morning, he walked past several available taxis and wandered into the heart of *la Rive Droite* — the Right Bank.

Stopping at a tiny mart that appeared to occupy a former narrow alley, he purchased Camembert, a package of Madeleines, yogurt, orange juice and a bottle of Beaujolais. At the cashier, he noticed the headline of the evening journal. The familiar Arabic word was rendered in French, but it captured his attention. "*ASSESSIN!*" it screamed. He continued reading. "*President Chambers est mort.*" Stunned, he picked up the newspaper and began to walk away. The clerk had to remind him to take his other items --- and to pay for the journal.

Hassim stumbled onto the sidewalk, walking mechanically. The green neon cross of a pharmacy beckoned, but he resisted the urge to acquire aspirin or ibuprofen, which would interfere with his blood's ability to clot. He was convinced he must have perforated something during the day, given all the opportunities. Then he found a tourist hotel that let one-bedroom units with kitchens by the week. Having no luggage, he prepaid for two weeks and stated simply that the airline had lost his luggage. The night clerk did not believe him, but feigned sympathy.

He was placing the yogurt in the mini-fridge when the doorbell rang. "What did they forget to tell me?" he wondered, thinking the night clerk was at the door. He was tired. He was no longer in the Mideast. He'd let his guard down. He simply opened the door to whoever might be there.

The tall American put his foot in the door before he calmly asked "May I come in?"

"*Je ne parle pas Anglais,*" Hassim tried.

"Of course you speak English, Hassim. You attended the London School of Economics." By now the American was in the living room, having gently pushed Hassim in front of him as he went. Reverting to Arab thinking, he announced, "I am neither your enemy, nor the friend of your enemy." Clumsy, but to the point.

"Glad to hear that," Hassim conceded.

"Good. Relax. Let's open that bottle of Beaujolais and become acquainted." The American's eyes took in the room and then scanned the kitchen. "And don't bring a knife from the kitchen unless you're ready to die." His eyes indicated that he meant it.

"Never bring a knife to a gun fight," Hassim recited. "With whom am I drinking?"

"James. That's all you need to know for now. It's not like I'll be a permanent fixture in your life," he replied as Hassim entered the kitchen to open the wine. "Don't bother to decant it. It's table wine."

Hassim was a flexible thinker. He had already concluded that the American probably meant him no harm on this occasion. "From the Embassy?"

"The one in Paris, in fact."

Hassim set the open bottle and two all-purpose, generic goblets on the dining table and poured. "Alcohol may be taken by Muslims to reduce physical pain," he explained, to head off the question that always came when he drank. He handed James his wine.

"Works for me. You in pain?"

"Only when I breathe."

"*Santé*, then. To your health."

"Thank you. *Shucran*. To yours too, although you appear to be robust at the moment."

"It's a condition of my employment." The American was not a sipper. Either that or he was in a hurry. He had finished his wine. "Not bad. Can't be last year's vintage. Bitter swill."

"Only the first sip is bitter."

"That's what they say." The American looked straight into Hassim's eyes. "Time to chat. Tell me the whole story. Leave nothing out."

Hassim hesitated. "I must determine if you know the identity of the lady in hospital who was on the plane with me."

"Fair enough. But I can't tell you unless I know that you already know it. Let's approach it in steps. What is her real name?"

"It begins with the letter M."

"This could take all night. The second letter is E."

"The third letter is G and she is married to an officer of the government of the United States."

"Is that man an elected official?"

"Yes. He's from Texas, but he works in Washington."

"Hmm. Is he in charge of his office?"

"He wasn't yesterday." It was the best Hassim could do under the circumstances.

"Well put. What is his name?

"It also begins with an M. What are the other letters?"

"A."

"R, C and O," Hassim finished. "So we both know who the lady is. Now I will relate the events."

Forty-eight minutes later, Hassim was finished. So was the Beaujolais. He'd omitted only the tattoo. It was not James' affair. The American had seldom interrupted. He seemed satisfied. He said "I am instructed to tell you that you are now a special advisor on Mideast Affairs to the President of the United States of America. This is a high honor which, in my opinion, fell into your lap. Don't take it lightly just because it came easily. Not only are you entitled to the protection and privileges of this office, you are also bound to keep secret everything you just told me. If you fail to do so, you will be punished for treason. It is a capital offense. Do you understand?"

"Yes I do. It is quite clear. And, as you say, it was an unlikely opportunity which came my way, but it was my decision to pursue the correct course --- which allowed the lady to escape."

The man who called himself James shrugged off that version of the events. "Your first assignment is to remain in Paris and monitor her progress for so long as she is receiving medical treatment here. I will be in contact, but here is my cell phone number in case of emergency." He produced a cell phone. "This one is yours. My number is programmed into it."

Hassim took the phone. "Thank you."

"Report only to me. If I don't answer, you can leave a detailed message. Do not attempt to contact any other person anywhere in the world."

"Will you be watching me?"

"You're on probation; so I'll be close by. Keep a low profile. Don't get into trouble. Do you need money?"

"Not yet."

"Let me know when you do. I'll bring the wine next time. Good luck."

"*Bonne chance.*"

The American let himself out. Hassim drank some of the orange juice. Then he fell asleep immediately.

And did something he rarely did. He dreamt of a woman. The woman was tall, thin, smart and brave. She was Meghan.

CHAPTER 54

The White House, Washington, D.C.
Friday, January 25, 8:03 PM EST

"Major Fox and Second Lieutenant Herrera are here, Mr. President." Marco rose to greet them.

"Send them in."

Major Fox waded right in. "Where are you bunking tonight, *compadre*?"

"Hadn't given it any thought. Been too busy, I guess."

"Place has lots of bedrooms. Maybe you should try one out."

Yolanda spoke for the first time. "You need your sleep, sir." It was a frank, open statement with no overtones.

"No argument, Lieutenant. I'm just not sure I'll be able to after today."

Yolanda opened her small purse and removed a bottle of *Hornitos Tequila Sauza*. There couldn't have been room for much else. Major Fox produced three shot glasses from his pockets. He announced "Time for the first Presidential Nightly Briefing."

The President played along. "Let's start with an assessment of Blue Weber agave distillation."

Major Fox held the three glasses in his left hand and

poured from his right, saying to Yolanda "I told you he received a copy of the agenda for this meeting."

"Confusion to the enemy!" toasted the President.

"It's certainly their turn," the Major responded as they raised their drinks, and emptied them.

"I already prefer this to the Presidential Daily Briefing," Marco admitted. "What's the next item for consideration?"

"We need to set up some simple parameters for future meetings of this nature. Yolanda has the list of suggestions."

After stating "I am not the author," Yolanda read from a sheet of copy paper. "We will not attempt to replicate the Presidential Daily Briefing. The issues discussed will be limited to those we deem most significant at the time. The use of first names to address each other is encouraged, provided no one else is present. Snacks are to be available. No more than one bottle of liquor is to be consumed. Neckties may be loosened and shoes may be removed."

"I think that covers it," Major Fox added.

"Looks like you've thought of everything. Let's proceed to the issues."

"We propose two for this evening's consideration: the assassination and your wife. Let's start with the former." Major Fox turned to Yolanda.

"Until the assassins of the real President Chambers have been located, there is not much the three of us can do. Our attention must be focused on the shooting of the actor portraying the President. At present, most of the world believes that he was the actual President, as we had hoped. We should anticipate that someone will discover that this is not the case. What will be the response?"

Marco did not hesitate. "To respond at any official level would be seen as an admission of the possibility. If he fooled the White House Press Corps, he must have fooled the rest of the world."

"That should work unless they find his body --- or his DNA," the Major declared. "Or if there was a credible eyewitness...."

"None of our people in the region were aware of his identity." Yolanda added "President Chambers was going to reveal it when he met with the Israeli Prime Minister, but that never happened."

"Mossad?" asked the President.

Major Fox shrugged. "That's one reason all knowledge was confined to select agents of the Secret Service. The FBI is riddled with Mossad informants. The CIA is practically a branch of Mossad." Yolanda's face expressed shock; so he expanded. "Yes, it's so bad that the only monument to an American in Israel honors a former CIA chief."

"So far, we don't believe Mossad has found out," said Marco, "although we can expect them to investigate if allegations surface."

Major Fox was thinking it through. "Can't imagine what the Israelis would do if they did find out."

"The Rose Garden Assassination," Yolanda intervened. "That's what the newspapers are calling it."

"Catchy phrase," Marco admitted. "Secret Service brought me the autopsy results. The actor was dying of metastatic cancer. Might not have known it yet. He was spared a long, painful death. At least that's the way it was presented."

The Major recovered from that revelation first. "The body?"

"Fortunately, President Chambers' advance directive specified cremation. That has already been carried out."

"But it wasn't President Chambers...." The Major's thought sputtered out. It had already been done. This was no time to begin questioning the ethics of one minute aspect of the deception.

"He needs to be buried before anyone claims it wasn't really President Chambers," Yolanda pointed out.

"We're doing that as quickly as we can while still maintaining the dignity of the office," Marco assured them.

"Any word on who shot him?" the Major inquired.

"The FBI is combing its lists of known assassins. The CIA is supposedly cooperating. Meanwhile, the Secret Service has come up with something interesting." The President paused for effect. "It appears that the shooter could not have fired from the sniper's nest and disappeared in the time allowed. They simulated it. I don't have details yet."

Yolanda put it together. "You mean he didn't use the sniper's nest?"

"That's one explanation." The President was searching their faces for signs of guilty knowledge. To his relief, he found none.

"Then where was the shot fired from?" Major Fox didn't expect an answer. Sometimes it feels necessary to ask the obvious question aloud.

"You two are the experts. Any ideas?" He was looking at Major Fox.

Yolanda sighed deeply and began to unbutton her blouse.

"What are you doing?" Marco asked.

"I am showing you personally that I could not have fired the weapon."

"This isn't necessary, Lieutenant," exclaimed Major Fox.

Yolanda removed her blouse. "Yes it is, Major." She stepped between them both to permit them to examine her shoulders for signs of kickback. Then she turned one hundred eighty degrees to allow each to inspect the opposite shoulder. Both men were trying not to stare. "Look at me, gentlemen. That's why I took off my blouse."

Both men inspected her with their eyes. "Okay, Lieutenant. No bruises," said the President.

"Men!" She was exasperated. "I could have covered a bruise with make-up. You must touch me to make sure I haven't."

Neither man moved.

"Both of you."

Slowly and gently, each of them brought his hand to her shoulders to confirm that no bruise had been concealed. When they were done, she returned to her seat and announced. "If you've seen enough, I'd like another drink now." Then she put her blouse back on.

"So would I." The President agreed.

With the bottle in his right hand, Major Fox poured another round.

CHAPTER 55

Paris, France
Saturday, January 26, 3:17 Western European Time

In his dream, he was escorting her to a fine restaurant. She held his arm. Everyone noticed them. She was radiant. Then it was a *souk*, not a restaurant. They were out of place. It wasn't right. Smiling Arab children began to circle them, laughing --- closing the circle. It was so hot he couldn't catch his breath. His legs were heavy, unresponsive. But he knew he had to make them move. He looked at Meghan. Her eyes were frantic. Her lips parted, but the sounds came to him slowly at first. Then distinctly.

"Bzzzzz."

It made no sense. It wasn't her voice. Then it all vanished except the noise.

"Bzzzzz."

Hassim broke through the fog and answered the cell phone.

"Someone's looking for you in Blois. Any idea who?"

"No idea."

"Did you use your real name anywhere?"

"The hospitals must have it. I did not use it anywhere else."

"Why would French Arabs search for you?"

"There is no reason. Perhaps they seek my companion."

"She will be easy to locate once they know her condition. Did you tell anyone who she is?"

"Hah! That would be like asking to be killed."

"Then how could they find out?"

"Not from me."

"Don't leave. I'll pick you up in the morning. We've got to get both of you out of France."

"I'll be here. Asleep."

As his exhaustion relieved him of his burden of consciousness, the face of his servant Khalid flickered across his memory.

If they knew about Meghan, Khalid was surely dead --- or worse.

Hassim was wrong.

At this very moment, Khalid was scouting the *premiere arrondissement* for the haunts Hassim had described to him back in Palestine. He had kept a list on his computer for the day he himself would arrive in Paris.

If he found Hassim, he would be a hero to Islamic Jihad --- a dangerous, but potentially useful group. If not, he would at least identify the places Hassim had been known to frequent for them. If Hassim did not have the good sense to avoid those places, it would be his fault he would be caught --- not Khalid's.

Either way, he would start a new life in France. *Vive la France!*

CHAPTER 56

The White House, Washington, D.C.
Friday, January 25, 8:29 PM EST

The first Presidential Nightly Briefing continued. The speculation over the location of the assassin when the shot was fired was inconclusive. They moved on to the second item on the agenda.

"Meghan is paralyzed from the waist down," Marco announced. "They don't think her condition is permanent. Otherwise, she's healthy."

"That's a big otherwise, *amigo*," Major Fox observed.

"Nevertheless, we've got to bring her home as soon as possible. We can't protect her in a French hospital."

"What about an Air Force hospital in Germany?" asked the Major.

"Not without revealing her identity. Besides, once she's on a plane, she might as well come home."

"But, sir." Yolanda still could not bring herself to address the President of the United States by his first name. "How will you explain her injury?"

"I'm hoping she'll be able to walk by that time."

"Going to be difficult to explain if she can't," Major Fox observed. "How long is Agent Meghan available?"

"And do you think she'd mind having a crippling accident?" Yolanda added sweetly.

"Ahh. I guess we can wait a day or so to develop a plan," Marco conceded.

With that, the first Presidential Nightly Briefing ended.

CHAPTER 57

Paris, France
Saturday, January 26, 7:42 Western European Time

The smiling women with their uncovered heads and their revealing Western fashions returned his smiles and captured his eyes. Women with stylish hair you could actually see. Women with long, naked legs. Women with figures complimented by their clothing --- instead of concealed by it. Even in winter! How he enjoyed this stimulating display of pulchritude. He loved them all.

Had Khalid not been staring at every young woman he passed, he might not have walked right past Hassim leaving his lodgings in the company of a tall man in black. Both men continued without making eye contact, but something made Khalid look back. He'd recognized the tassel loafers Hassim always wore. He took one quick look to confirm, then reached for his cell phone.

"Are we going to America?" Hassim asked James when they were seated in the back of the Mercury Marquis.

"Negative. Your friend needs special treatment before she returns."

"She's leaving the hospital?"

"The three of us are flying to Sweden in an air ambulance this morning."

"Why Sweden?"

"That's where the neurosurgeon is."

"Can't he come here?"

"His clinic is in Sweden. He wants her there. Besides, Paris isn't safe. Remember?"

"Yes. Any more news on the people inquiring after me?"

"Your fan club," James said dryly, "has grown. The *Deuxiéme Bureau* reports that the entire Muslim population of Paris seems to have your description. One of your former employees provided a photograph."

"That would be Khalid," he assumed aloud. "He probably had no choice if they came around looking for me."

"Loyalty has a way of disappearing when the surgical instruments are produced," James observed.

"Well, they won't be looking for me in Sweden." Hassim hoped aloud.

"They'd better not be. You have become a liability, Hassim. Don't make this a habit."

"It is not my choice. I assure you."

"That's irrelevant. If you are deemed to constitute a sufficient danger to the patient or to the United States, you will disappear permanently. Do you understand?"

"Of course. And if you kill me, I will understand that it is merely your duty."

"Sure you will...."

After a moment, Hassim spoke. "Pardon me for asking, but has that decision already be made?"

"Not to my knowledge," the agent replied. "But if it were up to me, I'd consider you an unacceptable risk."

"I am worth it. You will see."

"I hope so."

CHAPTER 58

The White House, Washington, D.C.
Saturday, January 26, 1:50 AM EST

Agent Meghan arrived at the side entrance with trepidation. She was now the acting first lady, with the accent decidedly on "acting." If Camp David had been the tryouts, this was Broadway. She would be on stage full time, playing a role she didn't know. And she wasn't an actress. "More like a stunt double," she admitted to herself as the door of the limousine was opened for her. Showtime!

To her relief, she saw Marco standing several feet away. If she could make it to him, maybe she would be identified by association.

"Welcome to our new home," he understated, giving her a straight line.

"Is there room for a garden?"

"I checked that out for you," he improvised. "It's mostly roses now."

"That's a nice start," she conceded as she entered his open arms and kissed him on the cheek.

"It even has an office."

"Oh good. I hate it so when you spread your work out all over the kitchen table." People were chuckling. This wasn't so hard.

"You should have told me...."

Thus, they bantered their way through the awkward reception, thankful that the late hour had kept it somewhat private. Somewhat is a relative term at the White House. At least thirty persons had witnessed some aspect of her arrival.

Now she stood facing the Presidential bed, unable to speak. There was no way she could sleep elsewhere. She was trapped. And it wasn't his fault, she had to keep reminding herself.

Noticing her preoccupation with the horizontal furniture, Marco offered "I sleep in pajamas."

She looked up at him. "Thank you."

"I don't do it for you."

"Thank you anyway." He understood. She felt better.

"It's late. I'm going to sleep right away," he announced. "Kick me if I snore."

She managed a little smile at that. Imagine sleeping with the President of the United States and being invited to kick him. "I may kick you just for the Hell of it," she proclaimed as she went into the bathroom to shower.

"That's the spirit!"

When she came out, the lights were off. She closed her eyes for a count of sixty to adjust to the darkness. When she re-opened them, she could make out his pajama-clad upper body on the left side of the king-size bed --- wrapped in most of the covers. She entered the right side of the bed with maximum stealth, gripped the covers with her right hand, and executed a violent spin which moved the covers to her side of the bed.

The President slumbered on.

"I might survive this," she told herself.

CHAPTER 59

The Krister Clinic, Göteborg, Sweden
Saturday, January 26, 11:50 Western European Time

She opened her eyes slowly. There was Hassim. She found that reassuring. "Drugged?" Speaking was an effort.

"Very much so," he replied.

"Why?"

"Had to move you."

"Where?"

"Sweden. For treatment. Special clinic."

"Sweden?"

"*Ja*," he joked.

"*Ja?*" She was too groggy for humor.

"Yes. Southwest of Stockholm, place called Göteborg. They make Saabs and Volvos here. Who knows what else? One of the ports of the Hanseatic League in Napoleonic...."

"Touch my toes," she interrupted.

Hassim became wary. "The doctor hasn't seen you yet...."

"Just touch my damn toes, Hassim."

Hassim complied, one foot at a time. "Any feeling?"

"You sure you're touching them?"

"I am squeezing your large toe now --- like a grape in

a wine press."

"Nothing. Nothing at all."

"Maybe it is the drugs...."

"Hassim, I need for you to be honest with me. I really do. We both know it's not the drugs. I have a severe nerve injury somewhere in the lumbar region of my spine. It will take medical treatment or a miracle for me to recover. Maybe both. Well-meaning people will tell me I am getting better in a misguided effort to maintain my spirits. I, in turn, will resent them for this. Don't be one of them, I beg you. I am a determined person, not a cheerful one. I will deal with my condition without false expectations."

"What about bravado?"

"That's what I like about you, Hassim. You don't pander to me. You'll help me more by sarcasm than all the others will by sympathy."

"Then, to hear is to obey, *mumsahib*."

"I never got the chance to tell you how convincing you were when you offered to help the hijackers," Meghan said.

"That is because I was sincere."

"What?"

"Always be sincere — even if you don't mean it."

"Sounds like one of the satanic verses."

"Your President Truman said that."

A nurse's aide entered with a cartload of medical paraphernalia and shooed Hassim away.

CHAPTER 60

The White House, Washington, D.C.
Saturday, January 26, 9:10 AM EST

Major Fox and The President were returning to the Oval Office after the Presidential Daily Briefing. The Major was now included among the participants, but had kept silent. He preferred to listen. After all, he could discuss matters with the President one-on-one later.

"You didn't say much," Marco observed.

"It is better to remain silent and be thought a fool, than to speak and remove all doubt."

"Go ahead, remove all doubt."

"So how's your love life, Mr. President?" he asked.

"Non-existent," he admitted. "Agent Meghan stole the covers."

"Is there no respect for the highest office in the land?"

"Not in the Presidential bedroom."

"When's Meghan coming back?"

"Not soon. They moved her to a clinic in Sweden."

"Maybe she'll come back home as a tall blonde."

"She's already a tall blonde," Marco reminded him.

"You are a difficult man to cheer up, *amigo*. You get irritable when you're horny."

"That's true, *Zorro*. But I could use her political insights right now, too."

"Any idea when she can come home?"

"Not yet, but we should probably be planning for it."

"Want to hear an idea, completely out of the blue?"

"From you, always. If nothing else, it will be entertaining."

"I'll overlook that last comment. What about this? Meghan's father orders a Volvo for overseas delivery. That means he has to go to Sweden to pick it up. He takes his daughter with him and the swap is made there, where no one's looking."

Marco was stunned. "That might be brilliant!"

"Let me check it out. We can discuss it further at the nightly briefing."

"Make it a priority, but keep it between us for now."

"*Omerta*," the Major responded solemnly. "But you'd better run it by your father-in-law."

"He's waiting for us in the Oval Office."

Paul Carnegie considered the proposal to retrieve his daughter. He refused to call it a plan. "It's not completely baked," he explained. "But it could work under the right circumstances."

"Agreed," the President said by way of terminating that conversational subject.

"Marco, you may be the President, but you are not the elected President. You need to get the public behind you as soon as possible or your administration will be a charade."

"Sir, you don't beat around the bush," observed Major

Fox. "He's got a point."

"And how do you propose that I accomplish that?"

"North Korea," Carnegie stated flatly. "It's time for retribution. Quick and deadly. Surprise the world."

"I'm listening."

"No nukes," Carnegie added.

"No targets worthy of them," Marco responded. "And my predecessor already has a contract out on Kim. We've been told that the assassin is already in place. It's a private operation; so we don't have details."

"Glad to hear it. Doesn't change anything though." To Marco's surprise, Carnegie turned to Major Fox and asked "What would you do?"

The Major had a ready answer. "Take out their military, utterly and completely. Destroy their air force and naval installations in a coordinated lightning attack. Then go after their ships at sea and coastal defenses. Do it before the international community can react. Make sure everyone knows it's over."

Carnegie was pleased. "You've given this some thought."

"I prepared a detailed plan when Marco invited me to Washington."

"Who else knows about this, Major?" Carnegie asked.

"Just my staff of one."

"She's trustworthy," Marco assured Carnegie. "I think it's time to take a look at your plan, *amigo*.

"I'll have Yolanda bring it to us now, if you'd like."

"I've got time," Carnegie offered.

"Call her then," said the President.

CHAPTER 61

The Krister Clinic, Göteborg, Sweden
Saturday, January 26, 15:27 Western European Time

Meghan awoke at the center of a web that appeared to be the work of a demented spider. Various limbs hung at improbable angles and directions. She couldn't move. Except to scream, which she did with sufficient vigor and conviction to summon several nurses and a resident. By now she was ranting. They observed her from a safe distance, saying nothing. One of them was reading the various monitors attached to her, to make sure nothing was officially awry.

Then Hassim appeared. "The flower awakens," he announced as he entered the room.

"Do something!" she ordered.

And he complied. To the astonishment of all, his hand swooped down upon her left big toe like a bird of prey --- and pinched it.

"Ouch! That hurt, damn it!"

"Precisely the point," he replied smugly.

She blinked as it sunk in. "Do the other one!"

Wordlessly, he complied.

"It hurts good," she admitted. "So when do we leave?"

The hospital personnel began to drift away, to perform

other miracles for other patients.

"Not just yet, I'm afraid. You have to wait for the incision to heal. Until then, you'll remain in bed."

She glared at him. "Can you translate that into days?"

"Best guess right now is ten days. It may be fewer, maybe more. It's a small price to pay to be able to walk again."

"I guess it is," she sighed.

"Should I tickle your thighs? Just to be sure?"

She laughed a little. "Hassim, I was your captive. I was nearly naked. You could have done anything you wanted to me, but you didn't. You didn't even appear to be interested," she asserted as though it were an incomprehensible concept. "Now you want to tickle my thighs? I don't think so."

"We shall just assume then that your thighs are as responsive as your toes."

"Yes. For now." Then she added, coyly "Will you keep the offer open?"

"It is what any chivalrous man would do," he proclaimed solemnly.

"A chivalrous Muslim...."

"We are not so different. Muslims and Christians believe in the same Old Testament. It's the second set of instructions that followed which makes the difference."

"All the difference," she added.

"The differences have more to do with our cultures than our religions. My people have lived in tribes for too long. Everyone outside the tribe is either an enemy or a potential enemy. In the melting pots of the West, the tribal culture did not flourish. Nations replaced them. In the Middle East, the national boundaries were imposed by outsiders with little knowledge of the tribes. For example, three disparate tribes were combined to make Iraq."

"That certainly worked out well."

"They still don't trust each other. They may never trust each other."

"But you're not like that."

"True. I'm, neither tribal nor national. I serve myself."

"But you work for the United States," she reminded him.

"Loyalty to one's employer is part of the job."

"Am I part of the job?"

"Yes," he replied without hesitation. "But occasionally --- just every now and again, mind you --- you are a pleasant part of the job." It was not flattery, just truth. Meghan found it disarming.

"Smooth talker."

CHAPTER 62

The White House, Washington, D.C.
Saturday, January 26, 10:38 AM Eastern Time

Agent Meghan was in the President's private sitting room, awaiting her first appointment. A tall *mestiza* in military uniform entered. She was striking and confident. She spoke as the door closed behind her.

"I have news," she whispered. "She has regained feelings in her legs. They expect her to recover fully."

"My God. When?"

"No more than ten days."

"Does the President know yet?"

"He's been in a meeting. He'll be told when it's over."

"Why are you telling me?"

"I'm not here just to tell you. I'm Second Lieutenant Yolanda Herrera. I work for Major Fox. We're concerned about you. You have a difficult assignment. Failure is not an option. You must convince everyone that you are his wife."

"I already share his bed."

"That's a good start," Yolanda admitted. "I suggest you take the next step, but that's up to you. He is handsome and charming."

"Did he put you up to this?"

"No. He doesn't know I'm here. But think about it. I'm told his marriage is more of a political arrangement than a romantic one."

"That sounds right. His wife actually encouraged us to practice intimacy when we met at Camp David. Oh.... Did you know about that?"

"Yes, but not until later," Yolanda assured her.

"Good. I didn't want to spill any state secrets."

"You didn't.

"So why are you here, promoting adultery at the highest level of government?"

Yolanda smiled. "Is that what I'm doing? I guess it is. I hadn't thought of it that way."

"There's another way?"

"This is Washington. There's always another viewpoint."

"Granted. Let's hear it."

"O.K. Here goes. You are young and single. You presumably have hormones...." She let it hang.

"Yes," Agent Meghan admitted warily.

"The President of the United States is an attractive man with whom you could have an affair without having to hide it. It would be good for both of you."

"We grasp, grapple and gasp for the good for the country?"

"Absolutely."

"Then I should sleep with the President because it's my patriotic duty?"

"Who wants a sexually frustrated man to control the nuclear button?"

"I should sacrifice my body to prevent World War III?" Yolanda shook her head. "But you won't."

"I won't?"

"No. You won't sacrifice your body." Yolanda paused. "You'll enjoy every second of it and come back for more."

"Then I owe you my gratitude for setting me straight," Agent Meghan replied with sarcasm.

"You'll do it?"

"Probably," she admitted. "If the situation is right."

"Making it right shouldn't be too difficult," Yolanda opined. "You're already in his bed."

"Point taken."

"If you need something more stimulating, take him in the Oval Office."

"That does have a kind of kinky appeal...."

"Whatever."

"Really, now. Who sent you?"

"I came on my own, acting on my own convictions."

"Why?"

"Because one of us has to do it, and I want to --- but it wouldn't work out."

"What?"

"You heard me." Yolanda stood. So did Agent Meghan.

"Well, Yolanda, this has been the most stimulating conversation I've had in a long time. Do drop by again."

"You can count on it. And good luck with your new mission."

CHAPTER 63

The Palace
Pyongyang, Democratic People's Republic of Korea
Saturday, January 26, 16:25 Japan Standard Time

Jung was amazed she had gotten this far. But here she was, a girl from the remote mountains near the Chinese border. Now she was swimming in a private indoor pool in the seven-story pleasure palace of Kim Jong-il himself. She wasn't alone. The Dear Leader's physician and nurse were also in the warm water, both of them young, attractive women possessing dubious medical credentials. The Dear Leader himself tooled around the huge pool on a body board fitted with a small motor, challenging the artificial waves generated by the wave machine that cost more than five hundred times the average annual income of his unfortunate countrymen.

It had all been carefully planned, of course, by the Green Dragons from New Jersey, with the blessing of former President Carnegie. Jung had been recruited to infiltrate the palace several years before. She had accepted the assignment for the opportunity to avenge her boyfriend, who was tortured for showing disrespect as the Dear Leader's limousine passed by on parade. The fact that he had turned his head to avoid sneezing on the woman standing in front of him did not reduce his guilt in the eyes of the national police. In their zeal to please their master, the police had inadvertently killed him. This was merely one of several acceptable outcomes for them. They possessed latitude in the performance of their patriotic duties.

Of course, she had other qualifications besides hatred for the government. Among them was a natural beauty that brought Korean men to a dead stop when they saw her. But, most important, she had played the drums in the school band. Once she joined the cause, her repertoire was expanded to include jazz. She studied Gene Krupa from cracked 78 rpm records. Then they taught her to play a home-made electric guitar. Her opening came when the lead guitarist of the Dear Leader's favorite all-girl band became pregnant. Although Jung didn't know it, this had also been planned. So she had donned stilettos, hot pants and a bikini top to commence her musical career.

One night after the party was over, Kim had reappeared without warning while the girls were jamming. Jung threw herself into the opening riff of *Johnny B. Good©*, using her guitar as a percussion instrument to make it sound like Jerry Lee Lewis on the piano --- just as Chuck Berry had. That was the night she discovered that Kim was a closet rocker. He had the bar reopened and insisted they continue --- which they did until dawn.

Before the evening was over, Kim's 1977 Fender Stratocaster was brought out for her to play. She made the Candy Apple Red instrument sing. At the end of the evening, Kim had insisted she take it home so she could practice. The guitar was easily worth more than money than whole villages would see in a lifetime, but it was just another trophy to the Dear Leader. He had an original 1954 model, too.

When her mentor had first seen her "Strat," he had become delirious with joy. He immediately set the pickup selectors to make the "quacky" sound like Eric Clapton; then he had played for 45 minutes without pausing. Reluctantly he had handed it back to his student and revealed the instrument's secrets. Jung caught on quickly. The rock 'n roll after-party became a fixture in the Palace.

Of course, the lyrics could be problematic since the Dear Leader was nearly fluent in English. *Born in the USA©* was clearly not acceptable, but *Back in the USSR©* was. The space between those two was a minefield. Generally speaking, the British groups were safer, but vague songs like Dylan's *Maggie's Farm©* posed no threat. The Dear Leader would not tolerate Elvis, presumably because of his association with the United States military. But he perceived Chuck Berry to be an oppressed Black man taunting America with his Negro rhythms; so most of his songs were fine.

But Kim flat out loved the Rolling Stones.

With her natural beauty and great energy, Jung effortlessly made the transition from guitarist to performer. She danced, pranced and played as the front man for the band. She studied Tina Turner's moves from the Ike and Tina days. Once she became so enthusiastic that she failed to notice that the guitar neck had accidently uncovered her right breast. Kim had waited until song ended to admonish her, pointed his stubby finger at her while laughing with delight. It became a random part of her routine. Yet she had to pretend always to be surprised. She would feign embarrassment, giggle at her exposure. It was a delicate pose, undoubtedly supported by her innocent face and the fact that her name meant "chaste" in Korean.

For the Dear Leader was basically nothing more than a naughty boy. His arrested development had left him more voyeur than participant. He wanted pretty girls around him. He wanted them to pay attention to him. But there was no hormonal drive for sexual conquest. He simply never matured. Indeed, many wondered how he had spawned a son, but no one doubted the paternity. The son turned out to be as corrupt and ruthless as Kim himself.

Like the other party girls, she drank sparingly and only when required to do so by the Dear Leader. It was part of the appearance of purity she affected. Girls who became drunk were removed by the guards and never heard from again.

What was sauce for the goose was not for the gander. Copious quantities of the world's finest wines were consumed at dinner, to be followed by cognac. North Korea was the largest customer of Hennessy VO in the world. It was flown in from Europe by Ilyushin-76 cargo planes carrying sixty tons of luxury goods per flight, from silk wallpaper to gold-plated hand guns. And every drop of cognac was consumed by Kim and his guests. After that, the finest single malt whiskies had their turn. If there were foreign guests, bottles of Paekdu Mountain Bulnoju would inevitably appear around midnight. This fiery rice liquor was served in chilled crystal shot glasses and poured down the throat in one quick swallow, like ouzo in Mykonos or tequila at a USC frat party. The Korean words for "Eternal Youth" were shouted either before or afterwards. This ritual finished off the less practiced male guests, but Kim and the others would routinely drink until completely trashed.

To the extent there was something worthy of the name, that was the plan. Use the drunken revelry to eliminate Kim Jong-il forever. Her first assignment had been to find a way to implement the plan. She had decided upon poison.

It would not be easy. Like everyone else who wasn't a guard or an honored guest, she was stripped and searched each time she entered the palace. She was permitted to bring nothing in with her except her undergarments and her guitar. She was provided with clothes appropriate to the event and her function. That usually translated into the Korean version of a Dallas Cowboys cheerleader outfit. The food preparation area was highly guarded. The beverages all arrived in sealed containers. All bottle caps were removed by the guards and destroyed, so no bottle could be used again. Kim received only the first pour from each bottle as it was opened. Each time he wanted another drink, another bottle was opened. Each evening, a new case was opened. Whether it was his paranoia or his world-class phobia about germs, he never shared a drink.

Introducing poison into an individually sealed bottle in a sealed case that was stored in a guarded vault did not hold much promise. Since all but one of the beverages consumed by the Dear Leader were imported by his own worldwide import company, there was no way to introduce any substance before arrival at the Palace. The Paekdu Mountain Bulnoju was produced in North Korea, but the facilities were tightly controlled by the Dear Leader himself.

Jung resolved to open her mind to the solution, rather

than dwelling upon the obstacles. Shortly thereafter, what she had witnessed many times before revealed itself to be the instrument of Kim's destruction.

She only had to place the poison in his glass, not in his beverage.

Of course, all the glassware was imported. But the level of scrutiny was less. Often the stemware and beer mugs were rinsed and placed in one of the top-of-the-line German freezers before the beverage was introduced. This procedure provided chillier *Cristal* and frostier *Warsteiner* for the Dear Leader and his guests.

Perhaps, it also provided an opportunity.

CHAPTER 64

Hotell Plats, Göteborg, Sweden
Saturday, January 26, 15:57 Western European Time

As was his custom, Hassim had departed his taxi at the main entrance to Centralstation and wandered among the crowds there. Often, he stopped to purchase a book or a snack before exiting one of the West portals. Then he would walk across Hotell Plats to the wonderful Victorian hostelry where he lodged. This evening the wind was nothing short of ferocious, hurling the sub-freezing air through his garments relentlessly. He walked briskly, with his head bowed. It was dark. For that matter, he hadn't seen the sun since he'd arrived in Sweden. Daytime was simply when it was slightly less dark than at night. Automobiles used their headlamps all the time. It depressed him.

He entered the unassuming door and made an abrupt left turn for the lobby bar. "Wodka, *snella*," he announced as he sat at the bar. It would be ice cold, of course, but it would feel warm. He would settle for that.

From his right he heard another non-Swede order vodka. He spun as he recognized the voice. "Khalid?"

"*Bonsoir, monsieur.*"

Hassim followed Khalid's lead. "*Ah, bonsoir. Comment*

allez vous?"

"Il fait beaucoup froid." Khalid expressed his opinion regarding the weather, indicating that it was too cold for him. He felt constrained by his limited French and suggested they remove themselves to the lobby, where wing chairs and small tables would permit private conversation.

"What are you doing here?" Hassim immediately inquired.

"To assist in your capture by Hamas, of course," Khalid explained.

Hassim tensed and looked around the lobby. Satisfied they were not being watched, he continued. "Of course," he agreed. "Are you open to a better offer?"

"That is what I came to discuss." Khalid smiled. "You taught me well."

"And you want?"

"To attain an old age. That is paramount."

"Survival with benefits."

"I assume the deal you made would accommodate my needs as well."

"I had more to bargain with."

"Must I seize the woman? It might be difficult to arrange her return."

"You know where she is?"

"The Krister Clinic, third floor."

"Who else knows?"

"No one...yet. But they could discover her at any moment. I doubt that they are relying solely upon me."

"Are they here, in Göteborg?"

"At least two of them, perhaps more. They may have

Swedish agents in place, as well," Khalid speculated casually. "It is refreshing to see you disturbed, Hassim."

Hassim shook his head slowly. "Khalid, if you approach the Americans with your offer, you are a dead man. The only question will be who kills you first."

"Yes. That is part of my plan. I choose the Americans. Please tell them for me."

"You want to die?"

"No. I want to appear to die. It is the only way to be rid of Hamas."

At that moment, the American who called himself James entered the hotel lobby. As he passed their chairs, he dropped his *Herald Tribune*. Hassim moved to assist with its retrieval. As they accumulated the sections, Hassim whispered to him. "Seize the man I am with."

Apparently, James was accustomed to such improvisation. "Alive?"

The question horrified Hassim. "Yes! Yes!" he whispered back.

James smiled broadly at the two of them. "Thank you for your assistance, gentlemen." He pulled up a chair. "You here on business, too?"

"Yes," Hassim responded vaguely.

"I'm a business consultant from the States." James began his cover story. "I help companies understand the way business is conducted in other countries. Today I told an automobile manufacturer why it wasn't reaching its target customer base." He pulled a cellular phone from his jacket pocket. "Excuse me, I have a call." He hit speed dial and started talking. "Door facing Hotell Plats now. Park close by."

As James spoke, he wrote on the corner of the newspaper. When he was done, he handed it to Khalid, saying "I've got to be off. You can keep the sports page." Then he abruptly departed, as if late for an appointment.

Hassim said "Good-bye." He turned to find Khalid reading the note. It read "2 men. Long black coats. Orange scarf. Go with them."

Khalid struggled to regain his look of confidence. "I have to go."

"Where?"

"I don't know."

Two gentlemen were approaching the entrance. One wore a bright orange neck scarf. Khalid rose to leave.

"We'll meet again," declared Hassim.

"*In'shallah.*"

CHAPTER 65

The White House, Washington, D.C.
Saturday, January 26, 12:25 PM EST

The head of Secret Service entered. "Excuse me, Mr. President. We've found something." From a long cylindrical package he extracted a black umbrella by the top, instead of the handle. "It has no center shaft." he explained.

Marco came around his desk to examine it. "It had one," he concluded aloud. He wore a confused look.

"It was in an umbrella stand in one of the interior rooms; so it was brought in by a staff member. Guests are required to check theirs at the entrance. That also explains why the missing shaft wasn't noticed."

Marco hadn't grasped the significance yet.

"The upper part of the cloth portion is deformed, as if something was carried in it...."

It clicked. "Like a rifle?"

"Exactly, Mr. President. Like a compact rifle carried so that the barrel replaced the shaft. Probably had a fake handle, but we haven't found it yet."

"Could this have worked? Would it match the bullet?"

"Yes on both counts, sir. Now we know how the weapon arrived."

"But the umbrella is still here!"

"Yes. It wasn't used to remove the rifle."

"Does that mean the weapon is still here?"

"It might, Mr. President," he conceded. "We have a tentative plan, subject to your approval." He waited.

"Don't stop now."

"Yes, Mr. President. Since we haven't been able to find the weapon, we propose to replace this umbrella in the hope that the shooter may retrieve it to conceal the weapon for removal. We would have to attach a small device to let us know when that happens."

"What if someone else picks it up?"

"The device would only send a silent alarm if someone sought to remove the umbrella from the White House. That should eliminate anyone who wanted a working umbrella. Only the shooter would want this one."

"Who else knows?"

"One other agent. I don't want it to go any further."

"I agree. Get it back in place as soon as you can. What if he's looking for it now?"

"We have someone using the room temporarily, to discourage any retrieval attempt.

"Excellent work. Keep the FBI out of the loop on this."

"Of course, Mr. President."

CHAPTER 66

Outside Göteborg, Sweden
Saturday, January 26, 17:34 Western European Time

From the hotel they had taken Khalid by car over a high bridge, away from the city. The highway wound past modern factories, many bearing the name VOLVO in large blue letters, illuminated by floodlights. Then they had driven past what appeared to be small settlements on either side of the road. On the right, the sea had suddenly appeared just before the driver had stopped to wait for the car ferry. The crossing had taken about twenty minutes. It had seemed longer because of the pistol in Khalid's ribs. Once on the island, the rural homes of the city dwellers were soon replaced by working farms set amid the granite outcroppings. The only words spoken had been a few directives aimed at him to remain silent. Yet he had remained calm until the car had turned onto a small lane that apparently led nowhere.

"We have medical training," the man with the orange scarf assured him.

The other chimed in "We can amputate."

Khalid was standing in a field in the moonlight. The snow was up to his ankles, which were bare, as were his feet.

Unfamiliar with Northern climates, he was astounded to learn that cold could burn. But the astonishment had passed ten minutes before. Shortly thereafter his demeanor had changed. He no longer attempted to bargain. He was pleading.

His American captors regarded this as an improvement.

As he finished recounting the events which had brought him to Göteborg, he added "I'm not a member of Hamas. They kidnapped me. They only wanted me to identify Hassim and the lady."

"How much are you being paid?" It was a typically American question.

"Nothing, I swear!"

"Then you must be on their side...."

"No, no! I am a tool that they will discard when they no longer need me."

"Discard how?"

"They have promised that they will let me go."

"Do you believe them?"

"No. That is why I contacted Hassim. If you could help me escape, I will not tell them where the lady is."

"And if we don't?"

"I have another plan, but it may not work."

"What if we just kill you now?"

"Ahhh. That would not work as well as having me assist you."

"For free." It was not a question.

"And you would not have to dispose of my body," Khalid offered.

"That's not much of a bargaining chip...."

"It is to me," he admitted.

The two agents smiled at each other. One tossed Khalid's socks and shoes to him.

"Allah be praised! Thank you, gentlemen. You will not regret this, I promise you." He was sitting in the snow, concentrating on getting his shoes over his stiff feet when two muffled noises made him look up.

Both agents were lying on the ground. They were not moving.

A pistol with a long silencer was pointed at Khalid's chest. At the other end was one of his Hamas handlers. "Where is the American woman?"

"Don't shoot! I will tell you." Khalid's reserve of calm had finally been expended. He blurted out "She's on the third floor of The Krister Clinic."

The man waved the pistol barrel toward the lane. "Show me."

He scrambled to his feet and began to shuffle away, shoes still untied, in the direction the gunman had indicated. He might live long enough for his feet to thaw. Over his shoulder he asked, "Are they dead?"

"Not yet."

CHAPTER 67

Göteborg, Sweden
Saturday, January 26, 19:16 Western European Time

Hassim had expected his handler to return after Khalid had been taken away. After finishing his vodka, he had taken a coffee. He was warm and relaxed, determined to stay inside for the remainder of this brutal night. If James did not return soon, he would move into the excellent dining room for a light meal.

The first passing fire truck had made him uneasy, but he had tried to ignore it. Then he heard more, and then even more.

He bolted for the door.

Heedless of the freezing temperature, he ran towards the glow at full speed. With each step closer his fears were confirmed. Then, to his astonishment, he realized that the Krister Clinic was not engulfed in flames. The small building across the narrow street was, however. It was enough to cause the evacuation of the clinic. He knew immediately that it was no accident. Hamas was nothing if not devious.

Patients were being helped outside, the staff going back in for more each time. Firemen were everywhere.

Freezing water blasted the Krister Clinic and surrounding buildings to keep the fire from spreading.

Dodging the vehicles surrounding the entrance, Hassim made his way forward --- looking for Meghan. In the confusion, no one stopped him.

He thought he'd spotted her a half block ahead. Some men were rolling her Gurney into an ambulance, one of several private ambulances at the scene. As he ran towards her, one of the men noticed him and blocked his way. "This is not your business," he warned in accented English.

"Yes, it is!" he protested. "I'm with the American lady."

"Not anymore." His fist shot up, catching Hassim under the chin. Hassim's knees lifted, then buckled coming down. When he was able to look around, the ambulance was gone. That was when it occurred to him that he hadn't looked at the license plates. All he remembered was a long red rectangle with white letters --- just like every other plate in Sweden.

Hassim struggled to his feet and began to inventory his injuries. His legs quickly lost the initial wobbliness. His breathing was normal --- considering the temperature. His jaw hurt like Hell, but he didn't need to use it right then.

In desperation, he set off in the direction the ambulance had taken. Maybe he'd get lucky. Besides, he'd freeze if he stood still much longer.

Hassim found many of the narrow streets blocked by emergency vehicles. That might permit him to determine the escape route taken by the abductors --- who had undoubtedly encountered the same obstacles. He jogged along slowly, telling himself it was a sustainable pace for the weather.

Another voice in his head cursed him for being out of shape.

The blood brought him back to the moment. It was all over the cobblestones. If it was human, that person had little blood left. He began to follow the blood.

The wind whistled around the corners. The streets were deserted. Those foolhardy enough to venture out were watching the fire and the spectacle surrounding it. It was not a night for strolling. There were bloody footprints, undisturbed by traffic. Hassim followed them as best he could in the light from the brick buildings he passed. Even his untrained eye could not miss the fact that the person had been staggering. He expected to stumble across a body at any moment.

But that's not what happened.

"*Allahu akbar!*" It came from behind, like a stage whisper. Then something slammed into Hassim's lower back. Arms locked around his waist and he lost his footing. Even before he hit the pavement, he had twisted so as to land on top of his assailant. He wasn't sure this would improve his situation; it was simply a reaction. He applied his weight to the man's back to pin him down while he scanned the area for other attackers. Seeing no further threats, he returned his attention to the man. He wasn't moving.

He was wet! It was the wounded man he had been following. He hadn't expected him to still be alive. Without further thought, Hassim turned him over.

"Khalid!" The eyes opened slowly. There was a brief smile of recognition. "We need to get to hospital!"

"On fire," Khalid croaked. His throat was cut, but not deeply. Blood spurted from his left carotid artery. Hassim's hand moved to put pressure on the wound. "I am dead, Hassim."

"Not yet! Your throat is intact. You are not coughing blood. We could...."

Khalid interrupted."No *effendi*, I am dead. My life has flowed out into the gutters of this frozen Hell."

"Cursed Hamas terrorists!"

Khalid coughed, but there was no blood. "No. They are dead. Killed, like me."

Hassim was struck speechless. His circuits had overloaded. He couldn't even ask "Who?"

He didn't need to. It was the only question. "Infidels."

"Europeans?"

There was a pause while Khalid summoned the energy to reply. "Maybe." Then he began to recite a Sunni prayer which he never finished.

Hassim finished the prayer for Khalid, cradling his lifeless head in his arms as if it made a difference.

Khalid's death had forged a bond between them that he was never able to achieve during his life. Hassim found it strange and sad. Twenty minutes later, a passing police patrol found them in the same spot, nearly frozen together.

CHAPTER 68

The White House, Washington, D.C.
Saturday, January 26, 8:02 PM EST

The next Presidential Nightly Briefing began in the belief that the First Lady was safe. A misguided toast to the success of this venture opened the meeting.

Because the President declined to share the discovery of the umbrella used to smuggle in the weapon that killed his predecessor, the focus of the discussion was the removal of Kim Jong-il. All they really knew about that was that an agent was in place in his retinue, ready to act when the opportunity presented itself. They didn't have an inkling that the agent was a young girl or how she had achieved access to the Dear Leader. But at least they knew more than the CIA did.

After that, the conversation died down.

"These meetings just aren't as exciting when Yolanda keeps her shirt on," observed Major Fox.

"Permission to speak freely, sir?" Yolanda asked curtly.

Sensing that she had not found this remark humorous, he said "No way."

"Then Good Evening, gentlemen." She left.

When the door had closed behind her, Marco suggested "Now might be a good time to tell me more about her trial."

"Not much to tell. Never found a gun to match the fatal bullet. Yolanda had some gunshot residue, but she'd been on the firing range that morning, using the same type of weapon that killed her husband. The prosecutor tried to make that sound like an unlikely coincidence, but it was one of the guns she used every time she went there. There just wasn't a case against her. The jury deliberated less than an hour."

"Do you think she killed him?"

"I really don't know. She knew he wasn't worth the risk. She didn't inherit much. There was not enough insurance to bury him...."

"So there wasn't much motive for a premeditated murder."

"I guess that's what I'm saying, but...."

"But, what?"

"She was certainly capable of it."

"And she possesses a fiery disposition?" The President asked.

"That, *amigo*, is an understatement," Major Fox responded.

"Were you ever involved with her?"

"No. But I've been tempted. So far, my caution has carried the day. Either that, or she's not interested."

"I'll try to follow your lead on this."

"That would be wise. Well, I guess I might as well move on too. *Buena noche*, Marco."

It looked like the President of the United States was going to get a good night's sleep for a change. He tightened the cap on the *Cuervo* bottle and took it to the historic

Presidential desk made from the timbers and planks of the *H.M.S. Resolute*. The desk had been presented to President Rutherford B. Hayes by Queen Victoria in 1880. It only felt slightly improper to use the secret trap door to hide the tequila bottle.

After all, Nixon had hidden a tape recorder.

CHAPTER 69

The White House, Washington, D.C.
Saturday, January 26, 10:44 PM EST

The President was still thinking about Yolanda when he entered the bedroom. To his surprise, Agent Meghan was wearing very high heels. But that wasn't the first thing he noticed. It was the gown, all feminine and revealing. Her hair was down, and remarkably silky. Marco was speechless.

She wasn't. "We need to work on our intimacy, Mr. President. I have a plan." She produced two flutes of champagne, handing him one. "To undercover operations," she toasted.

He eyed her warily while they both drank, noticing that she held her glass in her left hand. She emptied her flute. He followed her lead.

"Now kiss me like you mean it."

"Are you sure about this?"

"No," She admitted. "But I sure as Hell can't try this alone."

Marco smiled at her. She returned it. "Love the One You're With?" he ventured. He was wondering whether he should transfer his desire for Yolanda to her or simply pretend she actually was Meghan. Then he realized he was overthinking it. It didn't matter. He was aroused.

"You haven't kissed me yet," she reminded him.

He took her in his arms. Their lips met, briefly at first.

When they finally disengaged, he removed his shirt while she poured more champagne. Then, instead of taking a glass from her hand, he took the opportunity to step behind her to untie her nightgown. She gasped as it dropped to her outstretched arms. He took both champagne flutes from her, leaving her with one obvious activity: to complete the removal of her nightgown. Draping it over a nearby chair, she turned to face him. She was wearing matching lingerie. "You got in the mood quickly," she observed drily. She did not move toward him.

"I needed to know if you were committed."

"Am I?"

"Come over here and kiss me while I remove your brassiere."

Agent Meghan hesitated. "In for a penny, in for a pound." She took the offered champagne flute and emptied it. Then she stepped into his arms to be stripped naked by the President of the United States. "Don't call me Meghan tonight." There was nothing more to say --- she thought. She was wrong.

Beneath the left strap of her brassiere was a bruise. Marco stopped. "How about Mata Hari then?"

She studied his face before replying. "I was not sent to inveigle secrets from you, Mr. President. We're on the same side."

"How long have you been with the Secret Service?" he asked.

"I'm on loan from the Company."

"The Central Intelligence Agency?"

"That company," she admitted. "Does that cool your ardor, Mr. President?" She batted her eyelashes theatrically.

"Who are you taking your orders from?"

"My CIA controller."

"Not the Secret Service."

"Only when they don't conflict."

"Are you following orders now?"

"The Company hasn't ordered me to sleep with you. Nevertheless, it has been made clear that I should do so."

"Why?"

"I haven't been told."

"You don't need to know?"

"Apparently." She paused, uncertain. "Do you want me to get dressed again, Mr. President?"

"Not just yet," he admitted. "You're not a spy then?"

"No. I'm a Solutions Specialist." She sighed. Removing any more clothing was out of the question at the moment. The mood was broken.

"Like providing a substitute wife for the Vice President?"

"Fits the job description."

"How about shooting guns?"

"It's a big job description. I can do that too."

"How well?"

"Adequately." Then she added "I have trophies."

"Who ordered you to kill the actor?" There it was. The President had skipped ahead conversationally.

She was surprised. "Who said I did?"

"I believe I just did. Why didn't I see you?"

"Meghan wasn't there."

It took him a moment. "You were disguised as someone else?"

"Well, that's an accusation that I committed a capital felony. I don't appreciate it."

"You were acting under orders. You'll never go to trial. Whose orders?"

"First of all, I categorically deny any allegation that I was involved in the death of the actor who was portraying President Chambers. Secondly, I am not permitted to divulge the name of my controller in this operation without his prior consent."

"Can you get his consent?"

"I don't even know who my controller is."

"Not a clue?"

"Not really. When President Chambers embarked on this mission, it was just a routine job. I didn't have a controller. That changed when he and your wife were attacked in East Jerusalem. There was no briefing, no introduction --- just this mysterious controller who contacts me in various ways."

"How do you know he's CIA?"

"Oh, there's no doubt about that. He has all the right information about me, all the codes."

"You're sure it's a man?"

"Not at all. The odds favor it though."

"I see," he said. It was an exaggeration. "Tell me why you think, just your conjecture, the actor impersonating President Chambers was shot in the head in a manner that obliterated his features, while leaving no doubt as to the time and place of his death."

Agent Meghan considered the proposition before replying. "It's not that simple, Mr. President. There were different objectives, which were not mutually exclusive."

President Redondo sighed. "Where did you go to law school?"

To his astonishment, she replied "Georgetown."

"Good school," he managed to say. "Break it down for me, agent."

"Well, the client wanted a head shot. Not a requirement, but something equally graphic and indisputable."

Marco was unable to remain silent. "The client?"

"Mr. President, you must know that the CIA is officially underfunded. There is no way it can operate on its published budget, which barely covers physical plant and employee salaries. To make up the shortfall, the Company has resorted to other sources."

"Like the midnight heroin operations of the Pepsi bottling plant in Saigon?"

She paused to consider this. "I can't substantiate that. Before my time."

"Please proceed."

"The Company will covertly take on projects on behalf of others; so long as the objectives of the Company are not compromised. One reason is to raise capital. The other is to infiltrate a target organization. Any questions so far?"

"Clear as day."

"In this case it seems that the client wanted exactly the

same result we did, a very public and decisive death of the President of the United States. Of course, the Company knew that President Chambers was already dead. I don't know any more, but I imagine that the killing of President Chambers established the *bona fides* of a Company agent or front with a real terrorist group, as well as providing income for the conduct of other clandestine activities."

"Without Congressional oversight," he added.

"Naturally."

"So you were ordered to shoot the poor actor...."

"I don't admit anything. But his name was Rogers, sir. Marshall Rogers --- presumably a stage name. And I do know that he had a terminal illness with a short and painful life expectancy."

"Who fed you that line?"

"He did, Mr. President. I believed him."

"That's not an excuse...."

"I never said it was."

"O.K. I've got the picture that a CIA operative offered to assassinate President Chambers on behalf of a terrorist organization in return for money, because it coincided with the CIA's own goals."

"Hamas," she whispered.

"What?"

"That's the word. It was Hamas that paid for the hit --- which means Iran."

It took him almost a minute to get his mind around it. "Any idea how much?"

"Billions. Billions that they can't ever use against us. Plus our agent has established himself as someone Hamas can rely upon. Care to drink to that?"

"I guess we will finish this champagne after all," the President replied.

She refilled their glasses and offered a toast. "The truth will make you free."

"Then ye shall know the truth, and the truth will make you free. *John 8:32.*"

"Also the Company motto."

"Really?"

"Yes, but some people there say it should be 'The truth will make you worried.'"

"Disrespect for the scriptures aside, I can see how that might apply given the work the CIA does." As an afterthought, he added "You wouldn't kill me, would you?"

"How much money are we talking about?"

Agent Meghan smiled at him as she removed her brassiere. She lowered her eyes to convey shyness, and to allow him to stare at her body unchallenged if he wished.

"One more item...."

Her eyes met his instantly. Exasperated, she chided him. "You are just the least passionate man I ever met! You do know we're getting to the good part, don't you?"

"Yes. I'm looking forward to it."

"So you are familiar with it....?"

"I've not studied it, mind you. I believe it's important to retain one's amateur standing in these matters. Nevertheless, I intend to make a decent account of myself this evening."

"But, first?"

"Tell me about the umbrella."

"What umbrella?" She was incredulous.

"There's no umbrella involved?"

"I don't know about any umbrella. What's it got to do with the assassination?"

"It's our best lead on the assassin," Marco offered, starting to smile as he said it.

"My money's on the assassin then."

"Mine too."

"Not to mention your hands...."

"I'm afraid I'll need to fully de-brief you."

"Finally."

CHAPTER 70

The White House, Washington, D.C.
Sunday, January 27, 7:17 AM EST

Agent Meghan was gone without a trace. He was alone in the Presidential bed. For a moment he thought it might have been a dream --- the revelations, the sex.

But not the scratches on his back. They were real enough. There was a bit of blood on the sheets where he had slept. How to explain that.

"Should the President of the United States be embarrassed that his ersatz wife clawed his back while making love?" he mused. Then he decided that just having an ersatz wife was strange enough.

Marco put on some casual slacks and a polo shirt, went to the bedroom door. When he opened it, the Marine guard outside snapped to attention. He hated that. It was amply unnerving just having a guard at the door who was awake and alert while he was unshaven and still a bit dreamy.

"At ease. Seen Mrs. Redondo this morning?"

"Went down to breakfast at Oh-Six Hundred, sir." Even at ease he was a coiled spring. Everyone was still jumpy after the assassination.

"Thank you." He started to close the door, then

remembered. "In about fifteen minutes, will you alert the staff that I'm awake?"

"Yes, sir!"

The President retreated to his bedroom. It was too early on a Sunday morning for snappiness. He would shave with cold water. That usually aligned his neurons properly --- or whatever.

As he shaved, he wondered idly how many times he would have sex with Agent Meghan before his real wife returned. There was something kinky about the arrangement.

CHAPTER 71

Near Etam, West Virginia
Sunday, January 27, 8:42 AM EST

Deep in the dense forest stand three dish-shaped microwave antennae, the largest being 105 feet across. They belong to the Communications Satellite Corporation (COMSAT), which employs them to harvest civilian communications from stationary INTELSAT satellites at the rate of seventy thousand words per minute.

At this moment a message was blazing through one of its 4,943 half-circuits that should not have been in private channels at all. It was a coded message from Göteborg, Sweden.

This message, along with all the others, was intercepted by the 150-foot microwave antenna operated by the National Security Agency's G Group in the Allegheny Hollow near Sugar Grove, West Virginia --- less than sixty miles away. This site is so secret that no aircraft are permitted to overfly it. The only access is by a single well-guarded, but nameless, road.

Because of a heightened state of awareness concerning Göteborg at that time, it was flagged and decrypted immediately. The code was no problem; it was low-level CIA.

The message read:

FUMBLE. OPPOSITION RECOVERS.

Unaware of its significance, NSA immediately forwarded it to CIA headquarters in Langley, Virginia.

Thus did the home office first learn of the latest abduction of the President's wife.

Dozens of agents were awakened and immediately dispatched to Scandinavia and told to await orders. Plans would be formulated while they crossed the Atlantic.

But Meghan would be out of their reach before the FASTEN SEAT BELTS lights were extinguished.

CHAPTER 72

The White House, Washington, D.C.
Sunday, January 27, 11:09 AM EST

President Redondo was in the Oval Office, wearing casual slacks and a shirt with the collar open. It was quiet. He was working his way through a pile of "non-urgent" correspondence. He had even managed to forget momentarily that the world awaited his selection of a new vice president, which had been promised by this week.

Agent Meghan slipped in the side door, went to him. From behind him, she began to knead his shoulders. He let the papers fall from his hands.

"Hope I'm not interrupting," she ventured.

"You are, but don't let that stop you."

She continued the massage in silence for a minute, then "There's been a development."

He sighed. "There's always a development, my dear."

She leaned forward and whispered "Not like this. Your wife is gone."

Marco stiffened. "Gone where?"

"Off the grid. I was just told to break the news to you." Then she stepped around the desk and added "Guess they figured you couldn't fire me."

"Who are they?"

"The Company."

"Your controller?"

"I still don't know who my controller is. But I do believe that we've spoken directly. He uses a device to distort his voice."

"Isn't that unusual?"

"A bit. It probably means I would recognize his voice. Usually they don't care."

"You mean you might know him?"

She considered the question. "Normally that wouldn't make a difference. This is a high priority black operation. Maybe it's a person of high rank or a covert asset."

"Covert asset?"

"Someone who isn't even known to be associated with the Company," she sort of explained.

"Can you give me an example?"

"Not a current one, but there was Howard Hughes."

The President considered that. "I get it."

"It could be a politician or foreign diplomat, as well."

"So you'll never know unless they tell you...."

"Unless he slips up, and I catch it. I listen pretty carefully to the exact words he uses. An unusual term or expression can reveal a lot."

"Like 'honey child'?"

Agent Meghan laughed. "That's the idea, but not so obvious. If he said that, I'd assume he was trying to throw me off."

"Anything stand out yet?"

"He's said 'Keep it simple' more than once. Not that

unusual, of course, but could be a clue."

"You're sure it's a man?"

"Not really. What I hear sounds like a man --- and the odds favor it. But we're digressing."

He met her gaze. "O.K. Tell me what you know about it."

"There was a fire across the street from the Krister Clinic. Arson suspected, but still too early to know. It was deemed prudent to evacuate nearby buildings. In the confusion, someone took her --- a team with an ambulance or similar vehicle that could accommodate a patient who had to be kept on a stretcher."

"No witnesses?"

"Lots of them. But what they would have seen would have seemed appropriate under the circumstances."

"So, no one reported an abduction." He could picture how it had happened. "Wasn't she being guarded?"

"I don't have the details. But the clinic has rather limited visiting hours, which it strictly enforces. This occurred after visiting hours. It appears that she was moved by someone dressed like an orderly --- could have been one. It was all done in plain sight. The agent watching over her accompanied her into the elevator."

"What does he have to say?"

"He's gone too."

"Without a fight?"

"Apparently."

"Too easy," the President observed. "Could he have been in on it?"

"Actually, there was another agent in the lobby."

"Did he see anything?"

"He apparently left with them."

Marco put his hands to his temples and closed his eyes for a moment. Then he looked back at her. "O.K. Could *they* have been in on it?"

"I mentioned the second agent because betrayal is less likely when there are two of them. The initial approach is much more complicated, and each agent knows that the other could expose him. Agents are purposely not assigned to work together often in order to keep them from becoming friends."

"Agents don't trust each other," he concluded. "I suppose the second agent is missing too."

"So far," she admitted.

"Any organization claiming credit?"

"Not a word."

"So she could turn up in another facility?"

"The only real hospital in Göteborg is Sahlgrenska. That's where all the bed-ridden patients were supposed to have been taken. It's been searched. There are other private clinics in the area. So it's still possible, but don't get your hopes up."

"Is it possible that the Company didn't like the security at this other hospital?"

"I'm sure they wouldn't, but...."

"So maybe they took her somewhere safer, but there was a communications failure."

Agent Meghan doubted it, but had to admit "It's possible, what with all the confusion."

"Wait! What do we know about the burning building?"

The question caught her off guard. "The burning

building?"

"Yes!"

"They extinguished the fire." She was trying to recall the details of the message she had received. "It was gutted, except for the first floor --- so it didn't start there. Surprisingly, it didn't spread to the adjacent buildings."

"What was it used for?"

"How would I know?" she snapped. "It was being renovated." As soon as she had said it, she realized the significance.

"Perfect. No tenants. Easy to get into. Place some incendiary devices...."

"And no carpet or furniture to feed the fire," she added. "The burn could be controlled."

"The renovation supplies were probably stored on the ground floor. That's why it wasn't burned."

"No way to control the length of the burn...."

"Did it start with an explosion?"

"It wasn't noticed until some windows blew out. That could have been an explosion."

"So we're sure it was arson."

"I'd bet on it."

"Sound like a CIA operation?"

"Oh, yes." She expounded. "Well planned for maximum effect and minimal damage. No tenants to be injured. For one thing, terrorists aren't that considerate." She thought they had arrived at the same place in their analysis. Agent Meghan was wrong. "Definitely Company *modus operandi*."

"The CIA doesn't have her," he stated with absolute

finality.

"Why do you say that?"

"Did the CIA need to start that fire to get Meghan?"

"Of course not. They already had her." She began to feel uneasy.

"If they didn't need to start the fire, then they didn't do it," he explained. "And if the CIA didn't start the fire, then it wouldn't have an ambulance standing by to whisk her away in the confusion."

She was stunned. After a pause, she conceded "They wouldn't. And there are no reports of anyone commandeering one."

"Exactly." The President ran his hands through his hair.

"We're looking for another intelligence service then."

"Any come to mind?"

"Not American."

"But a government agency?"

"Most likely. They were definitely professionals."

"Inform your people." It was an order, but spoken as if it was the only reasonable course of action. Agent Meghan played along.

"They need to know." She acknowledged that she would do as he had asked --- without the necessity of obeying his order.

The President had known better than to expect a snappy "Yes, sir!"

Agent Meghan came around the desk and kissed him tenderly on the cheek. He hadn't been expecting that either.

"What can we do?" he asked.

"After I make that call, you and I should be seen together in public today. Reinforce the impression that your wife is with you."

He looked outside at the falling snow. "Bit chilly outside for a stroll...."

"We could build a snowman in the Rose Garden."

"For target practice?"

"No, my pet." Her voice dripped with sarcasm as she said it. Then she recovered. "For the press to photograph."

"Not a bad idea," Marco admitted. "Is there enough snow in the Rose Garden?"

"You're the President of the United States. You ought to be able to get enough snow."

"I'll bet I can even get us some hot chocolate."

"Now you're talking like the leader of the free world."

CHAPTER 73

Outside Göteborg, Sweden
Sunday, January 27, 19:45 Western European Time

Her left eye opened just enough to let in the light. "Artificial," her mind registered. She fought against the chemicals she knew were in her system, determined to keep this portal open to the world. "Hospital?" her mind queried her vision.

From her vantage point on her back she saw a white room. There was an IV tube in the corner of her view. She presumed correctly that it was attached to her arm. There was something odd about the ceiling. Like most people, her right eye was dominant. Unlike most people, she knew this. With great concentration, Meghan resolved her right eye to open.

The ceiling above her had support beams, but they did not appear to be wooden. Indeed, they appeared to be metal. "Could this be an auxiliary building? Pre-fab?"

Nearby she heard a car door opened, then slammed shut. A moment later a large internal combustion engine roared to life. The lights blinked. Her world began to vibrate gently.

"A truck!" she realized. "I'm in a truck!"

Eighty-eight kilometers North of Göteborg, the First

Lady lay strapped to a hospital bed in the back of a Volvo delivery truck that was parked inside a barn on a tidy, but remote, farm.

"I'm cargo!" was her last thought before surrendering to the drugs again. Both eyes closed.

"Ouch!" Meghan awoke to the pain of her big toes being pinched.

"Good. There is still feeling in the extremities," a man wearing a blazer said aloud. "You are awake?"

"A reasonable facsimile," she mumbled.

"Excellent. Attend to her," he ordered a young woman whose attire was more punk rocker than nurse. Instead of checking the IV tubes and monitors, the girl unfastened the strap which imprisoned Meghan and raised the back of the hospital bed. After that she pulled Meghan's covers down and began to bathe her with cleansing tissues. The man took no notice of this. He was fiddling with photographic equipment.

Then, consulting a photograph of Meghan torn from a magazine, the girl brushed Meghan's hair to match the photo. After that, she applied make-up. "Should I apply rouge to her nipples?" the girl asked as if it were the most natural question in the world.

Meghan gasped. The man held up a digital camera and checked her through the viewfinder.

"No. They won't be in the picture," he instructed. "Place the newspaper on them."

"What do you think you're doing?" Meghan shouted at both of them.

"Marketing," the man replied. "Look at the camera lens," he ordered.

Realizing that the man was in charge, Meghan glared at him defiantly.

"Some models need an incentive. I will start breaking your toes until you look into the camera."

Meghan refused at first. But she turned her face to the lens when he produced a pair of pliers.

Then the girl placed the folded front page of the *Herald-Tribune International Edition* beneath her neck and stepped away.

He began taking pictures, starting with close-ups of her face. Then he backed away to include more of her torso, making sure her birth mark would be seen. The newspaper's date appeared in all the shots. Meghan stared in stony silence, a false smile in place.

Click-click-click.

"The camera loves you."

CHAPTER 74

The White House, Washington, D.C.
Sunday, January 27, 4:52 PM EST

The snowman had been constructed, photographed and forgotten. Marco sat in the Oval Office browsing a report from the GOP party chairman about mid-term election strategies. From his perspective, it seemed to require a lot of travel and backslapping.

The side door opened without warning. That was Agent Meghan's way. "She's back on the radar!"

"Where is she?"

Agent Meghan paused. "Don't know. But she's in play."

"Tell me."

"We received a message --- with a photograph. Today's newspaper was in the picture. She was alive."

"Are we sure it's her?"

"Does she have a small birthmark on her left hip?"

"Yes," he conceded. "But that could be faked."

"They said that DNA could be provided."

"Who has her?"

"Unknown."

That was unexpected. "What do they want?"

"The reserve is Ten Million Dollars."

"Reserve?"

"Minimum bid," she explained. "It's an auction."

"An auction...." All he really knew about auctions was that the highest bidder always paid too much.

"Online bidding. It closes Tuesday at 5:00 PM Eastern. The winning bidder has twelve hours to wire the funds to an account to be disclosed at the time. If the funds don't arrive on time, they'll notify the second-highest bidder."

"How do we bid without making this public?"

"I think the Company can arrange it."

"Naturally." In less than a month, his life and his presidency had become entwined with the Central Intelligence Agency. The last decision he had made was to build a snowman. And even that was at the suggestion of a CIA agent. But he couldn't see any way he could get his wife back without their involvement. These were uncharted waters for him.

"Well?"

"Tell me she's not on Ebay," he ventured.

She smiled. "No. Whoever has her doesn't want publicity either."

"How thoughtful."

"Not really. They understand that the degree and manner of publicity is a key component in the package under bid."

"My wife's been packaged," he acknowledged dully.

"She's actually a part of the package. It includes the right to humiliate her --- and, by extension, the United States government."

"And the President personally." He had fully grasped

the situation.

"Of course. In most societies there is a tradition of attacking a leader through his family members."

"And when that member is the attractive young wife...."

"The possibilities increase exponentially," she confirmed. "Especially if the goal is to embarrass."

"We can't let this happen," he declared. "We don't bid."

Agent Meghan pondered this for a minute, then said "If we bid, we confirm she is your wife. I see that. But if we don't, we're throwing her to the dogs."

"There's more," Marco announced. "We have to convince the world that you're the real Meghan." He was making it up as he went along, but it was sounding solid. "We have a day."

"The deadline's...."

He cut her off. "We have to accomplish this before the bidding heats up."

"How do we do that?"

"You get a tattoo tonight. A birth mark."

"Ouch!"

"Then we fly to Florida early tomorrow; so you can show it off in your bikini."

"Uh, that might be a problem."

"No bikini?"

"That's not the problem. You ask a lot of someone who has not given a thought to wearing a bathing suit since last summer."

"You'd prefer a nude beach?"

"I will if you will," she challenged.

"*Touché*." He acknowledged her spunk. "Tempting though that idea may be, I want our photographs to appear in the *Washington Post*, not the *Bareass Beacon*.

Agent Meghan chuckled. "There's such a publication?"

"I only read it for the articles," he professed with mock sincerity."

"O.K., pilgrim. If you say so. Anything else I should know?"

The President sighed. "To convince the press that you're the real Meghan, I may have to knock you up tonight."

"You can try, Tiger, but I take birth control pills."

"Keep taking them for now. If this works, you don't need to get pregnant."

"But the real Meghan will."

"Yes. That could be the trickiest part of the plan," he admitted. "But we'll announce your pregnancy tomorrow on the beach."

"So you make this announcement while I'm immodestly displaying my new birth mark. So, am I having a boy or a girl?" she asked. "Some reporter is sure to inquire."

"Right. Who knew procreation was so complicated?"

"Women," she stated flatly.

"We don't know yet." He added "Have to keep our options open on that."

"Then I'll tell them I'm having a politician."

"Perfect."

"O.K. So far the plan calls for burning my flesh, stripping me in public and falsely asserting I'm with child. Any other liberties you'd care to take with my body?"

"I'll think of something," he promised ominously. "In

the meantime, arrange for a tattoo and pack your bikini. Might hit the instant tan bottle too."

"First the diuretics, my sweet exploiter."

"I don't need the details."

"Men never do."

"I think we can pull this off. I appreciate your reluctant cooperation, snarky though it is."

"No matter how convincing we are, someone will bid for her," she reminded him. "One of the goals is to get Meghan back, isn't it?"

"Of course. But once we've scuttled the enthusiasm for the auction, we can get her back with a lower bid."

"Romance is dead."

"That just follows from discrediting her authenticity. No reason to ignore it."

"So we submit a bid anonymously?" she asked, already knowing the answer.

"That's where your chums at the Company come into the picture. They may have to pose as a terrorist group."

"One that doesn't see my photo in the *Washington Post* evidently."

"Not on the day of publication, at least."

"It's going to be all over the news. Are these phony terrorists in the Outback?" she asked.

"That's brilliant! They're in a time zone that has them asleep when the news breaks."

She was unconvinced, but had no better idea. "O.K. I'll get the ball rolling on your out-of-touch terrorists."

"Has a nice ring to it," Marco mused.

"Don't forget to make our vacation plans, dear." Agent

Meghan was on the way out the door.

He picked up the phone. "Time to wreck the Sunday evening of the Secret Service," he observed aloud.

That mission accomplished, he made another call. "Pack your Speedo, *Zorro*. We're going to Florida first thing in the morning. Let Yolanda know. She's going too."

"No Speedo, *compadre*. And I wouldn't be surprised if Yolanda's bathing suit didn't have a holster. What's going on?"

"Desperation, mostly. It's complicated. Meet me at 6:30 in the morning in my office. I'll have a continental breakfast waiting. I'll explain what we're trying to accomplish. Your sage advice is eagerly awaited."

"Here's some for right now. Scrambled eggs and sausage --- *chorizo* if you can find it."

"You've already proved your worth, *amigo*."

"*Hasta mañana, Señor Presidente*."

Now he was hungry.

CHAPTER 75

The White House, Washington, D.C.
Sunday, January 27, 8:13 PM EST

"Twenty-One Million Dollars?" Marco was incredulous.

"Plus $252.99. That's what he said," Agent Meghan added. "The Company won't help unless there's a credible offer. That's the figure they came up with for the initial bid."

"Where'd they get that number?"

"It's enough to beat the others who bid low just in case she's genuine. It's more than double the reserve, in order to beat anyone who bids double. The final $252.99 was added to win if someone else thinks like them. They're good at this."

"I guess they have given it some thought." he admitted.

"They made two other points. First, we are the only ones who know for sure that she is the real article."

"And...."

"It's not your money."

He sighed. "Good points."

"They're prepared to go higher if necessary. This is a high priority for them."

"They don't think we can pull off our charade?"

"For us to succeed, we have to convince terrorists, not

journalists."

"Maybe terrorists awash in Dollars, and willing to back a long shot...."

"Or worse."

"What could be worse?" he wondered aloud.

"Terrorists who are absolutely positive that she is your wife."

"As in a leak?" He was surprised the possibility hadn't occurred to him before.

"It's been known to happen."

"Tell them to proceed. Do whatever it takes," he instructed her. "We'll do our part to sabotage the bidding."

Agent Meghan didn't move.

"Anything else?"

"Hurt like Hell. Thanks for asking."

He was confused, then "You've already got it?"

"It's just henna for now, but I can go into the water. It won't wash off." She unzipped the top of her slacks and pulled back some gauze to reveal a red mark on her left hip. "It will look more natural tomorrow. Takes a few hours."

He moved closer to inspect it.

"Don't touch it!" she warned. "It's still sensitive."

"I'm impressed. Thank you."

"All part of the job." She restored the gauze and zipped up. "Have to contact my controller."

"Yes. Please do."

CHAPTER 76

Outside Göteborg, Sweden
Monday, January 28, 4:11 Western European Time

The restraints were off, but she was still in the truck. A quick inventory revealed that she was wearing pajamas. She pulled the draw string and tied it tightly.

"Free-range cargo," Meghan muttered to herself. Gingerly at first, she moved her legs. No pain. In fact, everything seemed to work. She worked her way to the edge of the bed and tried standing. To her surprise, it was rather easy.

"Maybe I'm cured."

She walked to the double doors and gave them a shove. They didn't budge. Then she put her ear to one. Voices. English!

She pounded on the doors. After a minute, the left one opened. A blast of frigid air stunned her, but sharpened her mind. She stared into a vast enclosed open space lit by three simple light bulbs dangling from beams. There was a round space heater with a cord that trailed off towards a new-looking Volvo SUV.

"What do you want?" the man who had opened the door inquired. Another man sat in front of the space heater, watching her intently. Both wore corduroy pants and wool shirts with down vests. Their hats had ear flaps that dangled. The clothes were new.

"L.L. Bean, I presume."

"Call me L.L.," he replied. "That's Bean over there." He who had been designated as Bean tipped his red plaid hat to her without actually removing it.

They were large, fit-looking men. She was convinced that they were professionals familiar with the United States.

"Where am I?"

"In a truck inside a barn."

"I could have figured that out by myself."

"Bean thinks we just might be on a farm."

"Splendid. Maybe I should be speaking to Bean, since he's so clever."

"It was the tractor parked over there set my mind off in that direction," Bean explained.

Meghan began to shiver from the cold. "Mind if I share the heater?"

"It won't be as warm as the truck, but you're welcome to join us," Bean said by way of invitation. L.L. opened the other door, revealing metal stairs leading down from the cargo area. He offered his hand, but she chose the railing --- which was like grabbing an icicle. She willed herself to put her bare foot on the top step. She stifled a scream, as her body tensed in reaction to the cold.

"Exercise sure is invigorating," Bean observed. Then he pulled another metal fold-up chair to the heater. He produced a large red handkerchief from his vest pocket and dusted off the seat.

At the bottom of the stairs, L.L. took her arm and escorted her to the chair. "Your throne awaits, m'lady."

Bean provided a milking stool for her to rest her feet off the ground.

Meghan allowed herself to adjust to this relative comfort. She could always return to the truck. For now, she was glad to be out of the confinement. "Thank you, gentlemen."

"We'd appreciate it if you didn't incinerate your toes on our watch. They'll warm up soon enough." She reluctantly pulled her feet back a few inches from the heat source.

"You know who I am?"

"You're the truck lady." L.L. smiled as though he'd just come up with the correct answer at a quiz show.

She sighed. "And you are?"

"Oh, you nailed that. I'm L.L. and he's Bean."

"We didn't fool you for a minute." Bean added.

"And you're from Appalachia, Eastern Kentucky maybe." She turned to L.L. "Montana, right?"

Both men froze. Then Bean said "We're men of the world, no longer tethered to any specific geographic location."

"Not even Langley?"

"That's in Nevada, isn't it?" Bean wondered aloud.

"Pretty sure it's Utah, Bean."

"Always get those states confused. Which one's got the Mormons?"

"Oh, that's Michigan," L.L. announced confidently. "They're the ones who have more than one wife, aren't they?"

"That's just crazy," Bean responded. "One wife is about fifty percent too many."

"Enough!" Meghan shouted. The men began to laugh softly, like mischievous teenage boys. She joined them.

"Watch out for Stockholm Syndrome," Bean cautioned her.

"I've been vaccinated," she said pleasantly. "So you consider me your prisoner?"

"That's harsh!" L.L. complained.

"Don't go spoiling the mood," Bean advised. "We're all caught up in the same time warp. Makes no difference how we feel about it. Might as well make the best of it till it's over."

"When's that?" she asked.

"We were hoping you knew." Bean answered with a straight face.

"If you knew, you'd tell me?"

L.L. spoke. "I'm not real good with abstract concepts. I don't have any idea if I'd tell you, if I knew. Which I don't."

"Hours, days or weeks?" Meghan pursued it.

"If it's weeks, I'm going to run out of elk jerky," L.L. announced with apparent dismay. "Want some?"

"Sure." She had put them off balance again.

"Damn, truck lady, you're just full of surprises." He cut off a big slice and handed it to her. They watched her eat it, licking her fingers when it was gone. "So how are you feelin' these days?"

"I can walk again. And it doesn't even hurt."

This apparently was news to the men. "Were you in an accident?"

Meghan thought briefly. "Actually, it was more of an intentional."

Both men waited for an explanation.

-266-

"That's all I'm going to say for now, unless you tell me who you're working for."

"That's kind of an ethical dilemma for us. If we told you, we'd have to kill you," Bean explained.

"And since our orders are real specific about not killing you, then we'd be disobeying orders, you see."

"Bottom line, truck lady, is that we'd have to kill each other if we told you. L.L. figured it out."

L.L. looked at his watch. "Time for you to get back in the truck," he announced.

"Why?" Meghan protested.

"Maybe I'll ask the people who make the rules."

L.L. hustled her back into the truck and locked the doors.

Meghan sat on the edge of the bed and wondered why she would be held captive by Americans. They had to be CIA. They were supposed to rescue her.

"Protective custody?" she asked herself.

Meghan lay down. She was surprised how good the bed felt. She fell asleep trying to make sense of her situation.

CHAPTER 77

The White House, Washington, D.C.
Sunday, January 27, 11:04 PM EST

Marco was still reading in the Oval Office when Agent Meghan came in.

"Apparently we can do what's required to make babies, but we can't actually make them," she announced.

"What?"

"No birth announcement, Marco. My controller absolutely forbids it."

"Why?"

"I can't ask why," she said. "He's my controller. But he did indicate that it could have unforeseen ramifications later on."

Marco thought about it. "He's right. It could get complicated."

"I also got the feeling that he didn't think it would be necessary. Just a feeling."

"He thinks we'll be the high bidders?"

"He sounds confident."

"I guess that's good news...," he offered.

"Let's hope he's right."

CHAPTER 78

Patrick Air Force Base, Florida
Monday, January 28, 8:36 AM EST

"They think they can do it," Major Fox said to the President.

"Good. We'll go into the meeting assuming they can."

They were jogging down the magnificent beach that makes up the Eastern edge of the air base. They were wearing khaki shorts and sunglasses. They had not come far, for they wanted to arrive looking robust, not pooped out. It was, after all, a photo op. Route A-1-A was devoid of the usual traffic. Instead, parked helicopters and limousines occupied the pavement. There was also an Air Force bus which had brought in the reporters and photographers.

A short ways behind them jogged Agent Meghan and Yolanda, wearing tankinis. They were plotting a photographic *coup*.

Ahead was a podium standing in the sand, some Air Force and NASA officers and the inevitable members of the press. About forty feet from the podium, the ladies sprinted past the men on the hard sand at the water's edge.

"Hey!" Marco yelled.

"Don't even try," the Major advised. "Better to look surprised than beaten."

The two men were laughing when they arrived, to show the cameras that they were good sports. "It looks like I've been hanging around fast women," Marco remarked into a microphone.

"Don't be a sore loser," Agent Meghan shot back. Then she kissed him on the cheek. He slapped her playfully on the hip, which guaranteed that the tattoo/birth mark would appear in the news. Cameras clicked.

The President moved to the podium. He appeared to be young and fit. He accepted a Hawaiian print shirt and slipped it on as he approached the podium. He struck a body builder pose and flexed a bicep. "No. This is not the first episode of our new fitness show," he joked. But we are here on business. This," he said as he swept his arm across the beach scene, "is Patrick Air Force Base, after all. So any rumor that we're here simply to thaw out must be dismissed as scurrilous --- even if true. It's always good to see the press, even if you are a bit overdressed this morning. Enjoy this beautiful day, everyone. We're going back tonight. They tell me the forecast high temperature for Washington is 43 degrees."

With that, he waved and ran into the ocean, where he knew they couldn't follow. Agent Meghan, Major Fox and Yolanda joined him. As planned, they swam South to avoid the cameras when they emerged. A limousine was waiting for them.

CHAPTER 79

Democratic People's Republic of Korea (North Korea)
Tuesday, January 29, 1:14 Japan Standard Time

The three B-2A Spirit Stealth Bombers from Andersen Air Force Base in Guam were joined by the rest of the fleet from Whiteman Air Force Base in Missouri. Each bore down on its target undetected. That was about to change.

It came down to seconds, but the 8th Air Division base at Orang on the Sea of Japan was the first to be attacked. 44 MiG-19 fighters were lined up on each side of the long runway. All were destroyed on the ground in two bombing runs which also left the hangars in flames. The B-2A was out of North Korean airspace before any meaningful response could be made.

Moments later on the West coast, the 3rd Air Combat Command at Hwangju was destroyed along with 43 Mig-19 fighters, then the air base at Hwangsuwon and all 44 of the MiG-21 fighters stationed there. At Wonsan, all but 5 of its 72 MiG-19s were reduced to burning metal. All 46 MiG-23s at Sunchon were caught in the open and destroyed. The MiG-21s at Iwon, Koksan and Kwail ceased to be.

The last fighter base to be hit was Pukch'ang, home of 24 deadly MiG-29s and 36 Su-25s. Nothing remained but rubble and smoke.

Then three of the B-2As returned to destroy the bombers at Toksan, Sondak and Kwansan. Because bombers are not rapid response aircraft, they were not able to avoid the onslaught despite having several minutes notice.

The remaining B-2As delivered AGM-129 advanced cruise missiles to targets in the major naval ports of the Yellow Sea and East Coast Fleets, where the fuel depots and service facilities were destroyed. A few ships were taken out as collateral damage. The remaining ships had no operating harbors or oil.

Twenty-three minutes after the first bombs dropped at Orang, Kim Jong-il no longer controlled one of the most powerful military machines on Earth. He still had one of the largest standing armies in the world, complete with tanks and artillery, but his offensive capabilities had been removed in one surgical strike.

CHAPTER 80

The White House, Washington, D.C.
Tuesday, January 29, 9:53 AM EST

"Our bombers are over the Pacific now ---
international waters. None sustained any damage. The
mission appears to have exceeded its objectives, Mr.
President. The aircraft were sitting ducks. The North Koreans
no longer have an air force. Nor do they have viable naval
facilities." The Secretary of Defense was beaming. "Will you
be calling a press conference?"

"I think I'll wait to hear what the North Koreans have
to say first. Kim's so crazy he might not even admit that it
happened. Why broadcast defeat?"

"You have a point Mr. President." The Secretary was
disappointed. "Let's see how it plays out." He managed to
sound like he was in full agreement before excusing himself.

"Does Seoul know yet?" Major Fox asked.

"At the last minute, the Air Force let them know we
would be in the area --- to avoid them thinking the South was
under attack. I imagine they're getting a picture of the
operation by now."

"They'll be tempted to attack."

"That's one reason we didn't give them time to think
about it. The South is in a defensive posture."

"By the time they could prepare an attack, the element of surprise would be gone," Major Fox said. "They couldn't defeat North Korea in a land battle anyway."

"The Department of Defense believes that the first thing the North would do is overrun Seoul, destroying the political and economic heart of the country. After that, it wouldn't matter what happened. South Korea has too much to lose."

"So if they attack the North, they're on their own?"

"We've told them repeatedly that we will not support the aggressor in any future war."

"I hope they believe that."

CHAPTER 81

The White House, Washington, D.C.
Tuesday, January 29, 5:17 EST

"We won the bidding!" Agent Meghan announced as she entered the Oval Office.

"Great! Any surprises?" the President asked her.

"Just one, but we should have anticipated it."

"What's the surprise?"

"They want me to trade places with Meghan until they get away."

"A hostage?"

"That captures the essence of the arrangement," she admitted.

"That wasn't the deal...."

"The deal is what they say it is," Agent Meghan responded in the manner of stating an obvious fact.

"I don't like it."

"I can't say that I do either, but I can understand their reasoning. It's when they want something that makes no sense to me that I wonder what they're up to."

"You think they'll let you go?"

"Can't see any reason not to. It's not like I'm some super spy they want to interrogate."

"When will this happen?"

"They're still working out the details of the exchange. We have to negotiate to show we hold some cards too."

"When will we know?"

"Soon. A few hours at most."

Marco wasn't comfortable with the new terms. "If you decide your life will be in danger, you don't have to go."

"It's thoughtful of you to say, but it is my job. Besides, I'm the one who's dangerous."

"But you won't be armed."

"I don't need to be."

CHAPTER 82

Centrala Polisstationen, Göteborg, Sweden
Tuesday, January 29, 4:04 Western European Time

The reinforced steel door clanged behind Hassim, but this time he was on the free side of it. His clothes were unkempt. His other belongings were in an unmarked plastic bag in his left hand. He had been interrogated off and on since the police had picked him up the night of the fire. Of course, he knew that being found with Khalid's bloody body on the sidewalk in the dead of night would have repercussions. They thought he had killed Khalid.

The second day, a new interrogator had appeared from Stockholm. The questions changed focus immediately. "Was he an arsonist? Was he working with Khalid? Was he a terrorist?"

Then the arrival of his passport from the hotel showed him to be a United States citizen. A list was consulted. The U.S. Embassy had notified the state security force that an American was missing. After Hassim had identified the passport as being his, the interrogator had left the room and not returned. After several hours, a guard had come to initiate the process of setting him free.

"James!" he exclaimed at the sight of his handler.

James ignored this and wordlessly hustled Hassim out

the door and down the steps of the Centrala Polisstationen. A Mercedes pulled to the curb and they climbed in back.

"I've reviewed the testimony you gave."James was all business. "I have one question at this time."

""What?"

"Did you say or do anything that would lead them to believe you were working with the United States government in any capacity?"

"I did not waver from my cover story," Hassim assured him. "I'm a business consultant."

"What is your business in Sweden?"

"A general assessment of the market undertaken for my own benefit to see if the Arab population was being served adequately or whether opportunities existed in that regard."

James smiled. "And what did you conclude?"

"The market is presently served well by Arabs dealing with Arabs and does not present any clear openings for new legitimate enterprises."

"Were they convinced?"

"Someone reported seeing an Arab at the Krister Clinic the night of the fire. I think they now believe that was Khalid. But they still wonder how I ended up with him."

"You're right. They do."

"Thank you for coming for me."

"You're welcome. We have work to do --- but you can clean up first at your hotel."

"The food was surprisingly good in jail, but I promised myself a lobster dinner when I got out. Do we have time for that?"

"We're on call. If we can do that before the call comes,

then why not? But no alcohol."

"I can be devout."

CHAPTER 83

The White House, Washington, D.C.
Tuesday, January 29, 7:21 PM EST

The President was talking to Major Fox and Yolanda in the Oval Office when Agent Meghan slipped in the side door. She stopped when she noticed them.

"Go ahead," Marco told her.

"The details have been finalized."

"And...," the President prompted.

"Well, they're kind of convoluted. I'm to fly to Heathrow and await further instructions."

"Why London?"

"Quick connections to any city in Europe for one thing. Also, I won't stand out in a crowd there. These are guesses, though. We really don't know."

"Makes sense," Major Fox commented.

"What about the ransom?" asked Marco.

"One Million Dollars has already been sent. I'll receive further wiring instructions when I meet them."

"When you're in their custody," Marco clarified.

"Yes."

"When do they release my wife?"

"I'll be told where she's being held as soon as the first half of the money has arrived."

"How can they be sure we will send the remainder then?"

"Two reasons. The place she's being held is wired to explode. Once our people verify she's alive, they'll authorize the balance to be wired. As soon as the balance has been received, the kidnappers will call back with instructions to disarm the detonator."

"You mean the place will be set to blow if it's not disarmed in time?" Major Fox asked.

"Yes. And the second reason is that they'll still have me."

"Diabolical," Marco said.

"And well thought out," she added. "A very good plan."

"Professionals?" Major Fox asked.

"No doubt about it."

"When do you leave?" the President wanted to know.

"Early tomorrow, from Boston. British Air has a flight that gets into Heathrow the same evening. I have to get to Logan Airport by 5:15 AM. I'll be traveling incognito."

"I'm going with you," Yolanda surprised them by saying.

"We can't change the plan."

"I'll just be a fellow passenger on the same flight. We don't have to talk to each other. You sit in the back; I'll be towards the front so I can get off first to observe you. I'll make my own reservations and reserve a car. Even if they can access the names of all the intelligence agents in the United States, they won't find mine."

"What if they meet my plane, take me away right away?"

"What if they don't?" Yolanda countered. "Besides, at the very least we'd know you had been taken and have a description of the persons who met you --- maybe even a license plate."

"That would be useful," Marco admitted.

"Will you need a gun?" Major Fox asked.

"Too many people would have to become involved. I don't want this to leave this room."

Major Fox nodded his assent.

"Why would you do this for me?" Agent Meghan asked Yolanda.

"Well, you did me ... that favor."

The men were baffled.

"Girl stuff," Agent Meghan offered.

"We'd better get started," Yolanda said as she rose to leave.

Agent Meghan turned toward the door. "Cheerio!"

"*Buena suerte,*" Yolanda responded.

When they were alone in the office, Major Fox asked "You going to stop her?"

"The potential benefits outweigh the risks," he answered.

"That's what I think too. What do we do now?"

"I've got to call Paul Carnegie and tell him the good news."

"Afraid he might interfere?"

"He knows he's too visible. He may not like it, but he'll sit tight."

"Going to tell him about the explosives?"

"Not if I can avoid it. I don't know if that's a credible

threat, anyway."

"Let's hope we don't find out."

CHAPTER 84

The White House, Washington, D.C.
Tuesday, January 29, 8:59 PM EST

The President hung up the phone.

"That took long enough. How did he take the news?" Major Fox asked.

The President looked puzzled. "Seemed pleased that things were working out."

"He should be."

"He didn't appear to be worried about his daughter."

"Well, he is a politician. I doubt that his emotions surface in public often."

"Maybe that's it...."

"You didn't mention the explosives," the Major reminded him.

"True. That could have made a difference. He apparently thinks we'll get her back if we follow the instructions."

"And you don't?"

Marco thought about that before answering. "I guess that I do. I'm just not sure. Maybe I'm overthinking it. Maybe it is just a business transaction."

"Did he say that?"

"Pretty much," the President conceded. "He said we

should follow the plan and not complicate matters."

"Keep it simple, huh?"

"Yes. That's what he said." The President thought about it and continued "That's exactly what he said --- word for word."

"I never claimed to be original."

"No. That's not the point. I have to talk to Agent Meghan."

"She left while you were on the phone. A driver took her in an unmarked car. She was booked on the nine o'clock US Airways shuttle from Reagan."

Marco looked at his watch and made a face. "I'll try to reach her anyway. See if you can catch Yolanda. It could be important!"

Major Fox pulled out his cell phone.

CHAPTER 85

Reagan Washington National Airport, Washington, D.C.
Tuesday, January 29, 9:01 PM EST

The Airbus streaked down the runway in a light rain. Agent Meghan, wearing a brunette wig and carrying two passports, was crammed into window Seat 26A, next to a large man whose girth spilled over the armrest. She pulled out a James Crumley paperback novel and tried to read. She wanted to appear occupied in case he became bored with the sports section. "Why do people board planes with insufficient reading materials?" she asked herself, not for the first time.

Her thoughts turned to Yolanda, whom she had walked past as she boarded. Yolanda was in the first row of the economy seats, facing the bulkhead that separated business class from the unwashed masses. Even the shuttle had succumbed to the desires of passengers who wanted bigger seats and an extra pretzel bag. Capitalism thrived at 30,000 feet.

Was Yolanda's participation as spontaneous as it appeared to be, or was there an agenda in place that dictated it? If her presence was required, why? And who was running Yolanda?

Finding no answers, Agent Meghan began reading the pages she had been staring at.

Neither of them had received a message before taking off. Now their cell phones were off.

A sound like a small bell announced that Agent Meghan had a voice mail message as soon as she turned on her phone at Heathrow. Marco's voice simply said "Your father says, and this is a quote, 'Keep it simple.'" She replayed the message, then deleted it.

"My father?" she whispered to herself. While waiting for the passengers ahead of her to leave, she worked out that, since Marco didn't know her parents, he must be referring to his wife's father. So Paul Carnegie had used the same phrase her controller did. Well, the expression wasn't that unusual. Could be a coincidence.

Except it didn't fit the situation exactly, which indicated that it was an expression used often by the speaker. That's what they'd taught her at the Farm, anyway.

Her thoughts were interrupted by the sounds of struggle. It was the oversized man next to her attempting to stand, then cracking his cranium on the overhead baggage bin when the seat released him.

Agent Meghan prepared to disembark.

CHAPTER 86

The White House, Washington, D.C.
Wednesday, January 30, 7:00 AM EST

"News agencies in South Korea are reporting that major air bases and naval facilities in North Korea have been attacked. If so, it is not known who might have been responsible. The President of South Korea has issued a statement denying any involvement, without confirming that any attacks have taken place. He has offered to extend humanitarian aid to North Korea if requested. Military experts we have consulted are all of the opinion that it is highly unlikely that South Korea is responsible, some stating that it would be suicide to attack the North. There has been no comment from the North Korean State News Agency in Pyongyang. We'll be keeping you updated on this breaking story; so stay tuned to CNN. After the break, another movie star adopts a foreign baby."

The word MUTE appeared at the bottom of the screen, just as the dog in the advertisement smelled bacon.

"Kim's press staff must be having a hard time spinning this," Major Fox suggested.

"If he's told them." The President was intrigued by the lack of a response. "Maybe he's trying to order more aircraft before the Chinese know how badly he needs them. He's crazy, not stupid."

"The Chinese must have figured it out."

"I agree. The Russians too. And the Japanese seem to know every time a Stealth bomber takes off from Guam. The British, the French, the Germans --- they must at least have strong suspicions by this time.

"MI-6 will be upset."

"I've scheduled a call to 10 Downing Street already."

"What will you tell the Prime Minister?"

"The truth. And I'll apologize for not warning him in advance. I'll also ask him to remain silent about it until such time as I have made a public statement, if ever."

"Wonder what Kim's doing right now...."

CHAPTER 87

The Palace
Pyongyang, Democratic People's Republic of Korea
Wednesday, January 30, 17:25 Japan Standard Time

Jung had dutifully stripped naked for the guards at the workers' entrance to the Palace. It was only after they had thoroughly checked her body that she was told there would be no activities that night. She was told to return the next evening. The Dear Leader was away.

Kim Jong-il was indeed away. He and his family, along with 73 trusted servants, had been driven North on a 10-lane "ghost" highway that went into China. There was no other automobile traffic on the highway, because private automobiles are unheard of in the Democratic Republic of North Korea. Hence the term "ghost" highway. The paltry 1,500 miles of paved highways are merely symbols of progress. This is a shining example of symbol-thing confusion. The citizens obviously take pride in these strange symbols, for they materialize from the surrounding countryside every Sunday with homemade brooms to sweep the pavement. In every spot along the highway where the Dear Leader had ever stopped, his statue had been erected to memorialize the event. The peasants polish these statues religiously.

In a concession to reality, several of these highways serve as the sole runways for at least a dozen air force installations located alongside them, such as Pyong Ni South.

Before reaching the border, the convoy had turned onto a two-lane road and continued into the hills for several miles to Kim's secret Mountain Retreat. The mountains of North Korea reach about two miles above sea level. Many, including the one hosting Kim, are quite dramatic. Rather than a rustic cabin, Kim had opted for a magnificent compound that puts the Timberline Lodge at Mount Hood to shame.

Nevertheless, he fretted at being away from the capital and his Palace. The Dear Leader was not cut out for quiet contemplation on a mountaintop.

He decided to send for his entertainers.

The rumors that military facilities had been bombed were whispered throughout the capital. Fearing a further attack, Kim had gone into hiding. Perhaps the security there would not be well established yet. Jung sensed an opportunity.

Her cousin in the Green Dragons had already provided the poison, a small vial with a push-top atomizer. All she needed to do was to spray some into the freezer where the chilled mugs and goblets were kept. Anyone who drank from one would die within a minute --- too quickly for an antidote to be administered.

Smuggling it in would be a snap because it was

fashioned from an actual part of her musical gear. It was a modification of the protective cap for the quarter-inch J15 jack that plugged into the Stratocaster electric guitar the Dear Leader had given her to practice on. Knowing to whom it belonged, the security people treated the instrument with reverence. A scratch on its Candy Apple surface could end a career --- perhaps a life. So it was safer to simply watch Jung remove her clothes.

Jung returned to the workers' entrance with the guitar to let them know that she would be available in case the Dear Leader wanted some music.

She was instructed to wait just inside the first set of doors, where the temperature was still near freezing. When she advised them that the cold could crack the guitar, she was allowed in the building.

She wondered if it were true.

CHAPTER 88

Heathrow Airport Terminal 5, London, United Kingdom
Wednesday, January 30, 21:42 Greenwich Time

Agent Meghan entered the enormous steel and glass terminal built for British Airways' exclusive use. A marvel of efficiency, it nevertheless made most passengers feel small, often insignificant. Not Agent Meghan. Her mind was engaged in anticipating the next step.

She watched Yolanda clear passport control, then observed with a touch of envy the European Union passport holders zipping through their special lines with hardly time for a "Good Day." The Yanks were taking longer to process.

On the bright side, it did give her time to review her identity cover.

She departed the customs area, towing her rolling luggage through an exit to the outside. The humidity manifested itself that evening as a persistent drizzle.

Nearby, Yolanda was apparently having a cell phone conversation and displaying mild disgust, as though her ride was going to be late. If you're going to be standing outside customs waiting for someone you're not supposed to be waiting for, it was excellent spy craft.

"Could Yolanda be my controller?" Agent Meghan wondered for the first time. It would be perfect. And the request that she sleep with the President would make more sense coming from her controller. Of course, she had never heard Yolanda say "Keep it simple."

Agent Meghan needed sleep --- the kind you get in a bed, not an airplane seat.

They made brief eye contact, but nothing else, In the event a message was to be relayed, Yolanda would have dropped something and Agent Meghan would have helped her retrieve it. No message was good news.

When the Holiday Inn shuttle bus pulled up, Agent Meghan boarded it. Yolanda waited for the Avis shuttle.

At the self drive car hire agency, Yolanda politely rebuked the determined attempt of the tall young Pakistani man to deliver the car in the morning to her hotel to save her 29 Pounds plus the considerable VAT, which she finally remembered was the Value Added Tax. "I need it tonight," she insisted, hoping that she wouldn't.

"Terrible driving conditions tonight. The motorways will be slick," he had advised, as if being a car hire agent made him privy to all the secrets of atmospheric conditions.

"I'll try not to bend your vehicle."

He smiled. "O.K., American lady. I'll have your car brought to the curb outside. We didn't have a black medium compact automatic in Group I, as you requested; so I upgraded you to a Group K automobile for no additional charge."

Yolanda sighed. "O.K. Thank you."

"You are most welcome." He wasn't coming on to her, but she knew he would if given a hint of encouragement. "I think you will be pleased with it."

"What model is it?"

"A Mercedes C 180, a magnificent car for a magnificent woman, if I may be so bold."

She leaned towards him, frustrated that the car rental gods had chosen this particular occasion to upgrade her to a Mercedes. She'd wanted a dark car that would blend into traffic in case she needed to follow someone. "Pay attention."

"Yes?" He thought she was grateful.

"Driving in London traffic on the left side of the road is challenging enough. I don't need six extra inches of steel to scrape off."

He grimaced at the very prospect. "You have an excellent point. Would a dark blue Group I Peugeot 308 be acceptable?"

"Automatic transmission?"

"Yes." His ardor had cooled. He simply wanted to return to the cricket match on the telly. He scribbled changes on the paperwork and made a call. "It has been arranged. Just sign here, and here, and I'll be wanting your initials here, and right there."

She sighed without reading like everyone else. If they tried to rip her off, she would contest the charge with MasterCard when the statement arrived. The worst case scenario was that she couldn't set foot in the United Kingdom again. She handed the papers back to him with a sense of weariness.

"You may have a seat over there until your car arrives."

There were four padded metal chairs.

"Thank you."

"You are welcome. Have a pleasant holiday." He returned to his stuffed chair in front of the television.

Then she wandered the access roads in the rain until she found the Holiday Inn Heathrow.

After she checked in, she roamed the upper floors until she found a door with a pale green envelope protruding from it. She bent down to confirm that the return address was in Arlington, Virginia. Then she rapped softly. Knock. Knock. Knock. Knock-knock-knock. Agent Meghan had explained that it was the Duke's Song from *Rigoletto*, which hadn't been all that helpful.

Agent Meghan let her in.

Agent Meghan affixed a button to the inside of the small closet, where it would not be detected. "It's basically a wireless doorbell with a range of up to 100 feet." This is the bell part. Keep it with you at all times. In five minutes, I will test it by ringing it five times in succession. If I ring any more or any less, it is not a test. If you do not hear any rings, come back here and we'll figure out something else."

"And if it works?"

"Three rings means suspicious activity. Check out the hallway and exits, but don't contact me. Two rings means someone's outside my door. Check it out and contact me if you can afterward."

"And one ring?"

"Scramble. It's urgent. Means I'm not alone. Follow me if I leave."

Yolanda considered the time it would take to retrieve her rental car.

Agent Meghan said "I'll delay as much as possible, but you can track me with this GPS." She handed Yolanda a compact global positioning system device, then displayed a metallic pill. "I'll swallow it when the time comes."

Regarding the devices she now held, Yolanda observed "This is like Trick or Treat."

"Let's hope so."

CHAPTER 89

Holiday Inn Heathrow, London, United Kingdom
Thursday, January 31, 1:37 Greenwich Time

They came for Agent Meghan with a master key card. She swallowed the tracking device when she heard the suitcase she had placed against the door topple over.

"Time to close the deal," a man's voice said as the light came on.

She was dressed in blue jeans and a sweater. She automatically slipped on a pair of boots. She wanted to be dressed for the elements in case they went outside.

There were two of them. Neither brandished a weapon. They gave her a moment to compose herself before the taller one handed her a note and a burn phone. "The wiring instructions for this installment," he explained. "Make the call."

Agent Meghan went through her pockets convincingly before walking to the closet before either could react. "Number's in my coat pocket," she explained. The pressed the button once firmly as she retrieved her long coat. She produced a slip of paper from a pocket.

She made the call. "The funds are on the way."

The same man took the cell phone from her and

removed the SIMM card, which he cut into four pieces with pliers. He wrapped two pieces in toilet paper and flushed them down the commode. The remainder he pocketed along with the phone.

"You're certainly thorough," she commented.

"Time to leave."

Yolanda watched the three of them leave and enter a sedan parked at the entrance. One of them got in the right front seat; so he was the driver.

She waited a bit before pulling out to follow. It was the dead of night, but there is always some traffic around Heathrow to provide cover. She wondered what she would do if they took a deserted country road. It would be simple to follow them, but hard to remain undetected. Maybe the rain would help.

The car she was following took the M4 Motorway West, but exited at Hungerford. It proceeded along paved secondary roads into the chalk hills of Wiltshire. There were no other cars; so Yolanda stayed nearly a mile behind, even when they passed through sleeping hamlets. Abetted by the glowing dot on the GPS, the tactic worked this time. The vehicle ahead bore on through the night.

Until it didn't.

She went past the vehicle when it pulled onto a lane in a place called Avebury, which seemed to be a small archeological park of some kind. She continued to the next intersection to avoid any encounter if they went further. But the dot that represented Agent Meghan had remained in Avebury.

There was no motel to provide cover for her in the tiny crossroads village that was Avebury. As she had passed through, she had noticed that the public car park displayed a sign forbidding overnight parking.

She pulled onto the narrow shoulder and opened an energy drink. She swallowed a caffeine pill with it. A Cadbury's hazelnut bar completed her snack. She would be fully alert for hours. She hoped the petrol would hold out until morning.

Yolanda familiarized herself with the County of Wiltshire as best she could on a rainy night.

She was grateful for the radio, once she got past the hip-hop stations. She was surprised to hear "Ay! Ay! La salsa añeja" coming from the speakers, about two elderly people dancing to the salsa beat.

CHAPTER 90

Outside Göteborg, Sweden
Thursday, January 31, 3:45 Western European Time

Meghan felt the truck engine stop. She was not alarmed. It was turned off whenever they refueled it. She dozed off again. When she next awakened, she realized that she had pulled the covers up to her nose. It was cold inside the truck.

She climbed out of bed gingerly, trying not to put too many centimeters of her bare feet in contact with the frigid truck bed. After putting on all her clothes, she went to the door and began to pound on it.

No response. She tried shouting.

Nothing.

She was alone, locked in a truck in a barn in the countryside, with the temperature dropping.

The lamp on the front wall began to dim.

She crawled back into bed fully clothed and pulled up the blanket to preserve her body heat.

A few minutes later, the light went out.

She began to sob softly.

Twenty-two minutes later, she heard vehicles arrive

and doors slam. She jumped out of bed and pounded on the door.

"Is that Meghan?" a voice shouted.

"Yes! It is!"

"Stop pounding on the doors! Remain still. We're here to rescue you. The doors have been welded shut. It will take a few minutes. Be patient."

She wanted to ask why, but decided that might slow them down.

"What do you call your husband?"

"What?"

"We have to verify your identity. Do you have a nickname for your husband?"

"Oh. It's Pecos."

"And your mother's maiden name?"

"Delaney!"

"Do you have a tattoo?" a different voice asked.

"Yes." She was surprised by the question. "Hassim?"

"Where is it?" Hassim's voice inquired.

"On my back."

"What does it look like?"

"You should know. You gave it to me."

"Make the call," the first voice growled to someone else. "Now!"

"No service in here, I need to go outside," came the reply.

"Stay there till he calls back with the bomb instructions."

CHAPTER 91

Fishlock's Cottage, Avebury, United Kingdom
Thursday, January 31, 3:12 Greenwich Time

Although called a cottage, the residence was large. Agent Meghan had been permitted to freshen up in the upstairs bathroom, next to a bedroom that appeared to have antique furniture. It was a pleasant place, despite the circumstances. Now she sat before an open fire in the sitting room, drinking tea. Her attempts at conversation had been rebuffed. "Don't make us remove your tongue."

The call came to a cell phone that was answered by the tall man. "Understood" was all he said before hanging up. To his partner and Agent Meghan he announced, "The lady has been found. The remaining funds have been received."

"You need to tell them how to deactivate the bomb," Agent Meghan reminded him.

"They will figure it out by themselves --- or not," the man joked.

"You have the money! Keep your side of the bargain!" Agent Meghan implored them.

Fearing she might attempt to flee or cause them trouble, the other man explained "The man who called us has already told them how to disarm the bomb. He's just tormenting you."

"Oh. Then we're done?"

"Not quite," said her tormentor. "Before dawn, though."

Without warning, the other man pinned her arms to the sofa, so she could not prevent duct tape from being rolled over her mouth and around her head.

"Don't touch that! Put on your boots and coat. We're going for a walk."

Walking through the small garden, Agent Meghan noticed large shapes standing in the misty darkness. As she walked among them, she realized this was the remains of a Pagan henge, probably constructed thousands of years ago. The village seemed to have been built inside the ring.

Yolanda had finally attracted the attention of the local constabulary, who had pulled her over.

"I flew in last night and wanted to see Avebury at dawn. I knew if I went to sleep, I'd never get up in time. So here I am, way ahead of schedule with nothing to do."

The old policeman sighed. "You tourists will be the death of me yet."

"Since you've already met me, can I park in the public lot at Avebury? I'll pay the fee when the man arrives."

"Sure. Do that. It's preferable to you driving around until you fall asleep. Keep your doors locked. Get some rest. You've got hours until sunrise."

"Thank you. I'll go straight there."

"And since you're a visitor, dawn is when the sky gets a bit brighter. Don't wait for the sun."

She smiled appropriately. "Useful information, officer. Thanks again."

She drove into Avebury, pleased with the outcome of the encounter. At the car park, she positioned her Peugeot so that it faced the cottage where the car she had been following remained parked.

She did not realize that Agent Meghan had left.

Yolanda cracked the windows to allow the icy air inside. Then she opened another energy drink.

CHAPTER 92

Outside Göteborg, Sweden
Thursday, January 31, 4:37 Western European Time

"How long can it take to break a lock?" Meghan wondered. "Or pick a lock?" She hadn't heard any sounds compatible with breakage. Then it hit her. She shouted "Are you looking for booby traps?

An interval passed before she received a response. "Just making sure."

When the final wire transfer had been confirmed, the kidnapper had called back to advise the team leader that the bomb was in a box under truck bed. "To disarm it, simply open the cover of the box and cut the green wire."

Unfortunately, the cover was frozen shut. Heat was being applied in discreet amounts without the proper tools. Removing the bomb was not an option because it had been welded to the underside of the truck bed.

"We have nineteen minutes left. Any other ideas? Now's the time, gentlemen."

"Let's cut through the top of the truck. Hear me out. The top is different from the side walls. It's solid metal. Difficult to run wires through. There are supports that could be rigged, but they're spaced far enough apart to get a person through."

"But how do we know where they are?"

"We ask the lady inside."

"Do it!."

Meghan had been listening. "What do you want me to do?"

"Do you have something to measure with?"

"Yes!" She knew that the distance between her elbow and her middle fingertip was just under twenty inches.

"Measure the distance from the front edge of the van to the center of the first roof support."

She stood on the bed and measured as best she could. "About eighteen inches."

"Could you get through that space if we made a hole?"

She didn't bother to calculate. "Yes! I can!"

"Stand in the opposite corner. We're coming in."

"Sixteen minutes!"

"What can I do to get ready?" she asked.

"Remove any clothing that might snag or hang you up. When you see our saw, give us directions. But watch out for flying metal chips."

"Got it!"

There was a terrible screeching sound as the power saw cut through the metal.

"Stop!" she screamed. "Stop!"

The saw stopped. "What's the matter?"

"The outside dimensions must be different. You're about to cut the first support."

"How far do we have to go to start cutting between that one and the second one?"

"Four inches. Maybe five."

"Five for good measure."

"Twelve minutes!"

The screeching resumed and the saw appeared, moving slowly toward the second support. After a minute, she cried out "Stop now!"

The saw was removed and reappeared at an angle of degrees. It continued for about two feet, then stopped. "Are we parallel to the support?"

"Yes."

The saw reappeared at 90 degrees from the last cut. It continued until she told them to stop. The saw was removed. Then the metal top was bent inward from above.

"Nine minutes! Prepare to leave!"

A pair of hands reached down. Meghan grabbed them instantly. Dressed in a shirt and jeans, she emerged into the barn floodlit by generator-powered lights.

"Eight minutes! All personnel not disarming the bomb leave now. Sit rep, bomb squad!"

Meghan was lowered to the ground and ushered into a car. Hassim was already in the back seat. James was up front. It left before she had the door completely closed.

"What are you doing here, Hassim?"

"Rescuing you, of course."

"How considerate of you."

"I thought it would look good on my resume," Hassim replied.

Meghan punched his arm hard. "What do you know about this?"

"Khalid told me the people who took you were Europeans or Americans, not Hamas."

"Do you believe him?"

"Yes. He was near death, and he knew it."

"Are you going back with me?"

Hassim looked at James, who said "We have a few more questions for Hassim before we turn him over to State. Some genius at Langley thinks he's the mastermind behind your abduction from the clinic."

"Oh. I guess not. That will give you time to prepare a large banquet to celebrate my arrival."

She punched his arm again.

Back at the barn, the commander of the operation received the situation report.

"Almost got it, sir."

"Pull out now! We've achieved our objective. The truck isn't worth the...."

Just then the truck exploded, blowing apart everything and everyone within thirty feet.

CHAPTER 93

Avebury, United Kingdom
Thursday, January 31, 3:58 Greenwich Time

Yolanda snapped fully awake when a car drove by. It parked at the cottage. The Moon had come out, making a ghostly appearance in the misty sky. It was not enough to notice anything except that one person, probably a man, entered the cottage. Assuming he would be staying, she decided to investigate. Lacking a real weapon, she half-filled a gallon plastic bag with gravel from the parking lot. She had a sap.

Before she could reach the cottage, someone came out. It appeared to be the same person, a man wearing a long coat with a scarf around his neck and a fedora --- a bit old fashioned. Until she had his name, he would be Scarf to her. She followed Scarf as he crossed the road and entered a field with large upright stones. It looked like Stonehenge, but not so concentrated. The shadows of the stones provided good cover for her.

Suddenly, two men stepped forward to greet Scarf. It became obvious that Scarf was in charge. Yolanda followed as they led him to a stone that was lying on the ground. In the hazy moonlight, she couldn't tell if it had fallen over or been placed in that position by design centuries ago. Opting for the latter explanation, she mentally dubbed it the altar.

The surface of the stone moved.

Scarf approached the altar. He removed an electric torch from his coat and shone it upon the altar --- illuminating the gagged and bound Agent Meghan.

After recovering from the shock, Yolanda reflected briefly on what a fine job of watching the empty cottage she had done. Then she moved her thoughts to the problem of rescue.

"Some privacy, please. Keep watch," Scarf commanded.

The men who had been guarding Agent Meghan moved away, in opposite directions. That marked them as professionals.

She hadn't devised a plan yet, but when one of these men walked right past her, she seized the opportunity. At the moment the plastic bag of gravel connected with the man's cerebellum, he dropped silently. Yolanda had seen enough slasher films to know that the disabled killer always gets back up. She immediately clobbered him again for insurance. Then she bound his hands behind him and his feet together with the long plastic baggage ties she always carried. She put a rock in his mouth before she gagged him with duct tape. A quick search revealed that he had no weapon. This was England, not Detroit.

"God save the Queen," she whispered to herself as she set off after the other guard.

"We are in the middle of a field. If you scream, no one will hear you but me," Scarf told Agent Meghan. "And that will annoy me. You don't want me to become annoyed. Do you agree not to yell for help if I remove your gag?"

Agent Meghan nodded in the affirmative.

"Very well." Scarf produced a hunting knife, which he waved before her eyes before cutting her gag in one rapid motion. "Now we can communicate like civilized persons."

"What in the Hell do you think you're doing, Mr. Carnegie?" Agent Meghan rasped.

"Ah. You recognize me. I thought you would."

"You're my controller." It was stated as an established fact.

"My. Aren't we sharp? When did you come to that conclusion?" He wasn't admitting it.

"Marco figured it out."

"Now that is a surprise. It ratifies my decision to remove your gag."

"What do you intend to do with me?"

"An appropriate question, given the circumstances." He paused to consider the optimal phrasing. "You have become a loose end, which is synonymous with being a liability in our line of endeavor. So I have planned this delightful misdirection to eliminate you. I suppose the delightful part doesn't refer to the nature of your participation, but I think you'll admire the cunning of it nonetheless."

"I'm breathless with anticipation. Tell me more."

"I appreciate your sarcasm. If it's any consolation, you'll be going out with a bang, as they say." He smiled down at her. "You are lying on the altar stone of an ancient Pagan henge known as Avebury. For the most part it is an archeological curiosity, a minor tourist destination. Perhaps because it is by far the largest henge in the British Isles, there are some religious cults that take it quite seriously though. They have gatherings and perform rituals here at odd times throughout the year. One of these rituals is the sacrifice of an animal."

"I get to play the animal?"

"Yes. That will be your role tonight. Unfortunately, my research discloses that this requires that your garments be removed and that your heart be extracted while you are still alive. Due to the passive nature of your part, no previous acting skills are required. There are some markings to be made on your flesh, as well, but I have instructed those playing the roles of Pagans to wait until you can no longer feel them."

"Whatever happened to 'Keep it simple?'" Agent Meghan asked, despite the fact that she knew it wasn't important.

"The opportunity for misdirection overruled it, I'm afraid. The authorities will race off at full gallop in the wrong direction and never guess the motive --- an important component of the plan. Besides, a little nonsense now and then is relished by the best of men."

"But you need me! I'm your agent inside the White House."

"You were always a substitute. You knew that from the outset."

It came to her from nowhere. "You don't know!"

"Know what?" He was tiring of her, but sought any information she might have.

"Your daughter is dead!"

"What?" Paul Carnegie had just been blindsided.

Agent Meghan pressed her advantage. "The bomb exploded before they could get to her. She's dead, Paul. After all she went though, she was murdered after the ransom was paid."

"You're lying!" he shouted. He couldn't bring himself to accept it, but he believed it was possible. And that was enough.

"It's true. Check it out for yourself."

His confidence had been eradicated. Paul Carnegie, political power broker and senior CIA operative had been reduced to mumbling as he considered what might have gone wrong.

"There's not even enough to bury, not that you can acknowledge that she was your daughter."

"No."

"Come on, Paul. We're wasting time. We need to get back to work."

He composed his features and raised the knife. He hesitated.

Agent Meghan sought to assure him. "It was a communication error. That's all. We got it straightened out in time. We can go back to business as usual. No hard feelings."

"That's a stretch," he said.

"Maybe it is but, damn it, we're both professionals. We know the rules and the risks. You made a reasonable tactical decision based upon incomplete information. Now that you have the whole picture, that tactic is no longer appropriate. We have to be flexible."

"She's right," Yolanda said as she wrapped her left arm around Carnegie's throat, pulling him back.

He dropped the knife. "I know."

CHAPTER 94

The Mountain Retreat, Chagang-Do Province,
Democratic People's Republic of Korea (North Korea)
Friday, February 1, 11:21 Japan Standard Time

The feasting had started early, a show of bravado by the Dear Leader, as well as an attempt to distract himself in this isolated mountaintop. The recent arrival of the band had prompted Kim to move his reduced entourage to the "relaxation area" --- a combination cocktail lounge and theater. The acoustics were terrible, but the sound system was world class. And the bar was well stocked.

The members of the band had not been strip-searched, merely patted down by shy, rural military men. This bode well for lax security elsewhere. Perhaps it was the lack of guests. Maybe it was the informal country setting. The atmosphere was friendlier, almost like a family reunion. The Dear Leader was relaxed, enjoying the show.

It was time.

Jung swung the guitar behind her on its strap and signaled the drummer, who applied the brushes to the cymbals in a 1-2-3 beat that conjured up a strip tease. Jung kicked off her high heels and stretched toward the ceiling with both arms, standing on tiptoes. At first she ignored the beat. Then she unfastened her pony tail and ran both hands through her long hair, at times covering her face. Her body began to move with the beat. Kim, like every other man in the room, was mesmerized.

Then the bass guitarist began playing low, funky chords as Jung ran her hands down her body. Her hips moved with the beat. She began to sing in a low sultry voice. "I wish. I wish I was a catfish. Swimmin' in the deep blue sea. And all you handsome boys come fishin' after me. Fishin' after me."

When she was done seducing the crowd with her version of Sylvia Fricke's *Catfish Blues*©, the band jumped right into their closer, *It's Only Rock 'n Roll*©. When she pointed to the audience for the responses, even the Dear Leader sang out "But I like it!"

The two rhythm guitarists stepped up to take over from her. Still wearing the Stratocaster, Jung pointed to her throat to indicate she was thirsty. Then she made a small bow to Kim as she went straight to the bar. She asked the bartender for a cold beer, but continued to the Bosch freezer without hesitation, quickly grabbing a chilled mug as she sprayed the contents of the small poison canister inside. She handed the mug to the man behind the bar and joked in a raspy voice. "I guess I'm in a hurry." She downed half of it, said "I'll be back." Then she left it on the bar and rejoined the band to finish the song.

She had just firmly established the alibis of the other band members --- perhaps implicating herself in the process.

But, if the poison worked, she might be excluded from suspicion by the fact that she had not eaten the same food as Kim and his entourage. And, even if anyone was clever enough to suspect that the poison had been administered via the chilled glassware, the fact that she had drunk from one of them would argue against it. They could test her half-empty glass.

Now she had to hustle the band members away before anyone offered them drinks --- especially the types served in chilled glasses. "Worst beer I ever tasted," she told the band. "Made me sick to my stomach."

That should do it, since Kim never shared his *Dom Perignon* with the help.

The members of the band retired, exhausted, to the quarters reserved for them in an adjacent building. They snacked from the well-stocked refrigerator there, finishing off a few bottles of rice wine as well.

None of them touched the local beer.

CHAPTER 95

Fishlock's Cottage, Avebury, United Kingdom
Thursday, January 31, 4:43 Greenwich Time

"I haven't been completely candid with you, Paul. The bomb did explode. People were killed, but your daughter is O.K." Agent Meghan offered a figurative olive branch.

"Lying bitch!"

"Psycho!"

Yolanda sighed deeply. "Neither of you is anywhere near the top of my favorite people list. So I could kill either of you --- or both for that matter." As the only person in the room who was armed, the threat was real. She had found a knife of considerable menace in the kitchen. The other two gentlemen presently resided in the boots of the cars outside. "You are both intelligence agents. You work with persons you don't like all the time. What's the problem?"

Carnegie started to speak.

"That was rhetorical!" Yolanda screamed. "Settle this now; so we can all go home."

"We need to work out the switch," Agent Meghan said. "You visit me at the White House, and I'll go home with you for a few days. Even with the Secret Service escort, it'll be easier to do it there."

"How does my daughter get into my house without

being seen?" Paul Carnegie was giving in slowly.

"Before I arrive. You park your car somewhere and she's lying down in the back seat when you return. You can work out the details between you. I won't be involved in that part of it."

"That's rather undignified for the First Lady."

"She's been kidnapped twice, fought hijackers and crashed in an airplane. I think she can handle it."

"She has a point," Yolanda said. "Maybe she can wait another day or so to restore her dignity."

"I suppose she can," he conceded.

"Good," Agent Meghan said. "We've got to catch a flight to back to the States. Keep your friends locked up for another ten minutes after we leave to avoid mischief."

"And Mr. Carnegie?"

He turned to Yolanda. "Yes."

"Be careful driving. Some of the tire stems seem to be missing from your vehicles."

"I didn't think you'd make it easy."

"Give you time to have a hot cuppa in this pleasant cottage."

"After you accompany us out to our car to see us off, of course," Agent Meghan added. "Yolanda, be a love and put the kettle on the boil for Mr. Carnegie."

CHAPTER 96

The Mountain Retreat, Chagang-Do Province,
Democratic People's Republic of Korea (North Korea)
Saturday, February 2, 1:52 Japan Standard Time

Jung had set the tone. Besides, there were no visiting
dignitaries to introduce to the dubious delights of Paekdu
Mountain Bulnoju. So Kim had ordered cold beer for
everyone after the show.

Most often associated with deaths caused by
consuming *fugu*, a Japanese delicacy consisting of the flesh
of the puffer fish, tetrodotoxin (abbreviated TTX) can be
found in other natural sources, including mollusks, horseshoe
crab eggs, certain newts and the skin of some frogs,
salamanders, octopi and fish. Hence, it occurs all over the
planet. (Haitians know it as "Zombie Dust" for its associations
with those insidious voodoo practices.) The Sea of Japan,
which borders North Korea, is a plentiful source of puffer fish.

Whereas, it takes up an ounce and one-half of puffer
fish liver, gonads or skin, as little as one milligram of the
purified toxin can be lethal. Tetrodotoxin binds to sodium
channels in the human body, blocking the electrical activity
that causes contraction of the muscles. When such activity
occurs in the atrium, the heart can't beat. The same
mechanism paralyzes the diaphragm, causing respiratory

failure. It is ten times more poisonous than potassium cyanide. There is no antidote. Ingestion of a sufficient quantity will kill within hours.

The Dear Leader was finishing his beer when his lips became numb. His tongue didn't feel right either. When he became lightheaded, he concluded he was exhausted. He experienced some difficulty walking to his suite, but nothing that couldn't be explained by a hard day.

His manservant and butler got him into his bed and wished him *"Annyeonghaseyo, Chin-aehaneun Jidoga."* His response was unintelligible, but that was not unusual.

Extremely fatigued now, Kim was thinking about Jung's performance --- especially her vampy blues number. He decided he would make her the Republic's first international rock star, bringing pride and prestige to his nation. He would call his manservant back to start the procedure.

He couldn't speak. That was worrying indeed. Perhaps he was coming down with laryngitis. He would have a look at this throat in the bathroom mirror.

That was when he discovered he could not move.

Kim Jong-il was fighting the terror of his situation when the convulsions began. He was struggling for his breath as his soft body jerked around uncontrollably. His mind could not evaluate his condition. There was only panic.

His heart went into arrhythmia, beating erratically and ineffectively for several painful minutes. Then it stopped forever.

The Dear Leader was no more.

CHAPTER 97

The White House, Washington, D.C.
Friday, February 1, 8:30 AM EST

"Nice to finally meet you, Mr. President." Franklin Bollings, the venerable Director of the Central Intelligence Agency smiled wearily as he entered the Oval Office. "And you too, ah --- Mrs. Redondo."

"It's a pleasure to meet you, as well. And I'll introduce you to the real Mrs. Redondo when you bring her back from Sweden," the President quipped.

The Director stopped cold in his tracks. "I beg your pardon?" The three of them exchanged confused glances. "She's been found then?"

"I was about to thank you for locating her. I see we need to talk."

The Director took a chair. "I've been a bit out of touch with the operation the last 24 hours or so. We've received intelligence that Kim Jong-il passed away." When he saw the President's obvious interest, he continued. "We're trying our best to confirm it. No details yet, but the sources are reliable."

"The Green Dragons?" Marco asked.

"Among others." The Director did not try to disguise his surprise. "How did you know?"

"My idea to use them," the President confessed. "Was

he killed?"

"Poisoned, I'm told. It's still pretty early in the game though."

"Understood. Keep me up to date on this. In the meantime, I'll bring you up to speed on my wife."

"I'd appreciate that," the Director conceded.

"How do you like your coffee, Director?" Agent Meghan asked.

"With milk and a little sugar, please. And let me take this opportunity to say you've done excellent work filling in for the First Lady."

"Thank you very much, sir."

"Any chance we could steal you away from the Secret Service?" He'd meant it to be a compliment wrapped in a joke. It did not have the intended effect.

"You could if I didn't already work for you. I'm on loan to the Service. They didn't have anyone who looked like Mrs. Redondo."

"Oh my. I'm embarrassed that I didn't know...."

"Well, it did start out as a low-key, short-duration operation. Probably not significant enough to be brought to your attention," she suggested.

Marco listened with interest as his ersatz wife told his top spy what was going on in his own agency.

"That's probably it," he agreed. "You were part of a brief domestic operation run by another agency. None of my business." The Director felt a bit better about himself. "Nevertheless, you'd think that I would have been told of your involvement before I arrived here."

"Nobody knew you were coming when your secretary

left yesterday," Marco pointed out.

"That's true," he agreed. But he still seemed troubled. "Still working with the Secret Service, then?" he asked Agent Meghan.

"No, sir. When the incident occurred in the West Bank, the Company assigned me a controller."

"Excellent. Nice to know someone was on his toes at Langley. Do you know who it is?"

"Paul Carnegie."

"Carnegie, eh. Your father-in-law, I believe, Mr. President. Strange choice on the face of it, but perhaps inspired. Don't believe he's run an agent for a while. What do you think? Does he still have the touch?"

Agent Meghan sighed. "He tried to kill me, sir."

"He what?"

"Told me I was a loose end that needed to be tidied up."

"You're quite sure it was him?"

"Beyond any doubt. I spoke with him at length after he was subdued by a friend of mine."

"That's preposterous! When did this happen?" the Director asked her.

"Right after the ransom was wired."

"Oh dear. You did say ransom."

"Twenty-One Million Dollars --- plus a couple hundred more in case there was another bid of Twenty-One Million," she advised.

"Bid?"

"It was an auction, conducted on the internet." When she noticed his alarm, she added "Discreetly. We were the high bidders."

"And the money?"

"I understood that it came from the Company."

"I see." It was clear that he didn't. "I need to check into this matter at once, if you will permit me. I'll contact you when I have it in hand."

"Today?"

The Director moved toward the door. "You can count on it, Mr. President."

"I shall, Mr. Director."

CHAPTER 98

The White House, Washington, D.C.
Friday, February 1, 1:28 PM EST

Director Bollings was ushered into the Oval Office a second time. Major Fox accompanied him. "Please consider this to be an interim report, Mr. President. There is still much to be uncovered, I fear."

"Thank you for getting back to me so quickly Director Bollings. I didn't expect you to come all the way back from Langley."

"I've found that I often accomplish more if I'm not at Langley, Mr. President. I've been right here, enjoying the hospitality of Major Fox and his capable assistant, Lieutenant Herrera."

"Please be seated, both of you."

The Director began speaking before his back hit the chair. "Here's what I have discovered. Your wife was rescued by a CIA team from a barn in Sweden where she was being held. She was the only person there at the time, which was according to the kidnappers' plan. She was in the cargo compartment of a truck inside the barn. The doors had been welded shut. There was a bomb under the truck."

"The truck she was in?"

"That was part of the deal, too. Once a positive

identification was made at the site, then the last payment was wired. When the payment was received, the kidnappers told them how to disarm the bomb."

"So it didn't explode...."

"Unfortunately, the case was frozen shut. It went off before they could open it --- after your wife was away."

"Anyone hurt?"

"Four agents dead, one wounded. He'll recover. They were just leaving."

Agent Meghan cut in. "You say kidnappers. Are you sure it's more than one person?"

"So far, every way we've analyzed it, the operation requires more than one person. Assuming that the same persons started the fire that led to the evacuation of the clinic, it was a precise, professional operation."

"Like a CIA black op?" the President inquired.

"Very much so I'm afraid. There is a strong possibility that a foreign intelligence agency was involved. It was that well run."

"But the explosion?"

"The forensic experts won't be able to tell us anything about the bomb for quite a while, but we know that it was in a proper case. It was not some amateur pipe bomb."

"Does the fact that the kidnappers failed to anticipate that the cover might freeze shut tell us anything?" Agent Meghan asked.

"It would tend to move Scandinavians to the bottom of the suspect list. Russians, too. The problem with that conjecture is that the bomb maker may have had no idea where it would be used."

"Yes. Inconclusive," the President agreed.

"Why didn't the kidnappers disarm it remotely?" Major Fox asked.

"It didn't have that capability. It was on a timer."

"Doesn't that indicate a lack of technical proficiency?" the Major wondered.

"No. Cellular service inside the barn is not reliable. The team had to go outdoors to contact the kidnappers."

"Did you look into Paul Carnegie?" Agent Meghan asked.

Director Bollings glanced at the President, who nodded for him to speak.

"Paul Carnegie is a remarkable man. He was trained as a civil engineer, but he always saw the bigger picture. He bought the first company he worked for from an ailing owner in what would today be called a leveraged buyout. When the former owner died, the key man life insurance policy not only extinguished the balance of the debt, but provided enough capital to expand the firm. Then he took it public, receiving enough unregistered shares to make him a millionaire many times over on paper. When the corporation was large enough, Carnegie sold it to an investor from Omaha in exchange for stock and continued to run it until he retired at age fifty-five. By then he was working for us as well, using his international connections as cover for operations."

"Like Howard Hughes," Marco commented.

"That's what we initially thought, but he insisted upon going through training at the Farm and became a full-fledged agent, although he was never put on the payroll."

"Why not?" the President asked.

"He didn't want to be. Felt it might expose him. And he certainly didn't need the money."

"I assume that's still the case...."

"Not necessarily. We're still looking into that. Like many others, it appears he was worried about the health of the investor from Omaha. Thinking the value of his stock would drop precipitously if the old man had a stroke, he liquidated his holdings roughly six years ago."

"He had all his eggs in one basket all that time?" Marco was incredulous.

"It appears that he did. When he sold out though, he must have realized the risk he had taken. He decided to diversify. He invested about one-third of his fortune through an aggressive real estate company which claims to have a formula for working with developers, buying unfinished condominiums in Florida, Arizona and California. It is a safe bet that today these properties are worth substantially less than his contract price. Any he has not already flipped have become liabilities.

"Ouch," Major Fox remarked.

"Ouch, indeed," the Director concurred. "About half of his money was invested with a gentleman with an impressive record of returns on investment. Unfortunately, that gentleman was running a Ponzi scheme."

"All gone?" Marco asked.

"So it appears. But Mr. Carnegie retained ample funds to invest on his own. Apparently unable or too busy to decide at the time, he placed it all in the securities issued by his broker, an investment banker."

"Please tell us it wasn't Lehman Brothers," the

President requested. "Nobody can be that unlucky."

"Yes. It was Lehman Brothers. Mr. Carnegie is not broke, of course. But I doubt that he will be able to pay the property taxes on his estate in Virginia much longer."

"He doesn't strike me as the type to downsize," Agent Meghan noted.

Director Bollings agreed. "I think he would do nearly anything to avoid losing that estate, not to mention his status as one of the richest men in America."

"Director, where did the ransom money come from?"

"You were right. It came from our agency." The Director paused a moment, then continued "I don't suppose Mr. Carnegie will offer to reimburse us for any of it."

"Where did the money go?" she pressed.

"We've been looking into that. So far it has vanished in an uncharted sea of foreign accounts. I doubt we'll ever track it down," he confessed.

"Try looking at the other end," Agent Meghan suggested.

Everyone looked at her in the same way as if she'd suggested the money was in a flying saucer.

"I'll be more specific. Let's say there was a person who suddenly needed a whole boatload of money. We'll call him Pablo."

The President and the Major smiled.

"And this Pablo knows of a valuable person that some company would be willing to ransom. He also knows exactly where that person is. Furthermore, he has the resources needed to take that person, while deflecting any suspicion from himself. Everyone with me so far?"

"I fear we are, but...." It was the Director.

"Sorry to interrupt, sir, but save your questions, please."

The Director nodded for her to proceed.

"Not only does Pablo have the resources to take her and keep her, but he also controls the conduit for information, including the vital approval for the amount to be paid. That, of course, is a problem."

"Why?" the President asked.

"He's greedy. He wants a ton of money, but he doesn't want to ask for so much that he ends up getting none. So he presents it as an auction, rather than setting the amount himself."

"Making it a competition --- a competition we don't want to lose." Marco saw the genius of it.

"Exactly, then this same kidnapper, wearing the hat of my controller suggests the amount we should bid in order to win. Comes up with a convincing story about how the amount was calculated by Company experts.'

"And we buy it," Marco admitted.

"Lock, stock and barrel. Because Pablo is our expert, manipulating us each step of the way through his marionette, yours truly!"

"Insidious!" the Director commented.

"And the threat doesn't exist. He won't harm his captive. She's his daughter." Major Fox was keeping up.

"Probably isn't any bidding either. He knows who's going to win," the Director observed. "No point. Could only complicate matters."

"And if we had bid less than he suggested, he could still

claim we were the high bidder," she reminded them.

"How could we know otherwise?" Major Fax remarked.

"Exactly. This Pablo covered all the possibilities --- except one," she said.

"What was that?" the Director inquired.

"His plan even provided for eliminating me, in case I figured it out and had this little chat with you. But he didn't count on Yolanda --- that's Second Lieutenant Herrera. She saved my life, Director." Her story was over, but she wasn't finished yet. "Marco, Luís, get her a promotion."

That broke the tension.

"She has a point, Mr. President," Major Fox agreed.

"Get the paperwork moving. Any rank you deem fit up to Major that will keep her around. I'll sign if it's necessary."

The Director rose. "This has been an extraordinary conversation. I'll put more resources on Mr. Carnegie, see if his cash crunch is easing inexplicably." He turned to face Agent Meghan. "If you're right, I need you at headquarters, on my staff."

"I'm right, sir." Agent Meghan paused a moment, then added "And I just realized why my controller was dead set against the First Lady becoming pregnant. He knew his daughter didn't want to be."

"I'm afraid you are. If we investigate along the lines you have suggested, we should turn up something."

"I have photographs of the two men who accompanied him in England, plus their identification papers." She retrieved them from her pocket, handing them to him. "Maybe MI-5 can help find them for you."

"You are just full of surprises, Agent."

"You're telling me," the President added.

CHAPTER 99

Above the Persian Gulf
Friday, February 1, 22:15 Iran Time

The Milstar strategic and tactical relay satellite communications system issued the instruction to all five B-2A Stealth bombers simultaneously. "Go cruising. Repeat. Time to go cruising."

Each bomber had been configured for this exercise to carry twelve AGM-129 advanced cruise missiles. Up to four could be launched at the same time. Each missile already had a preassigned target programmed into the guidance system.

The strikes had been timed to coincide with Friday evening Muslim religious services. This would reduce the number of personnel available to react and limit the human casualties.

Simultaneously, missiles slammed into the facilities at the oil ports of Bandar Abbas and Bandar-e Emam Khomeyni. They destroyed the refineries, the port facilities and tankers in port at the time. The lesser oil ports of Jazireh-ye Khark and Jazireh-ye Lavan and nearby tankers were blown apart. The artificial port of Jazireh-ye Sirri constructed in the middle of the Persian Gulf simply vanished beneath the surface.

The last bomber demolished the liquid natural gas

facilities at the port of Kangan with just four of the Cruise missiles. The fireball from the pressurized gas accounted for much of the destruction. The remaining missiles were dispatched North to the oil refineries at Shiraz and Esfahan.

The pipelines went dry. In less than ten minutes, the world's third largest petroleum exporter no longer had sufficient capacity for its domestic needs.

CHAPTER 100

North of Luray, Virginia
Sunday, February 3, 11:33 AM EST

They were headed North on U.S. Route 341. Meghan was driving. "You can appear any time now."

Agent Meghan popped up from the back seat, wearing a wig of long black hair, with ringlets. "Shazam!"

"Shazam?"

"My brothers read Captain Marvel comics. The word 'Shazam' was somehow associated with the conversion into a super hero."

"If you say so. I didn't have any brothers."

"Gender perspective can be difficult to achieve without growing up around brothers. I had a girlfriend in high school with no brothers. She thought mine were amazing."

"Were they?"

"No. They were just creeps, although sometimes lovable."

"Speaking of lovable, I take it you and my father didn't exactly bond...."

"We really haven't seen that much of each other, and the circumstances haven't been conducive. To the extent we have any relationship, it was built on tension."

"You seemed eager to leave."

"I can't wait to try my own identity on again."

"See if it still fits?"

"Don't even go there."

Meghan laughed. "O.K., but let me pull over so you can change seats. I feel like a chauffeur...."

"Make a hole!" Agent Meghan squeezed over the console and into the front passenger seat. Meghan regarded her a moment.

"Ever wear that wig with Marco?"

"No. Why?"

"I've always suspected he'd like to have a *latina* once in a while. I've seen the way he looks at Lieutenant Herrera."

"Yes. Yolanda is the real deal. Big, strong, smart and dangerous."

"You've become friends?"

"She knew I was an imposter. That made her safe. I tried to keep away from most people."

"Of course." The First Lady did not sound convinced.

"You want to borrow the wig sometime?"

"It occurred to me."

"Yes, we had sex."

Meghan sighed. "Thanks for telling me. I suppose it was inevitable. Not right away I hope."

"I did it to keep him away from Yolanda."

"How thoughtful," Meghan replied with sarcasm. "Who's idea was that?"

"Yolanda's."

The car swerved. "What?"

"You have nothing to fear from Yolanda. She doesn't do casual sex."

"Amazing."

"Shazam!"

CHAPTER 101

The White House, Washington, D.C.
Monday, February 4, 4:04 PM EST

The First Lady and her father were ushered into the Oval Office. Meghan went straight to Marco and threw her arms around him. "Miss me?" she asked.

"I may never let you out again."

"Kinky," she whispered.

"Later. We have guests."

Paul Carnegie had seated himself, waiting for them to finish. The President pressed a button on his telephone. The doors opened immediately. The Director of the Central Agency strode it.

Carnegie stood and offered his hand. "Franklin, what brings you here?"

The Director shook his hand, saying "Business, Paul. Sordid business."

Then Major Fox and Captain Herrera came though the door, closing it behind them. Carnegie became alarmed.

"Want to volunteer?" The Director asked Carnegie, as the two men sat down.

"What's going on?" Meghan asked Marco.

"You'll see."

"It was just an operational misunderstanding between

us. I thought we'd cleared it up," Carnegie explained. "Rather unprofessional to bother you with it. Especially since we'd resolved it."

"Not that, Paul."

"Well, what then?"

"Now is the time to come clean, old friend," the Director continued. "Right now, before the opportunity passes you by."

Carnegie squirmed in his chair as he considered his options, He remained silent.

"Please," Director Bollings asked.

"I'd like to help, Franklin, but I don't have a clue what you're talking about."

"I see."

"Daddy?" Meghan said involuntarily.

Yolanda quietly moved into position behind Paul Carnegie, who was still wearing his confused face.

"You are charged with the crimes of kidnapping, murder and embezzlement."

"That's ridiculous! That Arab Hassim is under investigation for kidnapping my daughter!"

"Is that all you have to say?" the Director asked. "Hassim has been cleared. It was an inside job."

"Franklin, I don't know why you think these things, but you couldn't put me on trial even if you had the proof. There are too many secrets."

"That's it?"

"Yes, it is!" Carnegie started to rise. Yolanda pushed him back down by the shoulders. "Get your hands off of me!"

"Just following orders, sir. If you do not attempt to get

out of that chair, I will not need to touch you again."

"Whose damn orders?"

"The Commander-in-Chief, sir."

"You'll regret this!" Carnegie hissed at Marco.

"Not as much as you, Paul," the President replied. "You disappoint me."

"I'll never stand trial," Carnegie stated with confidence.

"You're probably right," Director Bollings conceded. "You see, the crimes you've been charged with have been construed as acts of terrorism against Americans. They were committed overseas."

"No." The confidence had vanished.

"You're going to Guantanamo as an enemy combatant, Paul. Right now."

"Daddy, what did you do?"

"Nothing. Certainly not what they're accusing me of doing."

"Give the money back, and the embezzling charge will go away," the Director offered. "It won't do you any good in Guantanamo."

"How do I make Guantanamo go away?"

"I'll speak with the Attorney General about that. We'll send down someone from the Agency with a plea bargain agreement for you to sign. There will be no negotiations. You sign or you stay."

Carnegie sensed a bargain nonetheless. "I'm the father-in-law of the President of the United States. You can't just throw me in jail."

"That's why Guantanamo works so well. You just disappear. Let us worry about what happens to you if and when you get back from Cuba. We'll come up with something that doesn't bring shame on the President and the First Lady."

"It sounds like you intend to kill me...."

"That is only one of many options, Paul. Return of the money might take that one off the table."

"O.K., you can have the money back."

"That's a wise decision, Paul. I'll send a banking specialist along with you on the transport. If you need your computer or files, tell me how to get them."

"I can get them myself."

"I'm afraid not, Paul. You're on the way to Andrews Air Force Base."

"You can't do this!"

"Of course, I can. Now, shall I have Captain Herrera place you in handcuffs, or will you go peacefully?"

"No handcuffs," Marco said.

"Yes, Mr. President. Perhaps, the First Lady should accompany us to the car, to make it appear to be a normal leave taking."

"Yes," a shaken Meghan agreed. She walked over to her father. "I'll do what I can, daddy."

"I'm sure you will, honey."

CHAPTER 102

The White House, Washington, D.C.
Monday, February 4, 4:42 PM EST

"What in the Hell just happened?" the First Lady demanded when she returned to the Oval Office.

"It's been an interesting two weeks," Marco relied. "I'm not sure I could survive another term."

"You won't survive this one if you don't tell me what's going on. You can start by telling me why Yolanda is now a Captain."

"She saved someone's life."

"She jumped right over First Lieutenant. Must have been a V.I.P."

"It was the First Lady."

"Hell, Pecos, that's nothing new. It's been open season on me since I left Camp David."

"I refer to your stand-in."

"Really? Someone tried to kill her right here in the White House?"

"No. It happened in England."

"In England." That threw her. "Who was it?"

"It was your father."

"My father?" she gasped.

"Yes, but we need to start at the beginning. Let's have

a glass of wine while I bring you up to date. It could take a while." He walked to the cabinet and extracted a chilled bottled of *Veuve Clicquot Ponsardin Brut* and two flutes. She locked the door. "Then I want to hear about your adventures."

"Wait till you see my tattoo...."

"If that involves disrobing, we should probably wait."

"Spoil sport," she chided. "What shall we drink to?"

Their glasses touched just enough to produce a clear note.

"To all the targets," he replied.

"What?"

"That will be part of my address to the nation. I'll want your help with the speech."

"That's what wives are for."

CHAPTER 103

The White House, Washington, D.C.
Monday, February 4, 8:00 PM EST

There was a hum of conversation among the press corps. Rumors had been spreading about events in North Korea. And now there were reports about Iran. President Redondo strode up to the podium and began speaking without preamble, looking into the video camera.

"Less than one year ago, the first intercontinental ballistic missile in history to deliver an atomic warhead to a population center obliterated the City of San Francisco and devastated the State of California. This was the greatest single loss any country has ever suffered. Yet we did nothing."

"We knew that the Taepodong III missile came from North Korea. I happened to be at Cheyenne Mountain that afternoon. I watched it approach on the monitors, a red snake of a line stalking its unwary victims. I watched brave American pilots willingly forfeit their lives to intercept it. The experience was horrifying."

"But the real horror happened in California. The beautiful city that gave birth to the United Nations was literally blown away. Nothing remains. The warhead was designed for maximum radiation release. San Francisco is now just so much radioactive rubble. As are Oakland and the other surrounding communities. And the former capital of Sacramento — flooded and irradiated." He paused to let that sink in.

"There is an expression for what happened next. It is 'the luck of the devil.' Although it was not surprising that the atomic blast would trigger an earthquake, no one could have anticipated that it would spread South to spawn new tremors that would rip apart the City of Angels --- Los Angeles."

"Yet we did not respond. Why?" He let them consider the question before he continued.

"Well, we did respond to the attack. Actually the Taepodong Rocket Complex was destroyed by a Stealth bomber moments after the deadly rocket was launched. Before anyone even knew whether it would reach our shores. Before anyone knew the devastation that it would bring. But since then there has been no response to this barbaric attack upon America. Why?"

"I am the third person to hold the office of President since this tragedy happened. I discussed it with my predecessor, President Chambers. I am aware of all the options for retaliation. I am also keenly aware that there is no San Francisco in the Democratic People's Republic of Korea. No Los Angeles. In fact, when the International Space Station flies miles above that part of the world at night, North Korea is darker than the Sahara Desert, darker than the Pacific Ocean. The only light comes from the government buildings and parade grounds in the capital city of Pyongyang, not from the enslaved citizens of North Korea."

"Furthermore, the government of North Korea is essentially one man, the brutal dictator Kim Jong-il. What wealth exists is in his firm control. The people of North Korea had no part in the attack on the United States. To this day, they do not even know that it occurred!"

"Nevertheless, every country has targets --- places and things it would prefer to keep. Earlier this week, on my orders, our bombers decimated the North Korean Air Force and destroyed the naval bases. As fast as they can rebuild them, we will level them. We will not warn them first or negotiate. We will be relentless for so long as North Korea pursues a policy of aggression."

"Which brings up a related matter. It has been reported that Kim Jong-il is dead. Although there has been no confirmation from the North Korean government, we believe these reports to be accurate. Since we hold him personally responsible for the launching of the nuclear attack on the United States, this means the perpetrator has slipped beyond our grasp. We urge the regime which follows to alter the disastrous course that country has pursued for the past six decades and to join the community of nations. We extend our hand in greeting to the oppressed citizens of North Korea."

The reporters broke into applause.

"Now I have a secret to share with you all," the President continued. "The risk taken by Kim Jong-il in attacking America far outweighed any benefit to North Korea. You see, Kim Jong-il was crazy --- not stupid. He had to know that even countries which professed to hate America would be appalled by a nuclear attack upon our cities. If, as the saying goes, the enemy of my enemy is my friend, then we are all friends when it comes to the atomic bomb."

"So why did he do it?" he asked rhetorically.

"Once you get your head around the concept that the foreign policy of the Democratic People's Republic of Korea was no more than the whims and desires of a single madman, you can begin to answer that question. And the answer was simple, fit like a glove. It was greed."

"Kim Jong-il ordered the attack, but he was just a hired hand. A thug --- doing the bidding of someone else in return for money. Lots of it. More than One Billion Dollars. We have irrefutable proof."

The audience was spellbound.

"We also know beyond any doubt who paid this blood money. Again, it came from another country of oppressed people. The dictators of this wealthy nation have so much income that they fund terrorism all over the world --- Al-Qaeda, Hamas, Hezbollah, even the Basque separatists in Spain. With staggering petroleum export revenues, they could easily afford One Billion Dollars to inflict humiliation and suffering upon America."

"I am proud to announce that we have put Iran out of business."

There were gasps, then a few cheers which quickly faded. The press wanted details.

"Minutes ago, our bombers returned from the Persian Gulf. There are no longer any oil or natural gas tanker facilities in Iranian territory. In addition, five oil refineries and the only liquid natural gas processing plant have been destroyed. This will drastically curtail the revenues to the dictatorship for years. What they do receive will have to be spent rebuilding."

"I wish to point out that the four refineries which

actually serve most of the population were not targeted. Although it is difficult to be precise in these matters, we did not wish to punish the Iranian people for the acts of their unelected leaders. To minimize loss of life, these attacks were carried out at a time when the most of the workers would be away from the facilities."

"To further minimize casualties, no military facilities were targeted. However, that option remains on the table and will certainly be exercised if the government of Iran attempts to retaliate."

"We regret the inevitable loss of innocent lives inherent in operations such as these. But we are all targets when evil goes unchecked. Dictators can not be appeased for long. Those who harbor them will suffer the consequences eventually. I wish to remind the Iranian people that this was a measured and restrained response to a nuclear attack which killed millions of innocent Americans. It is no secret that the nature of people is to fight back when attacked. Your government certainly understood that a miliary retaliation was likely when they put their terrible plan into effect. It was your leaders who caused this. Remember that."

"It has been said that people get the government that they deserve. Iran is an educated nation with a proud history. Let us hope that you can get the government you deserve instead of one that places radical terrorism above the needs of its citizens."

"I concede that our actions have not begun to set the books in order. But America's losses from the barbaric attack of May 25, can never be compensated or adequately avenged. That is always the case when you have more to lose than your opponent. The fact is that we have been blessed as a nation with the resources --- both natural and human --- to pick up our burden and carry on. And while we have not quite turned the other cheek, we have chosen to lead by example in order to provide the rest of the world the opportunity to live as we do --- strong, united and free."

"Thank you, and God bless America."

EPILOGUE

Agent Meghan was assigned to interrogate Hassim upon his arrival in Virginia. At first, Hassim was strongly attracted to her, but soon found her to be too domineering. She was intrigued by his experiences. Their relationship lasted ten weeks. Both were relieved when Hassim was assigned to the Embassy in Cairo, where he promptly married a tall, blonde American. Agent Meghan now works at the top level of the Central Intelligence Agency. She is one of the candidates to succeed Director Bollings.

Jung and her rock band toured the Far East as cultural representatives of the Democratic People's Republic of Korea. At the first opportunity, she traded her Stratocaster to an immigration official in Ho Chi Minh City in return for asylum. After hiding out for two weeks, she presented herself to the United States Consulate there and told her story. After confirming her claims, she was granted a visa. She presently resides in anonymity in Koreatown, Los Angeles, where she owns a restaurant with her husband. They don't serve *fugu*. The Green Dragons provided the investment capital.

The strikes against North Korea and Iran made Marco Redondo a popular President. When the new leadership in North Korea failed to respond appropriately to his offer of peace, a Stealth bomber was sent to destroy Kim's Palace and the Ryu-Gyong Hotel, a 105-story hotel shaped like a pyramid which had been nearly completed after twenty-seven years. He served two terms. He wrote his autobiography. He was shot and slightly wounded by a Hamas assassin while on his book tour. Meghan Redondo became Secretary of State during his second term when the previous Secretary retired because of ill health. She plans to run for President in the next general election.

Luís Fox remained part of the administration, becoming Colonel Fox along the way. As the end of President Redondo's second term drew near, Major Herrera had approached him to ask what his intentions for the future were. He'd told her he'd like to retire to the mountains of New Mexico with a good woman and a *cerveza bien fría*. "You drive a hard bargain, but I'll bring the *Dos Equis*," she'd responded. They were married in the Cathedral at the Air Force Academy five months later. She hasn't shot at him once.

Paul Carnegie returned from Guantanamo after forty-eight days. He conveyed his Shenandoah Mountains estate to his daughter, who could afford the taxes and upkeep. Then he asked Director Bollings for employment. Carnegie is now the senior resident agent for the O'zbekiston Respublikasi (Uzbekistan Republic), where decent accommodations are so scarce that the CIA subleases its office space from the Russian Foreign Intelligence Service (SVR).

The whole history of the world is summed up in the fact that, when nations are strong, they are not always just, and when they wish to be just, they are no longer strong.

— Winston Churchill

THE END

ABOUT THE AUTHOR

Noah Bond was raised in Upper Arlington --- a suburb of Columbus, Ohio. He received a Bachelor of Science degree in Business Administration from Ohio State University, after which he immediately moved to Florida to attend the University of Florida College of Law. There he was a Senior Editor of the Law Review, in which an article he wrote was published. He practiced law in Fort Lauderdale until retiring in April, 2011, to devote his full time to writing.

He has co-written four screen plays, which continue to circulate in Hollywood, occasionally breaking the surface. He has also written dozens of songs, some of which have been recorded and released.

All the Targets is his fourth suspense novel to be published. You may learn more, read the reviews, find insights about the process of writing, and even listen to some of the songs at *www.noahbond.com.*

Coming soon —

The kids call it "Nekkid Lake." To the local police, it's the site of the massacre --- the greatest unsolved crime in the state. There are no leads. The forensic evidence makes no sense. The only survivor is in a mental hospital. She hasn't spoken a single word since it happened. Is it about to happen again?

Nekkid Lake by Noah Bond